WIND CHIME CAFÉ

A WIND CHIME NOVEL

SOPHIE MOSS

Sea Rose
Publishing

Published by Sea Rose Publishing

ISBN-13: 978-0615949253

For the memory of my grandfather
Rear Admiral Charles D. Nace, U.S. Navy
1917-2000

Submarine commander, World War II hero, one of the greatest
men I have ever known

ONE

"Taylor," Annie Malone whispered, reaching for her daughter's hand. "Wake up."

Taylor's green eyes fluttered open. "Are we here?"

Annie nodded.

Taylor sat up slowly, gazing out the passenger side window. Crickets chirped in the tall grasses around their new home. The crisp autumn air carried the scent of the Chesapeake Bay. "It's quiet."

"I know," Annie said softly. "But we'll be safe here."

Taylor's free hand drifted to her broom—the broom she hadn't stopped carrying since the day everything had changed three weeks ago. It was lodged between her seat and the door. She tugged it back into her lap.

"Come on." Annie kept her tone upbeat as she stepped out of the car. The sooner they put the past behind them, the sooner Taylor could begin to heal. "I'll give you the grand tour."

Taylor clung to her broom as they walked up the overgrown path. Moonlight slanted through the beams of the wide, wraparound porch. The steps creaked as they climbed them, and when a cool wind blew through the empty streets, the window-panes rattled.

Taylor jumped.

Annie laid a comforting hand on her eight-year-old daughter's shoulder. She didn't know how long Taylor would be skittish around loud noises, but it was one of the reasons she'd wanted to move her away from the city.

Heron Island would give them a fresh start, a place where they could build new memories and escape the ones that still haunted them both at night.

Pushing open the door, Annie found the switch on the wall, flooding the first floor café with light.

"It's pink," Taylor said, surprised.

Annie smiled, guiding her inside and closing the door behind them. "It won't be for long."

Taylor stepped into the small dining room, with its simple black and white checkerboard floor, silver counters, and glass display case. "We can paint the walls?"

Annie nodded. They'd never been able to paint the walls in their previous apartment. The Washington D.C. building had maintained strict codes, mostly to keep the dilapidated structure from falling any further apart.

She'd been working double shifts ever since Taylor was born, putting away a small portion of her paycheck each week so that one day they could get their own place.

A rush of pride swept through her. This house was theirs; it *belonged* to them. They could do whatever they wanted with it. "You can help me pick out a new color after school tomorrow."

Taylor's small hands squeezed the handle of her broom. "I don't want to go."

"It's only one day." Annie knelt in front of her. "Then we have the whole weekend to spend together."

The counselor had recommended Taylor start back to school

on Friday. She'd said it would be easier for her to make it through one day rather than an entire week. Annie waited for her daughter's haunted eyes to lift back to hers. "I'll go with you, and I'll stay as long as you need me."

"You promise?" Taylor whispered.

Annie nodded, brushing Taylor's red hair back from her face. She wished she had the resources to homeschool Taylor. She wished her daughter didn't have to set foot in another school ever again. But she needed to work. She needed to get her restaurant up and running soon or she'd never be able to make the first mortgage payment.

They'd find a way to get through this together.

She stood, taking Taylor's hand and leading her through the kitchen. The back door stuck, but it swung open after a few tugs. They walked out onto a lopsided deck overlooking a yard covered with weeds and wildflowers.

"It'll take time," Annie said, gazing out at the quiet cove where a flock of geese chattered on the water, "but once the renovations are done, we can plant a garden."

Taylor looked up at her. "With flowers?"

Annie nodded. "Any kind you want."

Taylor sent her a small smile and they walked back inside, through the kitchen and the dining room, to the worn wooden staircase that led to the apartment upstairs. Taylor paused at the top of the landing, peering in the doorway of the bedroom on the right. "Is this *my* room?"

Annie nodded.

Twinkle lights crisscrossed the low ceiling where several layers of cheerful yellow fabric gathered before draping around the bed like a tent. All her daughter's stuffed animals were piled up around the pillows. Silver stars and sparkly ornaments hung from tiny hooks fastened into the material, twirling softly.

"Do you like it?" Annie asked nervously. It was a lot of

changes all at once: a new town, a new school, a new home. She'd dropped Taylor off at a friend's house earlier that day so she could meet the movers on the island alone. She'd spent most of the afternoon decorating Taylor's room so it would look cozy.

Taylor walked over to the bed, parting the fabric and peering inside. "I love it."

Annie let out a breath. "Do you want some hot chocolate? With marshmallows?"

Taylor nodded, crawling over the mattress and reaching for a large webbed circle with feathers hanging from it. "What's this?"

"It's a dream catcher," Annie explained. "It's supposed to catch bad dreams before they find you."

Taylor played with the blue feathers dangling from the strings. "Do you have one, too?"

"No." Annie shook her head.

The only dream she'd ever had was this—a home for her and Taylor. A place to call their own. A place where they could put down roots and get to know their neighbors.

A place where they could stay forever, if they wanted.

She didn't need a dream catcher to remind her she'd waited her entire life for this. And no matter how hard she had to work to keep it, no one was going to take it away from her.

WILL Dozier steered his rented SUV over the drawbridge connecting Maryland's Eastern Shore to Heron Island. Moonlight reflected off the narrow slice of water below, where a row of workboats bobbed in the marina. He could hear the muted clang of a halyard striking the mast of a sailboat. The night air smelled of salt marshes, oyster flats, and home.

He hadn't been back in over ten years, but he doubted much had changed. It was only nine o'clock and Main Street was already deserted. Cruising past the darkened windows of The Tackle Box—an island market that served as post office, bait shop, and liquor store—he scanned the rest of the shops to see if anything was open. He probably should have picked up dinner on the road, but all the restaurants had been packed.

He had a thing about crowds now.

And lights, especially fluorescent ones.

Locust and magnolia trees lined the cracked cement sidewalks, where a few homes were nestled between the bookstore, ice cream parlor, and the island's only clothing shop. Heron Island was a far cry from San Diego, where he'd been stationed for the past decade, and where he'd much rather be now than back home to settle his grandparents' affairs. But his agent had already found a buyer for the place. In three days, he'd be boarding a plane to California, and he'd never have to set foot on this island again.

He tapped the brakes when he spotted a light on downstairs in the last building on the right side of the street. A faded sign advertising cupcakes hung from the roof, and the pale blue siding gave way to a wide porch with café tables. He'd never understood the cupcake craze, but at least they were open. If they served dessert, they might serve something else, something that could pass for dinner.

He pulled over to the curb and cut the engine. Stepping out of the SUV, he caught the faint chattering of Canada geese out on the cove and paused, just for a moment, to listen. He'd forgotten how much he missed that sound.

Rubbing a hand over his eyes, he shut the door. He hadn't come back to get nostalgic. He didn't waste time thinking about the past, or wondering what would have happened if he hadn't chosen a certain path or made a different decision.

That was what he did at night, in his dreams, when he relived the mission that had stolen the lives of two of his teammates, including his best friend, and blasted the leg off one of the SEALs finest snipers.

Fighting back the images he couldn't seem to shake no matter how hard he tried, he walked up the path to the cupcake shop. Through the screen door, he saw a slim woman with long red hair surrounded by cardboard boxes and piles of crumpled newspaper. At the sound of his footsteps on the porch, she straightened, turning to face him, and cupcakes took on a whole new meaning.

Rich, fiery locks framed a striking female face with wide set green eyes and lips that were full and lush. A pair of close-fitting dark jeans and a stretchy black top hugged her curves and narrow waist. She was barefoot, and from what he could tell, all alone.

"May I help you?" she asked warily.

"I saw the light on. I thought you might still be serving." His gaze swept over the boxes and newspapers. "I didn't realize you were moving in."

"I won't be open for a few months."

I, not we. She was definitely alone. He nodded to the stack of boxes. "Do you need a hand?"

Her gaze flickered to the stairwell that led to the apartment upstairs. "No, thank you. I'm fine."

Hmm. Maybe she wasn't alone after all.

He checked her left hand for a ring.

Nope. No ring. No husband.

But someone was definitely up there.

"If you're hungry, you could try the market." She lifted a stack of plates from one of the boxes and set them on the counter. "I'm not sure when it closes."

"It closed a few hours ago."

"There's a grocery store in St. Michaels," she suggested. "It's only twenty minutes down the road."

"I try to avoid grocery stores."

She paused, watching him curiously. "Nobody likes grocery

stores, but we still have to go to them when we need food."

Will opened the door and stepped into the café. What he *needed* was to get laid.

ANNIE'S protective instincts kicked in as soon as the man stepped into the room. She positioned herself between him and the stairwell, her ear tuned for the sound of her daughter's footsteps. The last thing she needed was for Taylor to wake up on her first night in their new home and find a strange man downstairs, especially one who looked like he could have been a member of the SWAT team that stormed into her school three weeks ago.

The man was nearly a foot taller than her own five-foot-four frame. He wore a black hooded sweatshirt over a faded cotton shirt that revealed a broad chest and strong shoulders. Worn jeans hugged his narrow hips and covered a pair of long legs that were as big and muscular as his upper body. Thick brown hair framed a rugged, strong-boned face and a thin scar cut a jagged edge through the dark stubble lining his jaw.

It was an attractive face, the kind of face that under different circumstances she might have taken a moment to admire. But when his dark eyes shifted to the piece of paper taped up on the door, she swore under her breath.

She'd forgotten to take the menu down.

The man leaned closer, trying to make out the tiny print covered in red wine and butter stains. "Is that...French?"

"It's nothing," she said, hurrying across the room. Several years ago, during a New Year's Eve celebration at the restaurant where she'd been working in D.C., she'd been printing out menus for a special event the following day. After a second glass of champagne, she'd decided to create a menu for her own restaurant—her *dream* restaurant.

That night, she had vowed to make her dream a reality. She had carried the menu with her every day since then, and over the years, it had become a symbol of everything she'd been working toward. Tonight, after Taylor had fallen asleep, she'd taped it up on the front door to celebrate the first step of her dream coming true.

But no one else was supposed to see it.

She grabbed for the menu, but the man was faster. He peeled it off the door and gazed down at it, letting out a low whistle. "I don't remember any place like this when I used to live here."

Used to live here. That meant he was from here, and that made him a little less of a stranger, but still... "It's nothing," she repeated.

"It doesn't look like nothing." His dark gaze lifted, fastening on her. "I don't remember you, either. Did you grow up here?"

Annie pried the menu from his hand and folded it carefully, slipping it back into her pocket. "No."

The man took a step closer. His deep voice wrapped around her, drawing her toward him. "I think I would have remembered if you did."

Annie's gaze flickered up, into a pair of dark brown eyes the color of molasses. She felt suddenly dizzy, as if she'd just downed three cups of coffee.

"I don't suppose you'd be willing to offer a pre-opening plate to a weary traveler?" he asked.

She laid her hand on the doorknob, making it clear he shouldn't come any further. She knew what it was like to be weary from traveling, to be so hungry and exhausted that all you wanted to do was eat and crash. But that was another life, her *mother's* life, a life she had put far behind her. "I don't even know your name."

He offered his hand. "Will Dozier."

"Annie Malone." She slid her free hand through his. His

palm was broad and calloused and a shot of warmth pulsed up her arm as he gazed into her eyes. "I'm sorry," she said, easing her hand free. "I wish I could help you. But it's late and I still have a lot to do."

"Then have dinner with me tomorrow night."

Annie's brows shot up. She hadn't worked at one of the hottest restaurants on Pennsylvania Avenue for the past eight years without getting asked out on a fairly regular basis. But most of the men had *at least* waited until after she'd brought them their drinks. "I'm not going to go out with a man who can't even take himself to the grocery store."

Will smiled—a slow, lazy smile that warmed his eyes. It was the smile of a man used to getting what he wanted.

"Wait here," she said, turning and walking back to the kitchen before she could do something stupid, like say yes. She had a weakness for men with incredible smiles, but every hour of her life was accounted for over the next several months. Men didn't factor into the plans right now.

Pulling a packet of chicken tenders from the freezer and a can of cream of mushroom soup from the cupboard—a few essentials she'd stocked in case Taylor had been hungry tonight—she walked back out and handed them to him. "This is all I have to offer."

Will's smile deepened. "Now you have to let me take you out."

"Why?"

"To repay the favor."

"You're doing me a *favor*," she said, angling her head, "by leaving and letting me get back to work."

Will grinned, taking the food from her hands.

She opened the door wider, indicating it was time for him to go.

"Fair enough," he said, laughing. "But can I ask you one question?"

"*One* question."

"The menu I saw earlier—is that the kind of restaurant you're planning to open?"

"Yes."

"I haven't been home in a while, but I can't imagine a single local who can afford those prices."

"It's not for the locals."

"Who's it for?"

"The tourists."

Will glanced over his shoulder at the deserted street. "What tourists?"

"They're not here yet." Annie rolled her eyes. "They're coming with the resort."

Will's smile faded. "What resort?"

"The Morningstar Resort," she explained, "the one that's going to be built on the island."

The faintest sound of copper wind chimes drifted into the room as Will held her gaze. "Who told you this?"

"My realtor."

"Did he happen to mention where this resort would be built?"

Annie nodded. "There's an old inn at the end of the island sitting on fifty acres of undeveloped land. The owners passed away six months ago and apparently the guy who inherited the property is anxious to sell."

Will looked down at the can of soup, testing the weight of it in his palm. His expression had gone carefully neutral.

"It'll take time," Annie said. "But things are changing. And I'm going to be right here, ready to take advantage of it when they do."

Will lifted his eyes back to hers. They were even darker now, the color of bitter chocolate. He kept his expression blank, but she sensed a shift in him, something simmering just beneath the surface. "It was nice to meet you, Annie."

He tipped his head and turned, walking out the door and down the porch steps.

Annie stood in the doorway, watching him walk away. The sound of wind chimes floated toward her again, and she gazed up at the beams of the porch, searching for the source of the sound. But there were only a few hooks and some wire. She turned, walking back into the café as the scent of falling leaves swirled through the autumn air, carrying the promise of change.

WILL DROVE down the long flat road leading to the western tip of the island. He passed soybean fields, white pine forests, and marshes until the paved road turned to gravel and the yellow farmhouse rose up to greet him.

As if he hadn't been gone for the past ten years. As if nothing had changed.

His grandfather's Ford pickup truck was still parked in the same spot, the same rust stains crawling along the bumper, the radio probably still tuned to the same local country music station.

His grandmother's gardens still took up half the back yard, and the same hackberry tree, with its sagging branches almost touching the ground, still marked the beginning of the path leading down to the beach.

Will slowed the SUV to a stop beside his grandfather's truck and cut the headlights. He sat in the driver's seat with his hands resting on the steering wheel, gazing at the house that had been in his family for five generations.

This was only supposed to have been a weekend trip. He'd planned to go through the house one last time, grab a few things from his past, sign the contract, and pass the deed to the buyer. He'd planned to walk away after this weekend and never come back.

But could he sign this house, his family's history, over to a developer?

He stepped out of the SUV. His boots crunched over oyster shells as he walked slowly up to the porch, past those same five wicker rockers that had been there since he was a child. They used to sit there in the afternoons—his mom, his sister, his grandmother, his grandfather and him—waiting for guests to arrive.

He walked into the foyer of his old home and breathed in the musty air with a hint of Old Bay Seasoning. A thick layer of dust clung to every flat surface, and he would bet the raccoons and possums were having a field day under the porches.

Across the room, a layer of pollen coated a framed picture of him in his first t-ball uniform, which still sat on the mantel above the fireplace, right beside the picture of his little sister in a pink dress blowing bubbles in the grass. Something twisted deep inside him, and he turned away from the photographs.

What was the point in looking back, when you'd lost everything?

He bypassed the hall leading up to the stairs and walked into the big open kitchen. Moonlight streamed through the windows, illuminating the worn wooden counters and gas range stove. A chopping block that doubled as an island sat in the middle of the room. The same wooden stools were lined up around the counters.

He remembered how this room had always smelled of his grandmother's cooking: fresh baked bread, homemade vanilla ice cream, oyster fritters, and steamed crabs. It felt wrong to be here without her, without everyone. This house had always been filled with people. Laughing, chattering, happy people.

Now it just felt empty.

Setting the food on the counter, he crossed the dining area to the back porch that ran the length of the house. He opened the screen door, letting it slap shut behind him as he wandered outside, down the sloping lawn, past the tulip poplars and the abandoned swing that still hung from the thickest branch of the black walnut tree.

He walked out onto the dock, strolling to the edge of the pier.

He had some time. Not much, but enough. It wasn't going to be easy. The house needed a lot of work. But he could roll over a few weeks of leave that he hadn't taken from the previous year, in addition to the two weeks he was already taking. If he could restore the inn back to a state where it would at least pass inspection, he might be able to attract a regular buyer, one who wouldn't tear it down.

He ran his hand over a rotted piling.

He'd have to clear it with his CO, but his new boss had already suggested that he take some time off to "get his head straight" before rejoining the teams for a pre-deployment training in November.

His CO wasn't the only one who'd issued a subtle warning. Some of his fellow SEALs were starting to make comments. He wasn't himself anymore. He wasn't focusing.

Will knew they were only looking out for him. They didn't want to lose him. He knew better than anyone that there was no room on the teams for an operative, no matter how skilled, who couldn't focus.

He dipped his hands in his pockets, listening to the sound of the water lapping against the shoreline.

Maybe all he needed was a project to sink his teeth into. At some point, the nightmares would have to stop. And if they didn't?

He was sure there was nothing wrong with him that a few weeks with a beautiful redhead couldn't fix.

TWO

*A*nnie squeezed Taylor's hand as they walked the three blocks to the Heron Island Elementary School. The village was slowly waking up. Islanders were sweeping their front steps, clipping laundry to clotheslines, and taking their dogs for a morning walk. A man sitting on his porch reading the newspaper lifted his coffee cup in greeting.

Annie smiled and waved back. *Act normal. Act like everything's fine.*

The wind whipped at the Maryland flag flying outside the entrance to the school as they fell into step beside the other parents and children. Across the street, sailboats floated in Magnolia Harbor. Sunlight sparkled over the surface of the Bay and ospreys rode the salty breezes, their sharp cries piercing the air. They followed the bubbles of happy chatter into the brick building and made their way to the principal's office.

A woman with curly gray hair pushed back from her desk when they walked inside. "You must be Taylor!" Her hazel eyes crinkled up in a smile. "I'm Principal Needham. It's so nice to finally meet you."

"Hi," Taylor said softly, edging toward Annie and clutching her broom.

"Annie," Shelley Needham said, keeping her tone light and friendly as her gaze flickered down to Taylor's broom then back up to Annie's face. "It's nice to see you again."

"You too," Annie said. She knew Shelley wouldn't say anything about Taylor's broom. She'd warned her about it two weeks ago when they'd had their first face-to-face meeting to talk about Taylor's enrollment. Shelley had cleared it with Taylor's teacher, but it wasn't the teacher they were worried about. It was the other kids. The last thing either of them wanted was for Taylor to be made fun of on her first day back at school.

Annie had tried to convince Taylor not to bring it this morning, but she hadn't had any luck. She didn't have the heart to take it away from her. Not until she was ready.

"How are you feeling today, Taylor?" Shelley asked.

Taylor looked down at the carpet. "Okay."

"Would you like to see your new classroom?"

Taylor nodded, without looking up.

Shelley motioned for them to follow her and they walked back out into the crowded halls. Annie put her hand on Taylor's shoulder as they wove through the clusters of students to the second-grade classroom. She tried to focus on the student artwork, the bright colors and bubbly shapes decorating the halls, instead of the sudden tightening in her chest.

"Here we are," Shelley said, pausing beside an open door filled with kids chattering and hanging up their coats in cubbies.

Annie felt the air grow thick. They'd arrived too fast. She wasn't ready.

"Mommy?" Taylor whispered.

"What, sweetie?" Annie looked down, ready to pull her back down the hallway and run. "What is it?"

Taylor lifted her hand, the one Annie was holding. "You're hurting me."

"Oh," Annie said quickly, loosening her grip. "Sorry."

Shelley waved to a young woman with shoulder-length chestnut hair and brown eyes heading toward them. "Here comes your teacher, Taylor. This is Miss Haddaway."

Becca Haddaway smiled briefly at Annie as she knelt in front of Taylor. Annie watched the scene unfold, as if she wasn't really a part of it, as if none of it was really happening. She saw their mouths opening and knew words were coming out, but she couldn't hear them.

When Becca stood and held out her hand, Annie lifted hers to shake it before she realized the teacher was reaching for Taylor.

To take her into the classroom.

Shelley laid a comforting hand on Annie's shoulder. "You're doing fine," she murmured.

But the principal's words did little to soothe her. Cold needles of fear pricked at the backs of Annie's eyes as she slowly released Taylor's hand. She watched helplessly as Becca guided her daughter through the maze of desks and children to the cubbies. Taylor took off her backpack—her brand new purple backpack they'd bought last week.

Because her old one was covered in blood.

The blood of all the other students who'd died that day.

Annie reached for the wall, her fingers curling around a construction paper swan as Becca steered Taylor to an empty desk in the front of the room. A few of the students grew silent, staring at the new girl. Taylor didn't seem to notice as she listened to the teacher explain what was inside the desk and point out the various projects they'd been working on throughout the room.

When Taylor sat down, Becca helped her lean the broom against the plastic chair so it wouldn't fall, as if it was perfectly normal for a second-grader to bring a cleaning tool into school. Then she stood, raising her voice. "Good morning, everyone. Let's find our seats. It's time to get started."

"There's a chair in the back for you," Shelley said quietly. "You're welcome to stay as long as you want."

Annie walked on rubber legs toward the chair in the back of the room as the rest of the kids filed into their seats.

Taylor turned and looked at her.

Annie paused when their eyes met.

Taylor shook her head and twisted back around, looking up at her teacher.

Annie's knees almost gave out. *'Kids are resilient. They bounce back faster. The first day might be harder for you than it is for Taylor.'* The grief counselor's words floated back. *'Let Taylor return to normal as quickly as possible. Don't make it any harder for her than it needs to be.'*

Annie backed slowly out of the room to the hallway, lifting her hand in a half wave. But Taylor wasn't even looking at her. She rounded the edge of the door, leaning a shoulder against the wall and letting out a long breath.

Shelley closed the door to the classroom. The click echoed through the hallway as she turned to face Annie. Her eyes were filled with sympathy. "Why don't you come back to my office? I could make you a cup of coffee and we could sit and chat."

"No." Annie shook her head. "I...thank you. I'm fine. I think... I just need some air."

WILL DROVE INTO TOWN. He felt like a live wire, ragged and fraying around the edges, ready to snap. He hadn't slept. Again.

He was running on adrenaline now—every sense heightened, every thought twisted and fragmented.

It wouldn't be the first time. He recognized the feeling. He'd experienced it on enough overseas ops. It had fueled him through Hell Week ten years ago when he'd first joined the SEALs. One of the reasons the instructors pushed them so hard in BUD/S was to see if they could carry out a mission in an exhausted haze.

He knew how to function in this state.

It was all mental.

He just had to get control of his mind.

Marshes and soybean fields gave way to the playing fields of the Heron Island Elementary School. Faded orange soccer nets flanked the flat stretch of grass, and he slowed when he spotted a woman with long red hair sitting alone on the bleachers.

Wasn't that the woman he'd met last night?

What was she doing at the elementary school?

Unless...

Shit. Did she have a kid?

That would explain why she hadn't wanted him to come in last night, why she'd kept looking back toward the stairs leading up to the apartment. He tapped his fingers over the steering wheel. Kids complicated things. He didn't do complicated.

But he wanted to see her.

He'd thought of little else while he'd lain awake last night, staring at the ceiling.

Turning the wheel at the last minute, he steered the SUV into the parking lot. He pulled into a parking spot facing the playing fields and cut the engine. Screw it. He had six weeks to figure out how to un-complicate things.

He climbed out of the driver's seat and walked across the grass to where she sat. When she lifted her gaze, he expected her to say something sarcastic about the chicken tenders she'd given him last night. He wasn't prepared for the pale face and haunted eyes that stared back at him.

Whoa.

There was nothing uncomplicated about that. "Is everything all right?"

"I'm fine."

Her hands were wrapped around the bench on either side of her, curled into a death grip. "You don't look fine."

"Thanks."

"No," Will said, backpedaling. "I mean, you look like you could use someone to talk to."

"Actually, I'd really like to be alone right now."

Will paused a few yards away from her. He hadn't risen to the rank of Lieutenant Commander in the U.S. Navy without recognizing that most of the time, when one of his men said they wanted to be alone, what they really needed was someone to talk to. He wouldn't let one of his men off that easily, and he sure as hell wasn't leaving Annie alone in the middle of a panic attack. Not until she told him what was wrong.

"Look," she said after several moments of silence when he made no move to leave. "I just dropped my daughter off for her first day at a new school, and I'm worried about her. I want to stay close by in case she needs me."

"How old is your daughter?"

"She's eight."

Eight? Will's gaze combed over Annie's face. She didn't look old enough to have an eight-year-old daughter. He'd pinned her as twenty-six, twenty-seven at the most. She must have been pretty young when she'd gotten pregnant.

He took a moment to study her. She was wearing a stretchy black top and dark jeans again. She wore her hair long and loose, spilling in red waves over her shoulders. The wind whipped a touch of color back into her cheeks, but her eyes still held a hint of fear.

What was she afraid of?

"You're not wearing a ring," Will said, "so I'm guessing the father's not part of the picture."

"No." Annie brushed her hair out of her eyes. "He's not part of the picture."

Will wondered if he'd ever been part of the picture. Or if he could have something to do with what she was afraid of. "If your daughter's eight, shouldn't you be used to leaving her at school by now?"

"It's a new school. She doesn't know anyone here."

Still, he thought. She seemed pretty shaken up for someone who was just dropping her kid off at school. "What grade is your daughter in?"

"Second."

"Who's her teacher?"

"Becca Haddaway."

Becca? No kidding? "I didn't know Becca was a teacher."

"I thought you said you grew up here?"

"I did." Will rocked back on his heels. "I haven't been back in a while."

Annie glanced back up at him, shading her eyes from the sun. "How long is a while?"

"Listen," Will said, changing the subject, "you look like you could use something to eat, and I bet your daughter doesn't want you hanging around when she comes out for recess. Let me take you to breakfast."

Annie shook her head. "I need to stay here."

"For how long?"

"Until I'm ready."

"You can't say no to a fried egg sandwich from The Tackle Box. I'll even throw in a bottle of orange juice." He smiled down at her, trying to put her at ease. "We can call it a date."

"I told you last night. I'm not dating you."

"Why not?" Will feigned a hurt expression. "Don't I look dateable?"

"Yes," she said. "You look perfectly dateable. For someone else."

"But not you?"

"No. Not me."

"Why not?"

Annie's gaze drifted to the brightly colored playground and row of swings near the school. "Because I don't date."

Will walked to the bleachers, lowering himself to the bench beside her. "Ever?"

"That's right."

"That seems close-minded."

"It's not close-minded. It's just easier."

Will's eyes widened in mock horror. "What's easy about not dating?"

"Well, for starters," she answered, "not having to explain to my daughter where I'm going and who I'm going with."

"Your daughter's busy with school right now, so you don't have to explain anything."

"But I'd have to tell her later. We don't keep secrets from each other."

Will studied her for several moments. "You tell your daughter everything?"

"Yes."

"Everything?"

"Yes."

Will leaned in and brushed his lips over hers. Before she could react, before she could do anything, he eased back and winked. "Let me know what she has to say about that."

～

ANNIE SHOT TO HER FEET. She didn't know what shocked her more, the fact that he'd kissed her, or how badly she'd wanted to kiss him back. Warmth flooded her system and something stirred deep inside her—something dark, desperate, and needy.

She didn't want to feel needy. She didn't want to feel weak. "Don't do that again."

"What?" Will leaned back, stretching his legs out and crossing his feet at the ankles. He was wearing the same hooded sweatshirt from the night before, with faded jeans and work boots. There was a gleam in his eye, like he'd just won a prize at a carnival. "Kiss you?"

She looked quickly over at the school. What if one of the children had seen them? What if Taylor had seen them? "Yes."

"Why?"

Because... Annie resisted the urge to reach up and touch her lips, where the taste of him still lingered. It had been far too long since she'd had a man's mouth on hers, and the sensation had left her feeling rattled. She couldn't afford to feel rattled right now. She was barely keeping it together as it was.

Besides, she had Taylor to think about. She knew what it was like to have a mother who paraded a different man into her life every few months. It was confusing and unsettling, and Taylor had enough to worry about right now.

Maybe once things settled down on the island. Once the restaurant was open and Taylor wasn't afraid of school anymore. Once they'd made a few friends of their own. Then, *maybe* she would think about dating.

But not now. Not yet.

Will rose and Annie took a step back, putting a safe distance between them. The expression on his face was so smug, she wanted to throw something at him. But then three things clicked into place. He'd said he was from the island. He hadn't been back in a while. And he didn't know Becca was a teacher.

During one of their first meetings, Shelley had told Annie that Becca had been working at the school for over five years, to reassure her that they could handle Taylor's situation.

Which meant...Will hadn't been home in five years.

Maybe even longer.

"Will," she began uneasily, "does your family still live here?"

He shook his head.

"Are you home visiting friends?"

"Not exactly."

"Then, what are you doing here?"

"Fixing up a home to sell."

"Which home?" she asked, already knowing the answer.

He pointed to the road leading west, where there was nothing but fifty acres of undeveloped land—the land where the resort was supposed to be built. "It's down that way."

"There's only one home down that road."

Will smiled.

"But last night, when I told you about the resort, you acted like you didn't know about it."

"I didn't."

Annie heard a faint whistling in the wind, like the sound of all her hopes and dreams on a train about to derail. "The sale's still going to happen, isn't it?"

He shook his head.

Annie stood, rooted to the ground, as Will turned, striding back to the parking lot.

"I hope you have a backup plan for that fancy restaurant of yours," he called back over his shoulder. "Because there's no way in hell I'm letting a developer tear down my grandparents' inn."

THREE

*W*ill drove down Main Street, thinking about the expression on Annie's face after he'd kissed her. For a woman as attractive as she was, he was surprised she didn't date. Even single mothers deserved to have some fun now and then.

He'd enjoy helping her get back in the game.

The traffic lights of the drawbridge blinked red as a tall sailboat navigated down the narrow curve of water. It was too bad the fate of her restaurant was tied to his plans for his grandparents' inn, but the way he figured it, he'd just saved her a lot of time and money by telling her the truth.

He might have to work a little harder to convince her to go out with him now, but there was nothing he loved more than a good challenge.

He turned into the parking lot of The Tackle Box as the heavy jaws of the drawbridge creaked open to let the sailboat pass. He rolled up beside a beat-up silver Chevy with Ravens decals and a bumper sticker that read, *"There's no life west of the Chesapeake Bay."* Two labs were in the back, wagging their tails.

Will grinned as a man with dark blond hair stepped out of the market. There were a few people he wished he'd done a better job of keeping in touch with. Ryan Callahan, his best friend from childhood, was one of them.

Ryan took one look at him and his face broke into a matching grin. He set down the two bags of ice he was carrying as Will stepped out of the SUV and walked toward him.

Ryan held out his hand. "It's good to see you, man."

"You too."

"How long are you here for?"

"Just long enough to get the inn fixed up and ready to sell."

Ryan released Will's hand and picked up the bags of ice again. "I heard you were thinking of selling." He walked to the back of his truck, setting the ice in a cooler. "You have any offers yet?"

"Only one, but it didn't work out."

The dogs barked, their nails scraping against the metal bed of the truck until Ryan lowered the hatch so they could jump out. They raced toward Will, barking and batting their tails back and forth. Will reached down, wrangling a wet stick from the chocolate lab's mouth.

The parking lot dipped into a marina filled with workboats and a boat ramp that led down to the water. He tossed the stick toward the water and the dogs took off after it. The yellow lab was faster and she reached it first, carrying it back and dropping it at his feet. He picked it up and threw it again, further this time so it landed in the water.

The dogs chased after it, splashing into the Bay to retrieve it.

"Why don't you jump in and give them a run for their money?" Ryan said, leaning back against the truck. "They teach you guys how to doggie paddle in SEAL training, right?"

Will laughed as the dogs swam back to the shore, climbing up the rocks and bounding over the pavement toward them. "Something like that."

The stick landed at his feet and the dogs circled him, barking for him to throw it. He picked it up again, tossing it back into the water.

He could do this all day.

A red-tailed hawk soared over the bridge, stretching its wings toward the sun. The bells of the drawbridge rang as it slowly lowered back into place. He glanced over his shoulder, noticing the cages stacked up in the bed of Ryan's truck for the first time. "What's all that?"

"Oyster restoration project," Ryan explained. "I'm working with the Department of Natural Resources to reestablish the species in the Bay."

Will snagged the stick from the chocolate lab's mouth when she brought it back. "I thought you were working at the lab in Baltimore?"

"I was." Ryan reached into the bed of the truck, adjusting one of the cages. "But I was bored out of my mind. I finally realized I wasn't going to save the Bay by testing water samples. I was going to save the Bay by talking to people and living near the ones who are still working the waters."

He dug in the back pocket of his bleach-stained khakis and pulled out a business card. "I moved home a few months ago and started a nonprofit on the island. I do more outreach and project work now." He handed Will the card. "But I get to keep the scientist title."

Will glanced down at the card, surprised. His friend had a Ph.D. in Marine Biology from Woods Hole Oceanographic Institute, one of the best programs in the country, and he'd moved home to live and work on the island.

"Listen," Ryan said, whistling for the dogs. "I've got to run, but I'll fill you in on the rest later." The dogs scrambled up from the water, racing over the pavement and leaping into the bed of the truck.

Will walked over to them, scratching the yellow lab behind the ears. He hadn't realized how much he missed these dogs. He wondered if Ryan would be willing to leave one with him for a few weeks. He'd like to have a dog around while he was working on the house.

Then again, it was probably safer not to get too attached. He had a tendency to get attached to dogs, and people for that matter, when he spent too much time with them. It was better to stay detached, to keep things light and simple.

That way, he didn't have to risk losing someone again.

Ryan closed the hatch and walked over to the driver's side. "Come by Rusty's tonight. We'll grab a beer, play some pool. It'll be like old times."

Will picked a wet leaf off the dog's dripping fur. He should have known he wouldn't make it through the day without someone asking him to meet up at the island bar. But it was Friday and Rusty's would be packed tonight. If he went, he'd run into everyone.

He wasn't sure he was ready for that yet.

The dogs shook, spraying him with water, and he dropped the leaf on the ground. He hadn't really thought about his decision to stay on the island for the next several weeks. Once everyone heard he was back, people would want to ask him questions. They'd want to know why he hadn't come home in so long, why he hadn't at least come back for his grandparents' funeral six months ago.

The answer to the last question was relatively simple. He'd been overseas.

But where he'd been, and what had happened in the mountains of Afghanistan while his grandparents had been laid to rest thousands of miles away, was another story. He couldn't have the nightmares creeping in while he was standing in a crowded bar, surrounded by dozens of islanders.

"Come by around five," Ryan said, climbing into his truck.

Will nodded, unable to come up with a viable excuse as to why he'd rather be back in BUD/S doing flutter kicks with his head in the surf than face all his old friends and neighbors tonight at Rusty's. He gave each dog one last pat on the head before Ryan backed away.

A white Mercedes turned into the lot, sliding into the empty parking space Ryan left behind. Will took one look at the driver and bit back the urge to haul Spencer Townsend out by his crisp, white button-down shirt and shove him head first into the water.

Spencer was the same age as Will and Ryan, but they'd never been friends. His father owned the local bank and had almost put Will's grandparents out of business twice by threatening foreclosure when they'd missed a few payments during the winter lulls.

The only reason Will had even considered hiring Spencer as his real estate agent was because he knew he'd work his ass off for the commission. If there was one thing that motivated the Townsend men, it was money. And before coming back to the island, the only thing Will had cared about was selling the inn as fast as possible.

Spencer flashed him a bright-white smile as he stepped out of the car. His light brown hair was slicked back and his hazel eyes were covered in a pair of aviator glasses. His white shirt was tucked into a pair of tailored khakis, and he wore loafers with no socks. He looked like he'd stepped out of a yachting magazine.

"Will!" he said, striding forward like they were best friends. "Long time no see. How are you?"

Will folded his arms over his chest. "It's not happening."

Spencer stopped in his tracks. "What?"

"The sale."

Spencer's smile faded as he pulled off his sunglasses. "What are you talking about? Why not?"

"You said the buyer was an experienced inn owner. I assumed you meant a person, or a husband and wife team, *not* a developer."

"What difference does it make?" Spencer asked, confused. "You said yourself you didn't want the place."

"It matters when they want to tear it down."

"Don't be ridiculous." Spencer waved him off. "This development will be huge for the island. Think of the jobs it'll create."

"It's not happening," Will repeated. He was done with this conversation. He turned, striding into the market.

Spencer trailed after him. "I guess that's not your problem, is it? You haven't been back in over ten years. You don't really care about anyone on Heron Island."

"You don't give a damn about jobs either," Will growled as he spun around. "You want this sale for the commission."

Spencer took a step back, knocking into a rack of salt-and-vinegar potato chips. "Look," he said, bending down to pick them up off the floor. "You asked me to help you with this and I found you a buyer—"

"Find me another one."

Spencer looked up. "You can't be serious."

"I'm dead serious."

Spencer stuffed the bags of chips back onto the rack. "You can't walk away from this offer, Will."

"I just did." Will turned, following the scent of fried eggs and bacon to the grill in the back. "If you still want the commission from this sale, find me another buyer."

"You don't know what it's like out there," Spencer called after him, raising his voice. "The housing market is dead. This might be the only offer you'll get—"

"Find me a family who wants to run it as is, someone who'll maintain the integrity of the place."

"Screw integrity," Spencer bit back. "No one else is going to offer you that kind of price. Think about the money, Will."

Will turned, looking back at him. "It was never about the money."

ANNIE GNAWED ON HER FINGERNAIL, glancing up at the clock. The contractor was supposed to be here over an hour ago. She had a million errands to run, but she didn't want to leave and miss him if he stopped by. He'd agreed to squeeze her in today, and she needed his estimate so she could start planning the renovations.

She wasn't sure how many changes she could afford to make before opening, and after the bomb Will had dropped about his grandparents' inn that morning, she feared it would be a lot less than she'd originally planned.

Breaking down an empty cardboard box, she added it to the growing stack in the kitchen. The way she saw it, she had two options: continue opening her restaurant as planned and have faith that everything would work out in time, or agree to go out with Will and try to seduce him into selling the inn.

But did she even know how to seduce a man anymore? She knew how to flirt, how to turn on the charm when she was waitressing to maximize her tips. But she hadn't had much of a love life since Taylor was born.

Apparently, she was so out of practice, she'd forgotten how to react when a man kissed her.

She groaned and walked over to the sink, fishing a wet rag out of the suds. She still couldn't believe she'd just sat there when

Will had kissed her that morning. She went to work scrubbing the grease spots off the walls over the stove.

The kiss had only lasted a second, but it was long enough to learn that his lips were the perfect combination of soft and firm, that when he was that close his skin smelled like the ocean and sunlight, and the rest of him...

Good God.

What would it have felt like to lean in and run her hands all over those hard muscles?

At the knock on the door, she stepped back from the sink. *Get a hold of yourself!*

The last thing she needed was to start fantasizing about the man who had the power to destroy all her hopes and dreams.

She dropped the rag in the sink and walked out of the kitchen, pausing when she spotted the woman peering in the glass with both hands cupped around her eyes. The contractor hadn't said anything about sending someone else in his place, but maybe he'd gotten hung up on another job.

The woman straightened and waved.

Annie crossed the dining room and opened the door.

"Hi," the woman said, holding out her hand. "I'm Grace Callahan. You must be Annie."

Annie nodded, taking in the woman's wide gray eyes and long blond hair tied back in a ponytail. She was dressed in running clothes and looked to be about her age. "Did the contractor send you?"

"The contractor?" Grace walked into the dining room, looking around at the bare walls and boxes stacked up on the floor. "No. I heard someone bought this place and I wanted to get a look at you before the gossip mill churned out its own muddled version later tonight."

"The gossip mill?"

"You'll get used to it." Grace flashed her a smile and strolled over to the empty display case, running a hand over the dusty glass. "There aren't any secrets on Heron Island. People here know everything about everybody." She looked back at Annie. "We make it our business to know."

"I see," Annie said warily. She realized people were naturally curious. She *wanted* Taylor to grow up in a town where neighbors dropped by unannounced, where people cared enough to ask questions. But she didn't like the idea of them gossiping about her later tonight, when she wasn't there to defend herself. And she especially didn't like the idea of them gossiping about Taylor.

Grace leaned against the counter, sizing her up from across the room. "I heard you moved here from D.C."

"That's right."

"Did you work downtown? You look vaguely familiar."

"I used to work at a restaurant on Pennsylvania Avenue, a few blocks from the Capitol."

"Which one?"

"Citron Bleu."

Grace nodded. "That's where I've seen you before."

"You've been there?" Annie asked, surprised.

"I've been there tons of times."

Annie's eyebrows shot up. Citron Bleu wasn't the kind of restaurant you went to unless you were made of money or had serious connections to the top players in Washington politics. She hadn't expected to meet someone on Heron Island who frequented her old restaurant.

She looked closer at the woman's running clothes—a threadbare T-shirt over nylon shorts and a pair of beat-up sneakers. The outfit didn't exactly scream money. "Do you work in D.C.?"

"I'm a reporter for *The Washington Tribune.*"

Annie's whole body tensed as Grace pushed off the counter and walked over to the stack of boxes along the far wall.

"My father and brother live on the island so I come home a

lot on the weekends," Grace said, picking up a picture lying on top of one of the boxes.

It was a wallet-sized picture of Taylor, taken about a year ago. The name of her school and her grade were printed on the back.

"Is this your daughter?" Grace asked.

"Yes," Annie said tightly.

Grace turned it over, her eyes going wide as she read the words on the back. "She went to Mount Pleasant?"

A reporter from D.C.'s largest newspaper wouldn't have any trouble recognizing that name. Taylor's school had made national news three weeks ago when a shooter had walked into the building and killed seventeen second-graders before turning his semi-automatic weapon on himself.

He'd murdered an entire class of children—all except for the one who'd been hiding in the broom closet.

Taylor.

"We're not doing an interview," Annie said coldly, striding across the room and taking the picture back.

Grace blinked. "What?"

"An interview," Annie repeated, tucking the picture into her back pocket. "We're not doing one."

"That's not why I'm here."

Annie turned away. She grabbed the nearest box, ripped the tape off and started pulling out dishes.

In the days following the shooting, every major newspaper and TV news network had called for an interview. They'd told her how sorry they were, that they couldn't imagine what she and Taylor were going through, but they needed a firsthand account from the sole survivor. They needed a statement from Annie.

Some had even had the nerve to show up at the restaurant, at her *workplace*, hoping for a comment.

It was one of the reasons she'd wanted to get out of there. She didn't want Taylor's childhood to be defined by what had happened at Mount Pleasant. She wanted a fresh start, for both of them. "We came here to get away from that."

"I don't blame you," Grace said quietly.

When Annie looked up and saw the compassion in Grace's eyes, she took a deep breath and set the dishes down.

"Listen," Grace said. "If you're not doing anything later, you should come to Rusty's. My brother and a bunch of our friends will be there. I'd be happy to introduce you around."

"Isn't that the bar at the end of Pier Street?" Annie asked.

Grace nodded. "The sign on the door says Rusty Rudder but everybody around here calls it Rusty's."

"I'm not sure I should bring my daughter to a bar."

"It's not like the bars you're used to in D.C. It's a family place. Lots of kids will be there. Your contractor will be there. In fact," she said, glancing down at her watch, "he's probably there now."

Annie turned slowly to face her. "Now?"

Grace nodded. "If you come in tonight, find me first. I want to watch you give him hell for standing you up."

The wind gusted through the streets, sending a flurry of leaves into a spin. "How do you know he's standing me up?"

"Jimmy Faulkner's damn good at what he does, but he never makes it to an appointment unless you drag his ass off the bar stool."

"You're kidding."

"Don't worry." Grace's sneakers squeaked over the tiles as she walked to the door. "You'll get the hang of how things work around here, but don't expect anything to operate on D.C. time." She laid her hand on the doorknob, glancing back at Annie. "When were you thinking of opening?"

"December."

"I'd plan for February or March, to be safe. You should

expect to open at least two to three months after the date he gives you."

Two to three months? She didn't have enough savings to survive with no income until March. She was barely going to make it to December.

Grace opened the door and a cold wind swirled into the room, carrying the salty scent of the Bay.

Annie walked out onto the porch after her. "You're sure Jimmy's at Rusty's?"

"I'd say it's a pretty safe bet."

Annie slammed the door behind them. "I think I'll go have a *chat* with him now."

ANNIE MARCHED INTO RUSTY'S, her gaze landing on the five men sitting on swivel stools at the wooden bar. "Which one is he?" she asked Grace, who'd insisted on tagging along.

"Second from the right," Grace said.

Annie's eyes locked on a man in a blue flannel shirt and ripped jeans. He wore a faded ball cap and his dark brown hair was shot with gray. He was probably in his mid-forties.

"Jimmy Faulkner," she called, raising her voice over the baseball game blasting from the flat screen TV behind the bar.

Jimmy turned, a lazy smile on his tanned weathered face.

Annie crossed her arms over her chest. "Did you forget something?"

He looked her up and down, raising a brow in appreciation. "Honey, whatever it is I forgot, let me make it up to you." He shoved playfully at the man on the stool beside him. "Move it, Robbie. The lady wants to sit down."

"I do *not* want to sit down." Annie walked toward him. "I

want to know why you never made it to our appointment this afternoon."

Jimmy took a pull from his Budweiser bottle. "So you're the one who bought the Peasleys' place."

"I am." Annie's blood boiled when she saw that his eyes were red-rimmed and bloodshot. "You were supposed to meet me there over an hour ago."

Jimmy tapped his fingers on the bar. "Dave," he said, his deep voice calling for the bartender. "How about a drink for our lady friend?" He swiveled back to face Annie. "What are you having?"

"I'm not *having* anything until you give me an estimate for my renovations."

Jimmy smiled and hooked his work boot under an empty bar stool, dragging it over so it was right beside his. "Why don't you hop on up here and tell me what you want done and I'll give you a number."

Grace walked up beside her, and Annie caught the angry look in the other woman's eyes as Grace opened her mouth to tell Jimmy exactly *where* he could put that stool.

Annie put her hand on Grace's arm, silencing her. *I'll handle this.*

"You know what," Annie said, smiling sweetly at Jimmy, "I think I will take that drink." She glanced up at the bartender. "I'll have a gin and tonic, with lots of ice."

"Coming right up," Dave said, glancing over at Grace. "You having anything?"

"I'm not sure yet," Grace said, looking back and forth between Annie and Jimmy.

Jimmy patted the bar stool beside him for Annie. "Listen, honey, I've done all the work at your place for the last three owners. I know that building as well as the back of my hand."

"Well, why didn't you say so?" Annie slid onto the stool,

edging close enough so their shoulders were touching and she could smell the beer on his breath. She lowered her voice. "I hear you're pretty good at what you do."

He took another pull from his bottle. "I am."

She reached across him to retrieve her drink from the bar and her breasts brushed lightly against his arm. When she leaned back, she caught the shift in his eyes. He was focused on her now, extremely focused. "I hear your crew is the best on the island."

"That's right."

She stirred her drink slowly, drawing his eyes down to the neckline of her shirt. "I don't want to waste my time with a crew who can't get it right the first time."

He swallowed, and she watched the Adam's apple bob up and down in his throat.

"But I've also heard that your crew can be slow." She lowered her lips to the straw, looking up at him through her lashes. "That they don't finish when you say they're going to."

"Slow means quality."

"I'm just wondering," she said, sucking a sip of gin and tonic through the straw and holding his gaze, "how slow are we talking about?"

He tipped the brim of his John Deer cap back, wiping at the sweat forming on his brow. "I've got a crew of guys at a house in Sherwood and another working on a renovation project in St. Michaels. As soon as they're done, you're next."

Annie fished a piece of ice out of the glass and rolled it around on her tongue. "When do you think they might be done?"

"December." Jimmy's voice was strained. "January, at the latest."

Annie's eyes widened innocently. "But when we spoke on the phone last week, you said you would be finished at *my* place by December."

"That might have been a tad optimistic."

"Oh." She looked away, running her tongue lightly over her bottom lip. When she heard his breath catch, she glanced back at him. "What are the chances of fitting me in sooner?"

"I'm not sure I can do that."

"No?"

He shook his head.

"That's too bad," she said, standing. Tipping her glass over, she poured the ice cold drink into his lap. "I was really looking forward to getting to know you better."

"Jesus Christ!" Jimmy scrambled off the stool, knocking over the one she'd been sitting on and stumbling over it.

The men at the bar howled with laughter as he cupped his hands over the front of his jeans and stared at the wet stain seeping into the denim.

"Fit me in sooner," Annie snapped, turning on her heels and stalking to the door. "And don't call me *honey* ever again."

FOUR

*A*nnie pushed out the door, inhaling a deep breath of fresh air. Her stomach roiled from the stench of cheap beer on Jimmy's breath. It reminded her too much of New Orleans and the run-down apartment where she and her mother had lived above a seedy bar on Bourbon Street when she was a teenager.

Those two years had been the worst years of her life. Her mother's drinking, which had always been a problem, had gotten completely out of control. All the money Annie had earned waiting tables had gone into supplementing their rent. Because, once again, her mother's muse had deserted her.

God forbid she ever got a real job to pay the bills.

It was much easier to rely on her resourceful daughter to find a way to make ends meet.

"Wait," Grace trailed after her, laughing. "Annie, come back."

"I need to start searching for a new contractor," Annie said, striding across the parking lot. "Immediately."

Grace caught up with her. "Jimmy will come around as soon

as his pants dry. Come on, let me buy you another drink. Everyone inside is dying to meet you now."

Annie shook her head. Jimmy Faulkner had deserved getting a drink poured in his lap, but she knew now that her chances of getting him to start on her renovations before the end of the year were close to zero.

She couldn't make it to next spring without opening the restaurant. She'd expected to be limping along for the first several months. She'd known things wouldn't really pick up until the resort opened on the island. But at least she would have been moving forward, making progress, building a name for herself in the area.

What if the resort never came? What if Will wouldn't change his mind about selling to the developer? What was she going to do?

"Annie." Grace put her hand on her arm, stopping her. "Is everything okay?"

Annie's phone buzzed and she reached into her pocket. "I need to get this. It might be my daughter's school."

She checked the number. It wasn't the school, but it was a local number that looked familiar. She lifted the phone to her ear. "Hello?"

"Annie," a deep male voice came through the line. "It's Chase Townsend from Choptank Bank and Trust."

The banker who'd issued her mortgage and business loan was calling her on her cell? This was not good. Annie walked a few yards away, signaling to Grace that she'd be back in a minute. "Is everything all right?"

"There's been a complication with the sale of the inn."

Annie's gaze fell to a trail of crushed oyster shells. "What kind of complication?"

"As you know, I took a gamble on your loan because my son was closing a deal with Morningstar to build a resort on this island. Your restaurant seemed like a good investment at the time. But we're not sure that sale is going to happen anymore. This is a small bank, Annie. We don't take many risks, especially in this market. I made an exception in your case, but after re-reviewing your finances today, I'm concerned."

Annie twisted the toe of her boot into the oyster shells. "I'm still going to make the payments."

"How?"

"I have a plan."

"Would you mind sharing it with me?"

"I'm still working out the details."

"Come by the bank on Monday. I'll review your new proposal and decide if we can still issue the loan."

The line went dead and Annie lowered the phone.

She heard Grace's footsteps coming closer.

"Is everything okay?" Grace asked again.

Annie looked up at her. "I think I could use that drink now."

"A RESORT?" Grace gaped at her. "On Heron Island?"

Annie nodded. They'd gotten a table outside on the deck, overlooking the water. Workboats bobbed in the slips in Magnolia Harbor. The gravelly voices of a dozen watermen sorting through the day's catch rose over the Bay. "I'm surprised Spencer didn't say anything. I figured everyone knew."

"Spencer!" Grace seethed. "That little weasel. I should have known he was behind this." She dug in her pocket for her cell phone. "We definitely did *not* know." She searched through her contacts, pressing a button before lifting the phone to her ear. "If we'd known, we would have been fighting to stop it."

"You don't want a resort here?"

"No," Grace said emphatically.

"But what about the jobs it would create?" Annie asked. "The tourists it would bring to the island?"

"That would only be the *beginning*," Grace said. "Within a few years, they'd be planning an eighteen hole golf course and a gated community that would cut the land off from the people who grew up here."

Annie twisted the stem of her wine glass. "That seems extreme."

"I've seen it happen before." Pulling the phone away from her ear, Grace cursed as she hung up. "He's not answering."

"Who?"

"Spencer!" Grace tossed the phone onto the table, narrowing her eyes. "I'm going to kill him."

"But you live in the city," Annie protested. "You know what it's like to want to get away, to escape to a place like this on the weekends."

"A place like *this*!" Grace swept her arm out, emphasizing the casual picnic table seating and salt-weathered siding of Rusty's, the marina filled with workboats and undeveloped marshlands beyond. "Heron Island is one of the last places on the Eastern Shore that still *feels* like the Shore. A resort would completely change that."

"What would change besides having a few more people here?" Annie asked. "A few more restaurants and shops on Main Street to cater to them?"

"Nothing, at first," Grace admitted. "But over the years, the businesses that moved in would cater *solely* to the tourists. The rents on Main Street would skyrocket and the current businesses would be forced out by chic restaurants, upscale decorating shops, and designer clothing stores—places no local could afford."

Annie looked out at the water, watching a blue heron stalk out of the marshes. She'd moved here to open a fine dining restaurant, but she had no intention of putting anyone else out of business. Yes, she had planned to cater more to the tourists, but she'd hoped to provide a place for the islanders to come on special occasions—anniversaries, birthdays, graduations.

When she'd first contacted Spencer about the building on Main Street and he'd told her about the resort, she'd researched the local area and found that the closest fine dining restaurant was twenty miles away from Heron Island.

She'd seen a need in the market, and she'd decided to fill it.

Across the table, Grace shook her head in disbelief. "I can't believe I didn't know about this."

Annie picked up her glass, taking a sip of her white wine. "If it makes you feel any better, it might not even happen now."

"It better not." Grace looked out at the water. "I can't believe Will even *considered* selling his grandparents' land to a developer."

"He didn't." Annie set down her wine. "He didn't even know about it until last night."

"Wait...what?" Grace's head swiveled back to face her. "You've *talked* to him?"

Annie nodded.

"Will's *here?*" Grace's mouth fell open. "On the island?"

"Yes."

Grace grabbed her phone, punching in a new number. She lifted it back to her ear, and the person on the other end answered immediately. "Hey...yeah, I just heard. Did he tell you he was coming home? No, me neither. He's having drinks with us tonight? What? You want me to be *nice?* It's been *ten* years, Ryan!" She shook her head at the voice on the other end of the line. "Yeah, sure...whatever. I'll see you at five."

Annie watched as Grace hung up the call and dropped the phone back on the table. "Were you and Will...friends?"

"Yeah," Grace said bitterly. "You could say that." She shook her head as the blue heron squawked and spread its long wings, lifting into a low glide over the surface. "We used to be *best* friends."

"Did something happen before he left?"

Grace picked up her beer, taking a long sip. "What *happened* is that he left, and never looked back."

ANNIE AND TAYLOR sat on Taylor's bed after school, surrounded by construction paper, colored yarn, and a box of trinkets they'd collected on their walks in D.C. over the years: feathers, beads, glossy rocks, jingle bells that had fallen off the floats during the Christmas parade, green glass bottles that had washed ashore along the Potomac, and—Taylor's favorite—shiny pink ribbons that had been left on the fences after the Cherry Blossom Festival.

"Look." Taylor held up a strand of yarn decorated with blue jay feathers and sparkling red beads.

Annie forced a smile, taking the strand of yarn and standing on the bed in her socks. If what Grace had told her that afternoon was true, that Chase Townsend wouldn't think twice about backing out on her loan if it wasn't a sound investment, then she needed to come up with a new plan fast.

She looped it around a hook and sat back down, watching Taylor pull out another spool of yarn from the box. "You still haven't told me how the rest of your day at school went."

Taylor dug through the rest of the trinkets, pulling out a charm bracelet someone had left on the floor of the S2 bus that ran down 16th Street. "I like my teacher. She's nice."

Annie threaded a piece of string through a yellow construction paper gingko leaf. "How about the other kids in your class? How were they?"

Taylor looped the yarn through the links of the bracelet and the charms jangled as she held it up, like a tiny wind chime. "They called me Cinderella."

Annie's heart sank. *Because of the broom.* "Did you tell Miss Haddaway?"

Taylor looked down, fiddling with the strings on the charm. "She overheard and made them apologize. She said I was supposed to tell her if they did it again."

"Good," Annie said. "I want you to tell me, too."

Taylor nodded and Annie added a silver bell to the end of the string. The quiet tinkling brought her back to the day, over a month ago, when she'd first seen the ad for this property online. It was the day after the shooting, and Taylor hadn't spoken a word since it happened. She'd been curled up on the sofa in their tiny D.C. apartment with this same box in her lap, picking out the bells and making a pile on the cushion beside her.

All Annie had been able to think about in the days following the shooting was getting Taylor out of D.C. and taking her somewhere safe and far away from that school and those memories. When she'd made the initial offer on the building on Heron Island, her co-workers had sat her down and told her she was overreacting. They'd told her to give it time.

But she'd already made up her mind.

Between the small amount she'd put away from each paycheck, and selling off the rest of her mother's paintings after she'd passed away last year, Annie had had just enough for the down payment. But she didn't have anything to fall back on now. Every future payment was going to have to come from income that she earned.

Annie ran her fingers over the ginkgo leaves in her lap. Chase Townsend had made it perfectly clear on the phone earlier that the bank had made a gamble based on the assumption that Will would sell his grandparents' property to the resort company and tourism would pick up on the island. If that wasn't going to happen, neither was Annie's dream restaurant.

"Taylor," she said slowly. "I've been thinking..."

Taylor glanced up.

Annie took a deep breath. "I've been thinking that maybe we should open a café instead of a French restaurant."

"Why?"

"Well," Annie said, reaching into the box for a piece of purple ribbon, "if we opened a café, I'd be free at night. We'd be able to hang out together."

Taylor's eyes lit up. "Cafés are only open during the day?"

"This one would be," Annie said. "We could keep the downstairs basically as it is now. We'd have to find some fun things to decorate the walls and maybe pick up a few more tables and chairs, but we wouldn't have to live through months of messy renovations."

"Can we keep the walls pink?" Taylor asked.

Annie sat back, surprised. "You want to keep the walls pink?"

Taylor nodded.

Annie wasn't in love with the color pink, but if it made Taylor happy, they could always repaint later. "I guess we could try it."

Annie's gaze shifted to the window, where the leaves of the giant oak tree were beginning to change from green to orange. She didn't know the first thing about opening a café, but she did like the idea of being home for Taylor at night. It was possible, if they worked fast, that they could open in two weeks.

They just needed to come up with an irresistible menu, a cute name, charming décor, and a fantastic chef.

"What should we name it?" Taylor asked.

"I don't know," Annie said. "It's got to be something cute and catchy."

Taylor held up her strand of yarn. The charm bracelet, three reindeer bells, and a silver whistle dangled from the yarn. They twirled in the wind blowing through the window, making a soft sweet sound as they knocked into each other. "How about Wind Chime Café?

A fishing boat cruised up the channel. Annie looked back out the window. Over the churn of the motor, she could hear a faint tinkling...but not from the chimes Taylor held. It was as if they were coming from outside. As if they were right under the window, hanging from the roof of the porch.

But she knew there weren't any wind chimes down there.

"We can decorate the porch with them," Taylor said.

Outside, the wind chimes sang louder. Annie turned back to her daughter. "Wind Chime Café it is."

FIVE

*W*ill strolled into Rusty's a little after five o'clock. The bar was already packed. Men in sun-bleached jeans and T-shirts sat on the barstools, drinking Budweiser and Miller Lite. Families with young children were tucked into the booths facing the windows and a group of women sat outside on the deck, sipping wine and watching the sailboats glide over the Bay.

He nodded at two men in their early twenties playing pool in the corner and headed for the bar. He made it three steps past the hostess stand when the cheerful jumble of conversation faded to hushed whispers. Bar stools squeaked as men turned. Women glanced up from their tables, their mouths falling open.

"Will Dozier?" Billy Sadler pulled his faded ball cap off his head. "Is that you?"

"Yes, sir."

"My God, son." Billy climbed off the barstool. His thinning white hair stood up around his ears in tufts and he hobbled on arthritic legs over to Will, holding out his hand. "Welcome home."

"Thank you."

"How long are you here for?"

"Just long enough to fix up the inn and find a buyer."

Billy released Will's hand and stepped back. The skin around his blue eyes, tanned and leathery from years spent working on the Bay, fell in deep creases. "You're really going to sell it?"

"I am. It's too much for one person. Besides, my life is in San Diego now."

"But what if you decide to leave the service? You might want to come back home, start a family." Billy's voice grew wistful. "That big house deserves a new family."

"I agree," Will said. "I'm going to wait until I find the right buyer, one who will appreciate it as much as I did."

Billy stepped back, and another man walked up to shake Will's hand. More men came, circling around him. The two younger men in the corner had stopped playing pool and were watching him now with something like awe in their eyes.

He felt a familiar prickling sensation crawl across the back of his neck. He shouldn't have come here. He forced a smile as Neil Johnson, another one of his grandfather's friends, pumped his hand enthusiastically and thanked him for his service.

These people didn't know the truth. There was nothing special about him, nothing noble. He hunted down terrorists in the worst hellholes in the world to get revenge on the people who'd killed his mother and sister in 9/11. That was it. End of story.

He'd joined the SEALs straight out of college because he'd wanted to be the one to put the bullet between Bin Laden's eyes. He'd known that if anyone was going to take out the bastard who'd planned those attacks, it would be a SEAL.

"Is that Will Dozier?" a woman whispered from behind him.

"I heard he was back in town," another woman whispered.

"I heard he looks even better than he did when he left," a third woman whispered.

"Is that even possible?" the first asked.

Will scanned the room for Ryan, acutely aware of every sound in the bar: the silverware and glasses clattering into the bus bins, the pots and pans clanging around in the kitchen, the bartender dumping ice into a blender, the whir of the blades drowning out the Hank Williams song playing from the speakers.

More people surrounded him, looking up at him like he was some goddamn hero. He ran a hand over the back of his neck. His fingers came back damp.

"We're all so sorry about your grandparents," Neil said sadly.

"Thank you," Will said.

"What a shame you couldn't make it back for the funeral."

Will nodded as boat motors revved up outside in the marina. Sails snapped in the wind like whips. The air grew thick. He tasted dust. Desert dust. Afghani dust.

Not now.

His muscles clenched as gunfire erupted inside his head. His hands, slick with blood, twisted a tourniquet around what was left of Colin Foley's leg. On the other side of the rocks, their youngest team member was fighting off the insurgents with one eye blown out. They were surrounded, ambushed.

The man bleeding out beside him fumbled with the radio, fading in and out of consciousness as he made the call for help. Will secured the cord around Colin's leg and shouldered his rifle, in time to hear his best friend's primal scream, in time to watch him fall as he took a round of bullets straight to the chest.

Something cold and hard pressed into Will's hand. He looked down at the Budweiser bottle.

"All right folks, that's enough for now." Ryan clapped him on the back. "We wouldn't want all this talk to go to Will's head, would we?"

Everyone laughed and Will lifted the bottle to his lips, taking a long pull.

"We've got the Rockfish Tournament coming up in two weeks," Neil said. "There's room for one more on my boat."

Will forced the dust down his throat, into his lungs. "Sounds good."

Ryan steered him away from the crowd toward the back deck overlooking the water. The cool salty air beckoned and they were almost outside when a woman with long blond hair and wolf gray eyes stepped into his path.

Grace Callahan crossed her arms over her chest. "Did you forget how to use a phone?"

"Grace—"

"What about email?" Grace asked. "Did you forget how to use email?"

He could still hear the gunshots, the faint echo of rotor blades in the distance. Grace let out a muffled protest as he hooked an arm around her waist and hauled her in for a hug. He held on until the last remnants of the flashback subsided and he was back in the bar, able to breathe again.

"How do you think it felt to hear that you were back in town from a woman who's only lived here for two days?" Grace demanded.

Annie. Will's arms tightened around Grace. *She must have met Annie.*

"Two days!" Grace dug her heels into the toe of his sneaker. "And she knew more about you than what I'd been able to squeeze out of your grandparents over the past ten years!"

Will looked down at her flashing gray eyes. Grace had been trying to find out what he was up to from his grandparents? He'd figured Grace and Ryan would have forgotten about him years ago.

She shoved at him. "You think you can walk back in here

after all this time and expect to pick up where we left off without a single call or email?"

She was right, Will thought. Grace and Ryan had been his closest friends when he'd lived here. How could he have let ten years pass without getting in touch?

He surprised her by releasing her and letting her step back.

She let out her breath in a huff, but some of her anger deflated with it. "I hate it when people leave and don't call."

"I know." He winced as he remembered that that was exactly what Grace and Ryan's mother had done to them. She'd left them when they were little kids and they'd never heard from her again. How could he have done the same thing to them?

"I'm sorry," he said.

She snatched the beer from his hand, narrowing her eyes. "I'll take your apology into consideration."

Will watched Grace take a long sip from his bottle. She had the same sun-streaked blond hair and pale eyes as her twin brother. They both sported the same lanky athletic builds. But while Ryan was easygoing, Grace's temper was legendary.

Ryan waved at someone across the crowded barroom and Will turned, spotting Becca making her way toward them. Her pretty heart-shaped face was drawn, her big brown eyes troubled.

"What's wrong?" Grace asked when she got to them.

Becca did a double take when she spotted Will standing beside them. "Will?" Her eyes went wide and her face brightened slightly. "What are you doing here?"

"I'm back in town for a few weeks."

She smiled, lifting up on her toes to give him a hug. "It's really good to see you."

"You too," he said as she drew back and a flash of light on her left hand caught his eye. He glanced down at the diamond ring, surprised. "Who's the lucky guy?"

Becca blushed. "Tom Jacobson."

"Tommy?" Will asked, shocked.

"He goes by Tom now," she corrected.

"I see," Will said, lifting his gaze to Ryan. His friend's expression had darkened at the mention of Tommy's name. Will didn't blame him. Tommy was a jerk. "Is he here?"

Becca shook her head. "He lives in D.C. now. He's a lawyer."

"But you live here?"

She nodded, her eyes shifting away. "I'm moving to D.C. when we get married."

Whoa. Becca was leaving the island? She was the last person in the world he expected to leave Heron Island.

Becca had dated Tommy for a while in high school, but he'd never thought they'd get serious.

"I'll get us a round of drinks," Ryan said, heading for the bar.

Grace and Becca went outside to grab a table on the deck, and Will walked over to join Ryan by the bar. He thought about asking his friend what was up, but decided against it. If Becca had a rock on her finger, it was probably too late. It was none of his business anyway.

They made small talk while they waited for their drinks, then walked out to the deck. As soon as they were settled around the picnic table, Grace turned to Becca. "Okay, spill it."

"I'm fine," Becca said, waving her off. She attempted a breezy smile but it didn't quite reach her eyes. "I want to hear what Will's doing here."

Grace shook her head. "Will's in the dog house."

"Already?" Becca asked.

Will nodded. "It doesn't take long."

Grace ignored him. "Come on, Becca. We've been best friends forever. I know when something's wrong."

"All right," Becca conceded, looking out at the water. "You know how I told you we were getting a new student—a girl from Mount Pleasant?"

Grace nodded and Will's senses went on high alert. *A girl from Mount Pleasant? In Becca's second grade class?*

"Her first day was today," Becca explained.

"But you were ready," Grace said. "You've been preparing for this day for two weeks."

"I know," Becca said, sighing. "I thought I was ready. The day started out great. When Taylor's mom dropped her off, Taylor didn't even want her to stay. She acted like it was a normal school day."

Will looked down at the cracks in the wood on the picnic table. Was it possible Annie's child was from Mount Pleasant, and that she'd been sitting on the bleachers outside the school this morning because she was afraid to leave her alone?

"I met the mother," Grace said, lowering her voice. "I stopped by the old cupcake shop on my way into town. I wanted to see who'd bought the place."

Will closed his eyes. It *was* possible. Annie was the mother of the sole surviving child of the Mount Pleasant school shooting. Instead of helping her get over her fear of leaving her daughter at school for the first time since the shooting, he'd kissed her. No, *first* he'd made fun of her for fretting over her daughter fitting in at her new school, *then* he'd kissed her.

He was a world-class asshole.

"Taylor's a smart kid," Becca continued. "She knew the answers to most of my questions, and she was happy to participate." She picked at the label of her beer bottle. "Then we went out to recess and I overheard some of the kids making fun of her."

"What were they saying?" Grace asked.

Becca took a deep breath. "This is going to sound strange, but she carries a broom around."

"What kind of broom?" Grace asked.

"A broom," Becca explained, "like the ones we have at our houses."

Will picked up his beer. "Why does she carry a broom around?"

"It makes her feel safe."

"Safe?"

Becca lowered her voice. "She survived the shooting because she was hiding in a broom closet."

Will set his beer down, the alcohol turning to acid in his stomach.

"She wouldn't let go of the broom when they finally found her," Becca said quietly. "She insisted on taking it home and Annie says she won't take it away from her until she's ready."

"But the other kids don't understand," Ryan said, finishing for her.

Becca nodded, looking up. "How do I explain to a bunch of eight-year-olds why the new girl in their class is carrying a broom? I mean, I talked to them about the shooting after it happened. It was all over the news. All the teachers talked about it with their students. When I found out Taylor would be in my class, I told them about her and what she had been through and that I expected them to be extra nice to her. But they're kids. They're second graders. They can't possibly understand what she's been through. None of us can."

That wasn't entirely true, Will thought, looking out at the water. One of them could. Annie's daughter was probably struggling with the same issues he was: flashbacks, nightmares, insomnia.

"What did they say?" Grace asked after several moments of silence. "How did they make fun of her?"

"Mostly by calling her names," Becca said, rolling the neck of her bottle around in her fingers. "Some of them called her a witch when her back was turned. I overheard one boy call her

Cinderella to her face and I made him apologize. But she withdrew after that and spent the rest of the time sitting under the tree, watching the other kids play."

Seagulls circled the marina, cawing overhead. Will watched them dip and dive, thinking he'd like to have a nice long chat with whichever kid had made fun of Taylor after what she'd been through.

"I can control the kids as long as they're in my classroom," Becca said. "But on the playground and in the halls, sometimes I can't always hear what's going on." She looked down at her hands. "It's my job to make sure Taylor feels like school is a safe place for her to be. It shouldn't be any harder for her than it already is."

"It was her first day back," Grace said gently. "There are bound to be setbacks."

"I know, but I still feel responsible." She glanced back at the crowded barroom and started to rise to her feet. "I think I'll go inside and see if I can track down some of the parents and ask if they'd be willing to talk to their kids tonight."

Will watched her walk away and he fought the urge to head straight to Annie's and ask her what he could do to help. He was probably the last person she wanted to see right now.

Ryan turned to Grace. "You said you stopped by to meet the mother earlier. What did you think of her?"

Grace smiled. "I liked her. She's probably about our age, maybe a little younger. She was waiting for Jimmy to give her an estimate on renovations. I told her he'd probably stood her up to watch the baseball game. She came straight here to confront him and poured a drink in his lap when he tried to hit on her."

Will watched a charter boat motoring in from a day of fishing. After what he'd told her about the inn this morning, and then spending all day worrying about her daughter, he could imagine

Annie's contractor not showing up would have been the last straw.

"I convinced her to stay and hang out for a while," Grace said, "but only after Chase Townsend called to tell her he was thinking of backing out on her business loan." She picked at a splinter coming loose on the table. "He's such a jerk."

Will's fingers curled around the bottle.

Ryan leaned back, stretching his legs out under the table. "What kind of business does she want to open?"

"She *was* going to open up a fancy French bistro," Grace answered. "I don't think she has a clue what she's going to do now."

IT WAS after dark when Will walked out of Rusty's. He'd waited around for a few hours in case Chase or Spencer showed up. He'd wanted to let them know exactly what was going to happen to them if Chase didn't approve Annie's loan.

The bank could afford to cut her some slack. And if Chase disagreed, Will had a few persuasion techniques he was happy to use on Annie's behalf.

Opening the door to the SUV, he climbed into the driver's seat. The last thing he wanted was to put a single mother out of business. He'd been so wrapped up in his own problems he hadn't considered how his decision might affect her.

Turning the key, he started the engine and rolled down the window. Inside the bar, Carrie Underwood was belting out a song about revenge and some of the women were starting to dance. It would be so easy to get one of them to come home with him tonight.

Part of him was tempted, and if this was San Diego, he would. But this wasn't San Diego. This was Heron Island. And he knew those women. He'd grown up with them. He'd gone fishing with their dads and uncles. He'd played sports with their brothers.

He wasn't going to use one of them to help him get his head straight.

He switched on the headlights and backed out of the spot. In the past, taking a woman home had always been the fastest route to get past the nightmares and the insomnia. But he'd had a flashback in a bar tonight, in a *public* place.

He'd never had a flashback in public before. They usually only happened at night, when he was alone. The tires crunched over gravel as he drove out of the lot. They were getting worse.

What the hell was he going to do if he couldn't find a way to control them?

He drove down the road in silence, not bothering to turn on the radio. When he got to the stop sign, his headlights shone over the two-story house with the purple shutters. He could see Annie through the downstairs windows, unpacking boxes.

Pulling over to the side of the road, he cut the engine and climbed out. He owed her an apology. Crickets chirped in the tall grasses as he crossed the street and walked up the steps to her porch.

She glanced up when he got to the doorway, and met his gaze through the glass. Sending him a look that said, *you have got to be kidding me*, she walked to the door and opened it. "I don't have anything for you to eat."

"I know. I wasn't..." He trailed off, gazing down at her. She'd taken a shower recently and her long red hair hung like fire-colored ropes over her shoulders. Her eyes, the color of wet leaves, looked haunted and tired. She was wearing a black wrap shirt over black yoga pants and no makeup.

He wanted to pull her into his arms and not let go for the rest of the night. "I thought you might need a hand."

"With what?"

He nodded toward the row of boxes against the wall.

Annie crossed her arms over her chest. "I'm not going to go out with you because you offered to unload a few boxes."

His lips twitched. He couldn't help it. "I'm hurt that you'd think I have an ulterior motive."

Annie rolled her eyes. "Fine," she said, turning and pointing to a box on the floor. "You can unload those dishes onto the racks behind the counter."

Will walked over to the box and picked it up. What was he doing? He should apologize and get the hell out of here. Annie didn't need any more baggage to add to the load she was already carrying. He should leave her alone and let her be.

But when he passed her on the way to the counter, she smelled like vanilla and apple pie. And the only place he wanted to be was right here, helping her unpack.

He set the box on the counter and started pulling out an assortment of mismatched plates and bowls. "Seems like a lot of dishes for two people."

"They're from garage sales," she explained, unwrapping a set of hand-painted wine glasses covered in newspaper. "My daughter and I collect them. It's sort of a hobby."

He set the plates on the rack. "Are you going to use them in the restaurant?"

Annie nodded.

Will glanced down at the chipped pottery. "In the fine dining restaurant?"

She looked up at him and he wished he could tell her he'd changed his mind. He wished he could tell her he'd decided to sell the inn to the resort company and she didn't have to worry about the bank pulling the plug on her loan. But he couldn't do it. He couldn't turn his grandparents' inn over to a developer. And a small part of him liked knowing they had that connection, that he had something she wanted, even if he was never going to give it to her.

When Annie looked away, Will set down the bowl he was holding. "Annie."

"Yes."

"I'm not going to change my mind."

"I know," she said, unwrapping a glass with tiny clusters of grapes painted on it.

Will watched her small hands methodically pull out glasses and set the crumpled newspaper aside in neat little stacks. "What are you going to do?"

She pulled out the last glass, lined it up next to the others, and bent down to retrieve another box. "I have a plan."

Will lifted a brow. "What is it?"

"It's a surprise."

His lips curved. He couldn't help admiring her spirit. After the day she'd had, he wouldn't blame her if she wanted to crawl into bed and spend the next few days there. Instead, she was down here unpacking as if nothing had happened and formulating a plan to move forward.

Will placed the last set of bowls on the rack and leaned back against the counter, watching her work. So they both had issues. Who didn't? He wanted to spend more time with her. He wanted to get to know her better. Hell, maybe he could even help her daughter get over some of her fears.

"Listen," he said, crossing the room to grab another box. "I was thinking of taking my grandfather's old sailboat out for a spin this weekend. You and your daughter should come with me."

"I told you," Annie said, looking up. "I'm not dating you."

"Don't think of it as a date. Think of it as a way for Taylor to learn something new."

Annie paused, her hand suspended over the box. She turned slowly to face him. "How do you know my daughter's name?"

Will carried the new box back to the counter and set it down. "I might have heard some talk tonight."

"What kind of *talk*?"

"Listen, Annie." Will leaned his arms on the box. "I didn't realize—"

"I don't appreciate my daughter being gossiped about," Annie said tightly.

"It wasn't gossip." Will straightened, pushing back from the counter. "Not in a bad way, at least. People are concerned. They want to help."

Annie scooped up the crumpled newspaper, shoving it into a trash bag.

"If you're going to live here," Will said, "Taylor should learn how to sail. It could be good for her, a way for her to find some courage and overcome her fears."

Annie's eyes flashed as they met his. "What do you know about Taylor's fears?"

Will gazed down at her. That was a good question. He knew what it was like to survive, to live with the knowledge that everyone else around you had died. He knew what it was like to live with that guilt, and fall asleep every night wondering why.

But at least he had the ability to go after the bastards who'd hurt his friends.

He couldn't imagine the helplessness Taylor must feel.

"I know," he said finally, "that sometimes the only way to get over your fears is to focus on something else, something as simple as learning to tie ropes and measure wind speeds."

Annie picked up the wine glasses; they clinked together as she gathered them into her arms. "Thanks for the advice. I think it's time for you to leave now."

"Annie—"

She carried them into the kitchen, setting them on the counter.

"Do me a favor," Will said, raising his voice so she could hear him. "Ask Taylor before you say no."

Annie walked back out to the kitchen doorway. "*I* will decide what I will, and will not, ask my daughter."

Will gazed back at her, at the fiery spark of protection and defensiveness in her eyes. "I wish you would let me help."

"You could help," she said, "by selling the inn."

SIX

The air was crisp and cool when Annie stepped out of
the bank on Monday morning. She'd managed to
convince Chase to back her new idea, at least temporarily. He'd
agreed that if she could open the café in two weeks, and as long as
it was a place for both locals and tourists, it could work. But he'd
tightened the terms of the agreement: there was no grace period
anymore, no second chances if she missed a payment.

She had to get it right the first time.

Across the street, a scrawny middle-aged man was climbing
the steps to her porch. She took in his white T-shirt and loose-
fitting black chef's pants and picked up her pace.

She'd had six responses to the online ad she'd posted on
Friday. At first glance, none of the candidates had popped out at
her, but she'd invited each of them in for an interview today. The
most promising one had been working as a sous chef at a hotel in
St. Michaels for the past seven years and was looking to
downsize.

"Carl?" she ventured, crossing the street.

The man turned, stubbing out his cigarette and tucking it behind his ear.

She climbed the steps, holding out her hand. "I'm Annie. Thanks for coming by before your shift."

"No problem," he said, shaking her hand.

She unlocked the door, leading him into the café.

"Would you like a cup of coffee?" she offered, walking around the counter to pour herself a cup. She didn't have much in the way of a budget for hiring staff, and she'd already decided to do most of the waitressing herself. If they were all going to be working closely together, she needed someone she could get along with, someone she could trust, someone who wouldn't mind an eight-year-old wandering in and out of the kitchen on the weekends.

"No, thanks," he said, taking in the pink walls and half dozen tables the previous owners had left in the dining room.

"Feel free to have a look at the kitchen before we sit down." She nodded toward the room in the back. "It's not much, but it should work for the café."

He walked into the kitchen and came back out a few seconds later. "There's only one oven."

"That's right."

"Are you going to add one?"

She looked up from spooning sugar into her coffee. There was no room in the kitchen or her budget for a second oven. "No."

"I can't cook without two ovens."

Annie lifted the mug, wrapping both hands around it. "I want to offer a basic café menu of soups, salads, and sandwiches. Can't most of that be prepared ahead of time?"

"What about desserts?"

"Actually," Annie admitted, "I was hoping to find someone

who'd be willing to make a few desserts at home in the mornings and bring them in when we open."

"I don't take work home."

"Oh."

"Sorry," Carl said, lifting a shoulder. "I was looking to downsize to a smaller kitchen, but this is a few too many steps down."

Annie winced as he reached for his cigarette. "Don't you at least want to hear what I'm offering?"

He shook his head, walking to the door. "I think I'll stay where I am for now."

Three hours and five interviews later, Annie was on the verge of a panic attack. None of the people she'd interviewed were willing to accept the salary she was offering. Four of them said they couldn't work in a kitchen that small. One of them said he couldn't work in a place with pink walls.

She had a fleeting thought about trying to cook herself, but the only dishes she could make were Campbell's soup casseroles. She laid her head on the counter. What was she going to do if she couldn't find a chef?

At the knock on the door, she glanced up.

A plump woman in her late-fifties wearing a gray pantsuit and black suede heels walked in. Her dark blond hair was streaked with gray and curled in cowlicks around her kind, round face. "I'm here about the job."

Annie flipped through the stack of résumés. Hadn't she already met with everyone? "Did we have an appointment?"

"No." The woman walked up to the counter carrying a single sheet of paper and a blue box with a pink ribbon around it. "I thought I'd apply in person."

"What's this?" Annie asked when the woman set the box down.

"It's a sample." She twisted her hands in front of her as she stepped back. "Of my cooking."

"You brought me a sample?"

She nodded.

Intrigued, Annie turned the paper around to face her. "And this is...?"

"My résumé."

Annie scanned the words on the page. There was only one job listed, a law firm where the woman had worked as a receptionist for thirty years. Her heart sank. "You don't have any cooking experience."

"Not professionally." She shifted from one foot to the other. "But I do all the cooking for the community events on the island. The ones at the church, the firehouse, all the festivals."

"You live on the island?"

"Born and raised."

Annie sat back. She was the first person who'd applied for the job who lived on the island. She thought about what Grace had said yesterday, about outside businesses moving in and pushing the islanders out. She'd like to hire someone from the island. But without any real cooking experience...

The woman pulled a second piece of paper from her pocket. "I have a letter of recommendation."

Annie took the paper, unfolding it. It was a handwritten note, consisting of one sentence: *Della's sweet rolls are to die for.*

"It's from the Fire Chief," Della explained.

Annie bit back a smile, peering at the pretty box on the counter. "Is that what's in the box?"

Della nodded.

Annie opened it, pulling out a perfectly shaped sweet roll dripping with sugary icing.

"Go ahead," Della urged.

Annie bit into it and her eyes almost rolled back in her head. She groaned as the perfect combination of butter, sugar, cinnamon and vanilla slid over her tongue. "Oh my God."

Della beamed.

"Okay," she said, setting the sweet roll down and laughing. "So we've established that you can bake. Can you cook?"

Della nodded. "Ask anybody on the island. They'll vouch for me."

"Could you cook a meal for, say, thirty people in that kitchen?"

Della walked over to the kitchen, glancing at it through the doorway. "Yes."

"Are you sure?"

Della gave her a strange look. "Yes, I can cook a meal for thirty people in that kitchen. It's no smaller than the one I have at home."

Annie let out a breath, glancing back at the woman's résumé. "Why don't you have a seat and let's talk a little bit about your work experience."

Della walked back over to the counter. She pulled out a stool across from Annie and eased her ample hips onto it. "What would you like to know?"

"Tell me about what you did at the law firm," Annie said, taking another bite of the pastry.

Della folded her hands in her lap. "I worked as a receptionist, mostly answering phones, taking messages, organizing schedules and calendars. I used to plan all the social events and parties for the clients."

"And you were there for thirty years?"

"That's right."

Annie glanced down at Della's résumé again, double-checking the dates. "Wait...your last day was Friday?"

"That's right."

"Did you retire?"

"Not exactly."

"Why the sudden change of heart?"

Della looked down at her hands. "The firm merged with another company recently, a bigger firm from D.C. The new manager wanted someone more qualified for my position."

"Someone more qualified?"

Della picked at the light pink polish chipping off her nails. "Someone who looked more like you."

"Oh." Annie's heart went out to her. She knew what it was like to be cast off, what it felt like to be forgettable and easy to replace.

Della glanced up, her blue eyes sad. "My husband, Joe—he's a waterman. He works hard, and has a second job working on Jimmy Faulkner's construction crew on the weekends, but it's still not enough for us to live on. We *both* need to have a job."

Annie gazed at the woman across from her. She knew what it was like to need a job, to wonder if there would be enough money to pay the rent or mortgage bill. It was risky to hire a chef with no restaurant experience. But Della had cooked for large-scale events. Even if they were only community events, they were still large-scale events. And if she'd worked at the same law firm for thirty years, that showed loyalty.

"I imagine," Annie said slowly, "if you grew up here, you probably know how to cook a lot of traditional Chesapeake Bay recipes."

Della nodded. "My grandmother taught me how to cook."

"Can you cook better than Don at The Tackle Box?"

"Don?" Della snorted. "I can out cook Don with one hand tied behind my back."

The sound of wind chimes glided over the salty breezes. It wasn't a deep rich coppery sound like Annie had heard the first night Will walked into her restaurant, or the delicate aluminum flutes she'd heard when she and Taylor had come up with the name of the café. These had a quirky, uneven cadence, like silver spoons suspended from tangled fishing line.

"I can't pay much," Annie admitted. "At least, not at first. If things start to pick up, we can talk about a raise."

Della's whole face lit up. "Are you offering me the job?"

Annie held up a hand. "I want to feature a seasonal menu of soups, salads, and sandwiches—local Chesapeake fare with a twist. The Rusty Rudder and The Tackle Box are our main competition. We'd need to offer a step up from that."

"A step up...?" Della said slowly.

Annie nodded. She and Taylor had spent the weekend scoping out the competition. The Tackle Box, which was a small dark green building at the bottom of the drawbridge, doubled as the island market and grill. Rusty's, which included an inn with about a dozen rooms, was known mostly as a family hangout and bar. They both specialized mainly in fried food.

"So," Della continued, "you mean something kind of classy? Like you?"

Annie brushed at her hair self-consciously. No one had ever called her classy before. "I guess...yes. That's what I'm looking for."

The woman sat up a little straighter. "I can do classy."

"I want to open in two weeks," Annie went on, "in time for the Rockfish Tournament. I've heard there will be close to a hundred tourists here that weekend. If we can find a way to get some of them to come to the café instead of going to Rusty's or The Tackle Box, we might be able to pull off a successful first day."

Della's eyes lit up. "We could offer to cook the fish they catch in the tournament, and I could get word out to the charter boat captains to put in a good word for us. It could give us an edge up."

"I'd want to see a menu by the end of the week, at the latest."

"I can get you one by tomorrow."

Annie smiled and held out her hand. "Then you're hired."

Della grasped Annie's hand in both of hers, pumping it up and down. "Oh, thank you! Thank you so much!"

Annie laughed, looking back down at the top of Della's résumé. "I forgot to catch your last name."

"It's Dozier," she said. "Della Dozier."

Dozier. Where had she heard that name before? A slow sinking feeling formed in the pit of her stomach and Annie drew her hand back. "You're not related to Will Dozier, are you?"

Della beamed. "I'm his aunt."

OF ALL THE *people on this island for Della to be related to.* Annie's boots scuffed through the fallen leaves beginning to blanket the sidewalks as she walked to the school to pick up Taylor. Was there no getting away from this man?

For someone who hadn't been home in years, Will sure had a lot of ties to this place.

Letting her fingers run through the golden leaves of a locust branch, she considered her decision to hire Della. In hindsight, it might have been wise to spend a few days verifying her references before offering her the job.

What kind of manager took a potential employee on her word and hired her on the spot?

A bad one, an evil voice whispered in Annie's ear.

No. She pushed the voice away. She was a good manager. At least, she had been when she'd worked as the assistant manager at Citron Bleu. But she'd never owned her own restaurant. She'd never had to worry about what would happen if she failed.

Taking a deep breath, she lifted her chin. Failure wasn't an option.

Passing several clusters of parents chatting and gossiping outside the entrance to the school, she was aware of several pairs of eyes on her. When she caught their glances of sympathy, she realized they must all know who she was now, and what had happened to Taylor.

She didn't want them to feel sorry for her. She wanted everything to go back to normal as quickly as possible. Walking inside, she made her way to Taylor's classroom. She spotted her daughter gathered around a craft table with five other kids, gluing wings onto construction paper butterflies.

Taylor glanced up when Annie stepped into the room. "Mom, look!" She held up her orange butterfly, its body suspended from a string. "It's a monarch!"

"It's beautiful," Annie said, smiling.

Becca waved to Annie from the front of the room. "Time to start cleaning up," she said to the class.

The organized scene dissolved into a fit of chaos as the kids grabbed handfuls of markers and construction paper and dumped them into the big plastic bins in the corner. Chairs scraped back from desks and their excited voices filled the room as they raced to get their things from their cubbies. Taylor ran over to Annie, carrying her broom and her butterfly. "Can we go see the monarchs, mom? I want to show you."

"Where are they?"

"Not far. There's a trail right across the road."

Becca wove through the desks, making her way to the back of the room. "The trail leads into the fields. You can't miss it. Follow it until you hit the weeping willow and then turn left. It takes about ten minutes."

Annie hesitated. "Isn't that private property?"

"Will won't mind," Becca said, waving goodbye to the kids heading out of the classroom with their parents. "It's his family's land, but it's always been open to everyone on the island. His grandfather made a walking trail through the marshes years ago. Everybody uses it."

Of course they do. Annie remembered Grace's reaction when she'd first heard about the resort. She'd said it would only be a matter of time before the developers expanded their vision to include a gated community and a golf course. This must be the land she was worried about losing.

Maybe it was time she saw what was so special about it. She looked back down at Taylor. "We can go for a short walk to see the butterflies."

Taylor grinned and ran to get her backpack.

Annie turned to Becca, lowering her voice. "She made it through the whole day?"

Becca nodded. "I think it was the nature walk. I've never seen a child get so excited about butterflies before." She reached behind Annie and pulled a small field guide off the shelf. "Taylor kept asking me about the wildlife while we were walking. I thought you might want to borrow this for a while."

Annie looked down at the field guide. The pages were worn and crinkled at the edges, like they'd been read and referenced hundreds of times over the years. If butterflies could help bring back her daughter's spirit, Annie would learn to identify every species in this book.

Taylor walked back over and Annie took her hand.

"Bye, Miss Haddaway!" Taylor waved as they walked out into the hallway. They made their way down the hall and out the doors to the parking lot.

"It's this way." Taylor marched past the cars with a sense of purpose Annie hadn't seen in a long time. "Miss Haddaway said the monarchs are only here for a little while and then they fly south. Their real home is in Mexico."

"Really?" Annie asked, flipping to the page on monarchs as Taylor led her into the fields.

"Miss Haddaway said they're in danger."

"In danger?" Annie asked. "Why?"

"She said their homes are being destroyed. They need special places like this one so they can survive."

Oh no, Annie thought as they crossed a small footbridge over a snaking finger of water winding through the soggy land. She wasn't just up against the islanders' resistance to sell to a developer; she was up against a natural habitat for endangered butterflies?

She stepped over a fallen tree trunk, following Taylor toward the weeping willow. "What is it about this place that they need?"

"The milkweed." Taylor pointed to the fields of overgrown weeds and wildflowers that wove through the marshes and painted the landscape in swirls of green and gold. "See the one with the fuzzy purple flower? It's the only plant monarch babies eat. Without it, they die."

Annie bit her lip. Maybe the resort would be willing to keep this land as a sanctuary for the birds and the butterflies. No, she thought. She knew better than that. Walking trails through a field of weeds didn't exactly spell out luxury.

"Look!" Taylor broke into a jog. "There they are!"

Annie could just make out a flutter of orange wings through the branches of the weeping willow. Her boots squished over the soft ground as she followed Taylor into the next field. When she saw them, she paused, awe struck. There must have been hundreds, or maybe thousands of butterflies.

Taylor's purple backpack bounced as she trotted toward them. "Aren't they beautiful?"

"They are," Annie breathed. She couldn't take her eyes off them. They flew over the marshes, drinking the nectar of the autumn wildflowers, stretching their wings in the afternoon sun. She'd seen butterflies before, but never so many in one place.

"Miss Haddaway said there's another field full of them if we keep walking that way." Taylor pointed to the west, where a line of white pines and dogwoods cut through the marshes.

Annie nodded, trailing after her daughter who was already heading for the next field. How could she say no?

She listened to Taylor chat about her day, occasionally flipping through the book to identify a bird stalking through the marshes or roosting high in the boughs of a tree. She drew back as a bramble bush tugged on the hem of her sweater, and looked down as Taylor ducked through an opening in an overgrown blackberry grove. "Wait, Taylor. I think we've..."

Gone too far.

The words died in her throat as she took in the gorgeous waterfront inn. It rose up against the water in shades of pale yellow and white. A hackberry tree sheltered the front porch, where a row of white wicker rockers sat facing the oyster-shell driveway. All the windows were open, and the gauzy curtains fluttered in the breezes airing out the house.

Annie drew in a breath as a butterfly landed on her shoulder, brushing its delicate wings against her neck. She took in the cluster of fenced gardens with charming red gates on the north side of the house, the old swing hanging from a tree branch in the back yard. Two red Adirondack chairs sat at the end of a long pier, facing the spot where the sun would dip into the water at night.

"Wow," Taylor whispered beside her. "Who lives here?"

Will.

Annie heard the sound of dogs barking, then the clang of boots on metal—someone walking down a ladder. She reached for Taylor's hand. "I think we should go."

"Why?" Taylor asked as two labs bounded around the side of the house and raced toward them with their tails wagging. Taylor giggled as the dogs surrounded them, jumping up and planting muddy paws on their jeans.

Annie tried to pull Taylor back behind the protective wall of blackberries. But she was too late. She spotted Will strolling around to the front of the house. A sweat-stained T-shirt hugged the broad muscles of his chest and shoulders. His long legs filled out a pair of worn jeans, and when he lifted the hem of his shirt to wipe the sweat off his face, she glimpsed a set of tan, washboard abs.

Taylor squealed as the yellow lab licked her face.

"Riley, down," Will ordered, his deep voice echoing over the water.

Both dogs sat, panting and batting their tails against the grass, cocking their heads at Taylor's broom.

"They're harmless," he said, his long strides eating up the overgrown dandelions and crabgrass as he crossed the yard to them. "But they think your broom is a stick. They want to play with it." He smiled at Taylor as he got closer, an easy, friendly smile—the kind of smile a woman could get lost in. "You must be Taylor."

Taylor nodded, giggling when the chocolate lab nipped at her construction paper butterfly.

"Here," he said, digging out a handful of treats from his pocket. "Feed them these and they'll do anything you ask."

Taylor handed her paper butterfly to Annie, taking the treats from Will and feeding them to the dogs. She laughed as they slobbered all over her fingers.

Annie folded the butterfly and tucked it carefully into Taylor's backpack. As soon as she'd zipped it back up, Taylor took off running down to the beach with the dogs chasing after her.

"She looks just like you," Will said, watching her grab a stick off the ground and toss it into the water for the dogs.

Annie nodded, her gaze slowly drifting back to the inn. She could picture the porches and steps covered in flowers, the gardens in full bloom. She wondered what it looked like inside, what the views were like from the upstairs bedrooms. Her eyes followed the curve of the driveway to the three private cottages nestled between two tall magnolia trees. Water lapped at the rocks behind them, a quiet coaxing lullaby. "I can't believe you grew up here."

"It was a great place to grow up."

Annie glanced up at him. In the afternoon sunlight she could see the tiny flecks of amber around his irises. Sweat gleamed off the muscles of his neck and shoulders. She resisted the urge to reach up and brush a bit of sawdust off his neck, just to feel the warmth of his skin on her fingertips. "What are you going to do with it?"

"Fix it up. Find a buyer who'll run it as is."

She looked back at the beach when Taylor squealed. The dogs had dropped the stick at her feet and were shaking their wet coats, spraying her with water. "You can't control what a buyer does."

"I can try."

So would she, if this was her home. She knew now why Will didn't want to sell it. This was the kind of house you wanted to raise a family in, the kind of house you held onto for generations. The kind of house you never wanted to let go.

But she needed him to sell it. She needed the resort and the tourists to come to this island so she could open her real restaurant. The café would hold her over for a little while, but it wasn't a long-term solution. She needed the stability of a resort, the income that a steady stream of tourists would generate so she and Taylor could stay here, so they could put down roots and build a life here.

She reached down, snapping off the top of a Queen Anne's lace. "It's just a house."

Will dipped his hands in his pockets. "How would you feel if someone tore down the home you grew up in?"

Annie turned away, picking more Queen Anne's lace and

winding them into a wreath for Taylor. "I wouldn't know. We've never owned a home before."

Will turned his attention back to her, watching her weave the stems. "Where did you grow up?"

"We moved around a lot."

"Military?"

She looked back up at him. "What?"

"Was one of your parents in the military?"

"No."

Will held her gaze. "I thought maybe that's why you moved around a lot."

She shook her head. "My mother was an artist. We moved every couple of years so she could find new people and places to paint."

"Every couple of years?"

"Pretty much."

Will's gaze dropped to where her fingers were twisting the stems into a tight, even braid. "How'd you feel about that?"

"I got used to it," she lied. She didn't need to tell him how hard it had been, how unsettling it had been to never know if her mother's muse would show up in the new city. To never know if they would be staying for two weeks, six months, or three years.

All she'd ever wanted was to stay in one place. To make friends she didn't have to say goodbye to. To live in a real home in a real town with neighbors who knew her name.

She looked back up at him. "Where do *you* live now?"

"San Diego."

"That's far away."

"It's almost as far as you can get from Heron Island and still be in the States."

"Why'd you move there?"

"I'm in the Navy."

"Oh…" She trailed off. She hadn't realized he was here on

leave. "That's why you asked if one of my parents was in the military."

He nodded.

"So you know what it's like to move around a lot."

"I do."

She looked back at the house. "How long are you here for?"

"Six weeks."

Her gaze lingered on the empty rocking chairs lined up on the porch, wondering what it would be like to sit there at the end of the day in the summer and watch the fireflies twinkle over the marshes. "What if you can't find another buyer in six weeks?"

He smiled. "I'll find one."

Taylor's carefree laughter rolled over the Bay and Annie looked back at her daughter. She couldn't remember the last time she'd seen her this happy.

"Do you want to come in?" Will asked, nodding toward the house. "I don't have much in the way of food, but I can offer you a beer. We could sit on the porch and see how long it takes until the dogs steal Taylor's broom."

Annie shook her head. She had to leave. It wasn't Taylor she was worried about getting attached to this time. It was herself. This was the kind of home she'd always dreamed of. It was the kind of place she'd learned not to wish for, because wishes were dangerous. Wishes led to hope. Hope didn't pay the bills, and it didn't put food on the table.

"We should be going," Annie said.

"It's just a beer, Annie."

And as soon as you sell this house, you're leaving. "I've still got a lot to do tonight." She turned, raising her voice over the wind. "Taylor, it's time to go."

Taylor dragged her feet, reluctantly climbing back up from the beach with the dogs.

Will smiled down at Annie. "You'll say yes, eventually."

Annie looked up at him. It would be too easy to say yes, to slip into a routine of saying yes to Will. But she refused to get involved with a man who was leaving, especially one who had no intention of ever coming back.

Grace had told her on Friday that the last time Will had left this island he hadn't looked back. He'd completely cut off his friends and the few family members he had left. If that was how he'd treated his family and friends, what would stop him from doing the same thing to a woman he'd only known for a few weeks?

Taylor walked up to them and Annie lifted the flower wreath, setting it on her daughter's head. "There. Now you're the Queen of the Butterflies."

Taylor smiled shyly and looked up at Will. "Can I come back and see your dogs again?"

"They actually belong to a friend who had to go to Annapolis for the day." He reached down, scratching the yellow lab behind the ears. "But I'm thinking of asking if I can borrow this one for a few weeks. If he says yes, you can come back and see her anytime you want."

Annie noticed that Taylor's broom dangled from her fingertips now, almost as an afterthought. All her attention was focused on the dogs, and patting them both on the head to say goodbye. She thought about what Will had said last Friday, 'Sometimes the only way to get over your fears is to focus on something else.'

Annie put her arm around her daughter's shoulders. "It's time to go."

Taylor gave each dog one last pat on the head and they turned to leave. Will walked over to the blackberry bushes, holding the brambles up so they could get through without their clothes getting snagged.

"How's the restaurant coming along," he asked.

She ducked under his arm. "I hired a chef this morning."

"Anybody I know?"

"Actually, yes," she said. "Your aunt."

Will smiled—that slow, easy smile that had her heart fluttering like butterfly wings. He was close, much too close. She could smell the salt on his skin and see the little spot of his pulse beating in his throat.

She forced her gaze up from the dark vee of sweat staining the front of his shirt.

"Let me know if you need a taste tester," he offered.

Her eyes flickered briefly down to his mouth. A rush of heat swam through her as she tore her gaze away, combing the fields for Taylor. She spotted her a hundred feet from them, catching butterflies with her broom. "I think we can manage."

Will laughed as she walked away. "If you change your mind, you know where to find me."

SEVEN

*S*he wasn't going to change her mind. Not now. Not after she'd seen that inn.

Annie lay in her daughter's bed, running a soothing hand over her hair. Taylor had woken up from another nightmare, the same one she had almost every night now.

Hadn't she suffered enough? Did she have to relive that tragic day over and over again in her dreams?

It was still dark outside, but Annie could hear the voices of the fishermen rising up from the water, the low hum of the work-boats motoring through the narrow channel that cut through the marshes to the Bay.

She wished there was something more she could do to make her daughter feel better, to make her heal faster. The grief counselor had said it would take time. It could be months before the nightmares went away. And the memories would most likely haunt her for the rest of her life.

All Annie could do was be comforting and supportive and take things day by day. She gazed up at the paper butterfly Taylor had made in class two weeks ago. They'd strung it up from the ceiling as soon as they'd returned from their walk and they'd made a dozen more since then. Paper butterflies in every color hung from tiny hooks now, their wings fluttering in the breezes that snuck in when they cracked the windows at night.

Taylor had insisted on going back to see the butterflies every afternoon, and Annie had taken her. But she'd been careful to keep her a safe distance away from the inn. Just like the monarchs that would leave in a few weeks, the inn wasn't going to be there for long. She didn't want Taylor getting attached to it...or to Will.

She'd done everything in her power to avoid him since that day.

There was a time, once, when she'd been young and naive enough to believe that a handsome man with a big home and a big family and everything she'd ever wanted could be hers.

The last time, he'd been tall and blond with blue eyes and a southern accent. She'd been seventeen when Blake Hadley had walked into the restaurant where she'd been working on Bourbon Street. She'd waited on him and a table of his fraternity brothers from Tulane. He'd been charming and flirtatious and when he'd invited her to come out with them after her shift, she'd said yes.

A week later, they were dating.

By the end of the summer, she'd fallen in love.

When he finally took her back to his family home, to the majestic mansion with the sprawling yard leading down to the Mississippi River with the Spanish moss dripping from the trees like jewels through the setting sun, she had slept with him.

His parents had been out of town at the time, but she'd seen their pictures on the mantel. She'd imagined herself in one of those pictures, wrapped in Blake's arms. Safe, protected, sheltered, loved.

Three weeks later, she'd found out the truth—she had been nothing more than a summer fling. His real girlfriend, the one that his family knew and approved of, would be returning to take her place as soon as the new semester began in the fall.

When she'd told him she loved him, he'd laughed.

In the end, the only thing he'd left her with was Taylor.

WILL SAT UP, his heart pounding, a cold sweat trickling down his back. It was dark out, but the TV was still on, flashing eerie bands of silver light through the den. He grabbed the remote off the floor and switched it off.

The silence pressed down on him.

The nightmares were getting worse.

Will rubbed his hands over his face. He'd fallen asleep in his clothes again, as he had every night recently. He'd been going to sleep later and later, trying to avoid the memories that would creep in as soon as he nodded off.

But it didn't matter what room he slept in, or what station he left the TV on; they still found him. Pushing to his feet, he walked out of the den. He'd been holed up out here for two weeks, pouring all his energy and frustration into fixing up the inn. But tearing up rotted plywood wasn't doing a damn thing to help scrub out the memories of his dead teammates.

He climbed the stairs to his room and pulled out a pair of shorts and a clean T-shirt from his bag. Lacing up his sneakers, he jogged back down the stairs and took off out of the house, the screen door slapping shut behind him as he broke into a run.

Voices drifted over the water—watermen talking to each other as they set their morning traps. An ebbing tide rubbed at the muddy shoreline, and the shadow of a blue heron stalked through the marshes.

He passed the dark homes and shops lining Main Street. When he spotted the small crowd gathered outside The Tackle

Box, he remembered that today was the day of the annual Rockfish Tournament. The shop was already packed with tourists buying bags of ice, beer, and bloodworms.

He crossed the street to avoid the crowds, picking up his pace over the drawbridge connecting the island to the mainland. Below, tourists and fisherman crawled over the docks of the marina. He ran until their voices faded. Until the wind swallowed the roar of boat motors. Until the sun peeled back the night, and the first hints of dawn painted the eastern horizon a pale muted pink.

By the time he turned around and crossed back over the drawbridge to the island, his shirt was soaked with sweat but he'd managed to chase away most of the nightmares.

At least, for now.

He jogged back down Main Street, slowing to a walk when he spotted the woman climbing onto a wooden stool outside the house with the purple shutters. He hadn't seen much of Annie over the past two weeks. The few times he had seen her she'd been in a big hurry, too busy to stop and talk. He cut quietly across the grass to where she stood. "You've been avoiding me."

Annie jumped, almost dropping the sign she'd been trying to hang.

He steadied the stool, gazing up at her. Her long red hair hung loose around her shoulders, but her green eyes were guarded. She was wearing a pair of black leggings and an oversized National Zoo sweatshirt. She looked like she'd just crawled out of bed and gotten to work.

She went back to hanging the sign. "I've been busy."

A gust of wind blew through the street and a soft tinkling sound filled the air. Will turned, glancing at the porch. Dozens of wind chimes hung from the beams. Silver spoons, aluminum flutes, and oyster shells spun in circles, catching the early morning sunlight.

Annie stretched up on her toes, hooking the left side of the sign to the metal ring drilled into the roof. "There." She leaned back. "Does it look straight to you?"

Will looked up at the sign, at the words, *Wind Chime Café*, painted in purple across the sanded plank of driftwood. A strange prickling sensation crawled across the back of his neck. "How did you choose that name?"

"Taylor came up with it." Annie glanced down at him. "Does it look straight?"

Will nodded as he steadied the stool for her to climb down. As soon as she was on stable ground, he walked over to the steps where more boxes of wind chimes sat beside the freshly potted yellow mums and purple pansies. "Where did you get these?"

"I made them." She walked to the end of the sidewalk to look back at the sign and confirm that it was straight. "Well, Taylor and I made them."

Will picked a set of wind chimes out of the box. It was a tiny teakettle with silver sugar cubes hanging from the spout. "You made these?"

Annie nodded, walking over and taking them from his hand. She climbed the steps to the porch and dragged a chair over to an empty hook to hang them.

She acted like it was no big deal, like it wasn't something special, almost like it wasn't something she was particularly proud of. He looked down at the box full of items strung together so carefully, put together with so much love. "My sister used to make wind chimes."

Annie glanced down. "Really?"

Will nodded, pulling out a long string knotted with feathers and bells.

"I'd love to see them," Annie said. "Does she live on the island?"

"No."

"Where does she live?"

"She died a long time ago."

"Oh." Annie paused, her voice softening. "I'm so sorry."

Will laid the string of feathers and bells carefully back inside the box. Not a day went by that he didn't miss her, that he didn't wish he'd been on that plane instead of her, that he didn't wish there was some way to bring her back.

He walked up the steps, peering in the open door of the café. The tables and chairs had all been painted white. One pink wall was covered in silver netting woven with sea glass and driftwood. The others held photographs of marshes, beaches and workboats. A shiny silver espresso machine sat beside the glossy dessert case. Inside, little printed name cards labeled where the pastries would go.

How had she managed to pull all this off in two weeks?

"I had to use what we had on hand to decorate," Annie said uncertainly, watching him for a reaction.

He turned, looking back up at the wind chimes strung across the beams of the porch. "You and Taylor made *all* of these?"

"Actually, I made a lot of them before Taylor was born. I've been making them since I was a kid. They're one of the few things my mother used to let me bring with us when we moved. "

Will watched her twist the loop of the wind chime around a hook in the beam. He tried to picture her as a child, packing up her boxes of wind chimes every time she was forced to move to a new place. She'd said she'd gotten used to her mother's gypsy life-style, but it couldn't have been easy on her.

He had chosen an uncommitted, unattached lifestyle as an adult because he couldn't deal with the pain of losing someone he loved again. But he couldn't imagine not having had a home when he was growing up. "You said your mother was an artist." He crossed the porch slowly to where she stood on the chair. "Did she make wind chimes, too?"

"No." Annie laughed, but it sounded forced. She busied her fingers by working out a knot in the string. "Making wind chimes was something I did to get out of her hair."

He surprised her by taking her hand and helping her down from the chair. "What do you mean?"

Annie started to pull her hand back, but Will held on. He liked the feel of her small hand in his.

"My mother never considered my chimes real art," Annie explained. "She was a classic oil painter, mostly landscapes and portraits. She would sell her paintings in galleries for thousands of dollars. This," she said, gesturing to the chimes with her free hand, "was just junk I found on the street."

Junk? Will tightened his grip on her hand.

"My mother was very talented, but her inspiration came and went. When it came, she needed a lot of space to paint, so I would leave and take long walks through the city and look for things on the streets to bring back. I'd wash them and string them up in the windows, over the beds, in the doorways."

She gazed up at the wind chimes. "I can't remember when I first started making them, but the sound always made me feel like I was home. Every time we left, I brought them with me, like I was bringing a little piece of that place with me. I know it's silly, but I used to dream of living in a house with a porch so I could hang wind chimes all over it."

"It's not silly."

She looked back at him.

"Is that why you moved here?" he asked. "To put down roots?"

"I moved here to get Taylor out of D.C.," Annie said. "I wanted a place where we could start over. But, yes, I want to stay here. I want us to build a life here, to make this island our home."

"I like the café," he said quietly.

Annie blew out a breath. "Thanks, but it's only temporary."

"It suits you."

"You don't even know me."

He reached up, cupping his hand lightly around her small chin and tipping her face up to his. "I would like to get to know you."

"I told you," she said, trailing off when he slipped his other hand around her waist.

Will watched something flicker deep in her eyes. He could feel it, the tension simmering between them.

She wanted him as much as he wanted her.

He had no doubt about that now.

"Come over tonight at sunset." He pulled her closer. "Bring Taylor. I've got fifty acres of shoreline we can walk. I bet you'll find all kinds of things to make wind chimes out of."

She started to shake her head, and he bent down until his lips were a breath away from hers. "Say yes," he murmured.

"Will—"

He touched his mouth to hers.

He couldn't help it.

He needed to taste her, to feel her soft lips mold with his.

It was only supposed to be a persuasion tactic, a little tease to entice her to say yes. But when her palms skimmed up the muscles of his chest and her fingers curled around his shoulders, he felt something inside him shift out of balance.

The wind chimes danced, singing their sweet song as her lips moved under his, warm and soft and eager.

He deepened the kiss, and inhaled the scent of her—vanilla, apples, cinnamon.

Annie.

He wanted more of her, *all* of her. Her soft breasts pressed into his chest. He could feel the warmth of her thighs in those barely-there leggings brushing against his. He dipped his fingers into her silky red hair. He wanted her out of this sweatshirt, out of these clothes. He wanted to run his hands over every inch of her body.

Annie pulled back, suddenly. Cold air filled the space between them. But when she lifted her eyes back to his, and he saw the desire swimming in them, he was lost.

"Say yes," he breathed.

She unwound her arms from his neck, placing her palms on his chest. His heart pulsed into her hands. He felt desperate and thirsty, like he'd been traveling for miles and all he wanted was to stop. Right here. And rest. With her.

He kept his arms around her waist, holding her against him, unable to let her go. "Say yes."

She wanted to say yes. He could see it in her eyes. Why was she being so stubborn?

"I can't."

"Why?" He needed a reason. He wasn't walking away until she'd given him a reason.

"Because you're leaving," she said quietly.

"Because I'm leaving?"

"In a matter of weeks." Annie stepped out of his arms. "I can't do that to Taylor. I won't bring a man into her life who I know isn't sticking around."

"That's why you won't date me?" Will asked. "Because I'm not sticking around?"

She nodded.

"What if I was...sticking around?"

"Are you?"

No, Will thought. And it wasn't fair to lead her on. She didn't do casual, and he didn't do serious for the same reason: because he *was* always leaving. He'd decided a long time ago not to get married, not to get serious with anyone because there was always a chance, on any given mission, that he could die. Every time he left this country, he put himself in the most dangerous situations imaginable. He knew what it was like to lose the people he loved most in the world. He wouldn't put anyone through that.

But he wanted this woman. He wanted her for more than just one night.

Where the hell did that leave them?

Will looked down into her pretty green eyes. "What if we took things one day at a time?"

Annie shook her head. "I'm not okay with that. I can't start a relationship with a man who I know is leaving. I need a commitment, or at least the possibility of one."

He couldn't give her that.

But he couldn't let her go either.

He reached for her, pulling her close again. He bent his head back to hers, kissing her slowly this time. He wrapped his arms around her, wishing he knew what to say to convince her to spend some time with him, that everything didn't need to be planned out.

"Will Dozier!"

Annie jumped, twisting out of his arms.

Della Dozier stalked across the street with her hands full of baked goods and an expression of murder on her face. "*What* do you think you're doing?" She set two giant plastic containers on the steps and turned to face him, her hands on her hips. "This is our opening day! We are busy women! We cannot afford any distractions this morning!"

Will fought back a bubble of laughter as he caught Annie frantically smoothing out her hair. A blush crept up her pale cheeks as she stared at the floorboards. He resisted the urge to pull her close again and wrap her up in his arms one last time. Instead, he reached over and picked a leaf out of her hair.

"Get out of here!" Della ordered, pointing to the street. "Right now!"

Will walked over to his aunt and gave her a kiss on the cheek.

"Yes, ma'am," he said, reaching into the paper bag in her arm and pulling out a sweet roll.

"Will!" Della smacked his hand.

Will laughed and jogged down the steps. When he got to the street, he looked back at Annie and silently mouthed, "*Say yes.*"

EIGHT

I swear," Della huffed, carting the baked goods inside the café. "Give that man an inch and he'll take a mile."

Yep, Annie thought, she'd given him an inch all right. She'd practically crawled into his lap and asked him to carry her upstairs to her bedroom. Right next door to where her daughter was peacefully sleeping!

What was she thinking?

Della turned sideways to fit her plastic containers through the narrow door leading into the kitchen. "How long have you been dating my nephew?"

"We're not dating," Annie said quickly.

Della raised an eyebrow. "That didn't look like a first date kind of kiss, if you know what I mean."

"We're not dating," Annie repeated, walking into the café. "We have not been on a date. We are not dating." She switched on the espresso machine and grabbed two mugs from the rack behind the counter. "Do you want a cup of coffee?" she asked, desperate to change the subject. "How about a latte or a cappuccino? I could use another practice run before we open."

"Here," Della walked out of the kitchen, handing her a big slice of coffee cake covered in brown sugar. "Eat this first. You're too skinny. Look at those legs." Della clucked her tongue at Annie's leggings. "And, yes, since it's opening day, I'll take a latte."

"Coming right up," Annie said, fitting the scoop of dark coffee beans into the machine and snagging a quick bite of the cake. "Wow," she added, gazing reverently at the sugary topping of cinnamon and pecans. "This is amazing."

Della beamed, walking back into the kitchen. "I cut an extra piece for Taylor to have when she wakes up. By the way," she added, raising her voice so Annie could hear her over the hiss of frothing milk. "When you *do* go out with Will, tell him to take you to someplace nice in St. Michaels. He's more likely to ask you to join him and his friends for a beer at Rusty's."

Annie watched the steam rising off the bubbling milk in the metal beaker. "I'm not going out with him."

Della stuck her head out of the kitchen. "If it's Taylor you're worried about, I'd be happy to watch her."

"It's not Taylor." Annie turned off the heater and wiped it down with a towel. "He's leaving."

Della looked at her curiously. "Well, of course he is, Annie. He's in the military. That's part of what he signed up for."

"No, I mean when he sells the inn and goes back to San Diego, when he leaves for good." Annie set the towel back on the counter. "What you saw earlier—that was a one time thing. It just...happened."

"Sure it did." Della ducked back into the kitchen.

"You don't believe me?" Annie asked, following her into the kitchen.

"I *believe*," Della said, "that you're about as stubborn as he is." Parchment paper rustled as she unloaded the rest of the baked goods. "Once Will sets his mind to something, he doesn't give up."

"I'm sure Will has his mind set on plenty of other women on this island," Annie said, walking back out to the counter and pouring the hot milk over the espresso shots. "I'll do us both a favor and scratch myself off the list."

Della walked out of the kitchen and eyed Annie curiously. "Will's been at my house every night for dinner for the past two weeks. When he's not at my house, he's working like a mad man trying to fix up that old inn. If you're worried about him dating someone else, then you've got nothing to worry about."

Annie passed the latte to Della. This wasn't exactly the picture of Will she'd imagined. He didn't seem like the kind of man who sat at home pining after one woman. She'd figured when she hadn't seen much of him these past two weeks, he'd moved on. She'd given him enough reason to.

In her experience, there weren't many men who had the patience or persistence to pursue her once they found out she was a single mother. Most lost interest as soon as they heard she came in a package deal. But Will had already invited Taylor to join them three times. First for the sail, then to play with the dogs, and this morning right before kissing her, to come over tonight and watch the sunset.

That had to count for something.

"What about ex-girlfriends," Annie asked. "Didn't he used to date anyone on the island?"

"The only woman on this island Will has a history with is Hannah Elliott. They dated all through high school and most of college. Everyone thought they'd get married. But then...9/11 happened."

A shadow passed over Della's eyes.

Annie set her coffee cup down. "Did something happen to her on 9/11?"

Della shook her head slowly. "Nothing happened to Hannah. Will's mother and sister were in the plane that crashed into the Pentagon."

"No," Annie breathed.

Della's gaze drifted out the window, where yellow leaves swirled down from the willow oak. "Will changed after that. He and Hannah went their separate ways. She's married to Ronnie Faulkner now and pregnant with their third child. So, to answer your question," she said, sending Annie a sad smile, "you don't have anything to worry about in terms of ex-girlfriends."

"Was Will's mother your sister?" Annie asked, still trying to wrap her head around the fact that Will had lost both his mother and his sister on 9/11.

"My husband and Will's father were brothers."

"Where's Will's father now?"

"He passed away when Will was five."

He'd grown up without a father, Annie realized. Just like Taylor. Just like her. "Is that why he lived at the inn with his grandparents?"

Della nodded. "After his father died, Will's mother moved him and his sister back to the inn. She needed help caring for Bethany."

"Bethany?"

"Will's little sister."

The one who used to make wind chimes, Annie thought.

"They were five years apart, but I've never known a brother and sister who were closer than the two of them," Della said quietly. "Bethany was born with Down's Syndrome. Life wasn't always easy for her. But she was always smiling, always laughing. And she loved her older brother more than anything in the world."

Annie felt a lump form in her throat.

Della lifted her coffee cup, taking a long sip. "She was never supposed to live past the age of fourteen, but she was seventeen on 9/11. Will still blames himself for not being able to protect her from what happened."

It wasn't his fault, Annie thought. There was nothing he could have done to prevent it. She looked down at her coffee cake, not hungry anymore. "How did he change, Della? What was he like before?"

"He was happy," Della said simply. Her coffee cup clinked as she set it back in the saucer. "Don't get me wrong, I'm proud of him. I'm honored to be able to call him family. But I'm not surprised he made it into the most elite team of warriors in the world. Nothing can stop Will when he sets his mind to something, and joining the SEALs became an obsession after 9/11."

Good God. Will had said he was in the Navy. He hadn't said anything about being a SEAL.

Della rubbed her thumb over a stain on the counter. "Sometimes I wonder if this obsession, this thirst for revenge on the people who killed his family, is ever going to go away. I keep thinking that one day, maybe we'll get him back...the *old* Will. That one day, maybe he'll realize it's time to let go and live a normal life again."

"How could anyone ever let go of something like that?" Annie asked.

"He could move on if he had a family," Della said firmly, looking up at her. "A wife to love, and children to raise in that big old house. What he needs is a reason to come back home and build a life here on the island. That man belongs here, Annie."

WILL CLIMBED THE ATTIC STAIRS. The air was dark and musty. Dust motes floated in the thin beams of sunlight that peeked in through the two small upper windows. He walked slowly through the cluttered maze of boxes—boxes his grandparents had kept for him even though he'd told them to get rid of them long ago.

When he found the one he was looking for, he knelt beside it. His fingers brushed at the layer of dust and then snuck under the tape, snapping it open. He lifted the cardboard flap, and the memories of his sister released like butterflies into the wind.

All her chimes were still there, tangled up in knots, the colorful ribbons faded and crinkled from years of neglect. He swept a scattering of mothballs aside, and carefully unwound a long string of pink ribbons and bottle caps.

Bethany used to spend hours combing the marshes for feathers and driftwood, for oyster shells and glass bottles that would wash up after a storm. Her chimes were simpler than Annie's. Sometimes they were only painted ropes knotted together with a sprig of dried herbs and pop tops at the end. It was the sparkles that mattered most to Bethany. She especially liked the pieces that shined.

He reached into the pocket of his running shorts, his fingers closing over the yellow ribbon entwined with silver thread. To anyone else, it looked like a simple square knot tied into a faded ribbon fraying at the ends.

But it was the first knot he'd taught his little sister how to tie.

She had kept it, and given it to him as a present before he left for college. Back before 9/11, when he was only planning to serve the obligatory five years to repay the military for putting him through the Naval Academy. Back before those four planes went down on U.S. soil and his whole life changed.

He let the faded yellow ribbon roll through his fingers. He carried it everywhere now. On every deployment. On every training exercise. It went with him on every mission to every God forsaken place on this earth.

Will gazed down at the silver threads running through the ribbon. The shine had worn down long ago, except for the smallest sliver inside the protected center of the knot. He peeled it back, wanting to see it, wanting to remember his sister. Wanting to remember the way everything had sparkled when she was around.

Outside, doves cooed on the rooftop and a warbler sang from the branches of the hackberry. The wind rustled the leaves of the tulip poplars, only just beginning to change colors. Will pushed to his feet, picking up his sister's box and carrying it toward the stairs.

He'd come home to get rid of the things in this attic, to clean the house out and erase the memories. But the longer he stayed, the more he remembered and the more he wanted to keep.

NINE

Spencer Townsend leaned against the railing of Bob Hargrove's charter boat. The wind whipped over the Bay, spitting saltwater over the bow. His clients—three men from the Western Shore who were each in the market for a weekend home—had their lines in the water, waiting for the rockfish to bite.

When the phone in his pocket buzzed, Spencer welcomed the distraction. He'd never really understood the appeal of fishing. He'd much rather be out on a sailboat, cruising sleek and fast through the open water.

Walking back to the helm, he ignored Captain Bob's eye roll as he pulled out his phone to answer the call. "This is Spencer Townsend."

"Spencer," a deep southern voice came through the line. "Lance Hadley here."

Lance Hadley? Spencer stood up straighter. Up until now, he had only dealt with the regional acquisitions team. He hadn't expected to speak directly with the CEO and owner of Hadley Hotels. "Yes, sir? What can I do for you?"

"I understand there's been a delay with the purchase of one of our resort properties."

"Yes." Spencer cleared his throat. "There's been a slight delay."

"Is someone bidding against us?"

"No." Spencer stepped behind the plastic wind cover, lowering his voice. "The current owner is dragging his feet."

"Why?"

"He has an emotional attachment to the place."

There was a long pause at the other end. "An emotional attachment?"

Spencer winced. "Yes."

"I believe one of our acquisition managers discussed setting up an arrangement for you to keep an eye out for similar properties in the Mid-Atlantic, an arrangement that you would be compensated for."

Spencer swallowed. "That's right."

"I like the idea of having someone in the area to keep us apprised of valuable pieces of real estate before they go on the market. With your connections and your father's position as owner of a bank, you seemed like an obvious choice. But if you can't convince a man to let go of a piece of land because of an emotional attachment, you can consider that offer rescinded."

"I'll talk to him today," Spencer said quickly. "I know he'll come around. I was just giving him a little time to get used to the idea."

"I want this deal closed within the next two weeks, before one of our competitors gets wind of it," Lance said. "This property is perfect for Morningstar."

"I understand." Spencer glanced up at the raised voices coming from the bow. One of his clients had a fish on. From the strain in the line and the bend in the pole, it looked like a big one.

"Spencer?"

"Yes, Mr. Hadley?"

"How strong is this emotional attachment?"

Spencer thought back to Will's initial reaction to the resort company's offer, and his own failed attempts to talk him into the sale over the past couple of weeks. "It's pretty strong."

There was another long pause at the other end of the line. "Do I need to up the offer?"

Up the offer? Spencer watched Bob reach for the net, dipping it into the water as his client reeled the fish in closer to the boat.

Will had said he wouldn't accept a buyer who planned to tear down his grandparents' house, but surely there was a number that could change his mind, if it was high enough. "Potentially."

"How much?"

"I'm not—"

"How *much*?" Lance bit out, his impatience coming through the line. "Give me a number."

Spencer gave him one off the top of his head.

"Fine," Lance said brusquely. "Do it."

Spencer calculated the new percentage he'd get from the commission. He had to find a way to convince Will to take the new offer.

"If you can't close this deal, tell me now. I'll send someone else up there to persuade him."

"That won't be necessary," Spencer said, knowing that if Lance Hadley sent someone else up to the island to close the deal, any future working arrangements between them would be off. "You can count on me."

"DELLA?" Annie asked, stepping into the kitchen. "What are you doing? I thought you finished the desserts hours ago?"

"I did." Della dashed from the fridge to the stove, where a

saucepan of melted chocolate was threatening to boil over. "This is a new recipe I wanted to try out."

"A new recipe?" Annie scanned the crowded counters and overflowing dishes in the sink. Before she'd gone upstairs to change half an hour ago, everything had been on track. Now, it looked like a tornado had hit. "I thought we agreed on only four sweets today?"

"I know, I know." Della scooted bowls and plates out of the way to roll out a circle of sugary dough. "I got excited."

Annie looked fleetingly at the rockfish stations Della had set up earlier: one with bowls of egg, flour and bread crumbs for frying; one with a lemon zest and thyme marinade for broiling; and one with lemon wedges and slices of butter for sautéing.

She peered down at the chocolate, which was starting to burn. "Are you sure you have time for all this? It's almost eleven o'clock."

"Of course!" Della said, but her face had gone pale and beads of sweat were forming along her brow. "I have everything under control!"

It sure didn't look like she had everything under control.

Annie grabbed Della's hand, pulling her away from the cookies. "What's going on?"

Della's panicked eyes flickered up to hers. "I think you made a mistake."

"A mistake?" Annie's heart rate spiked. Had she forgotten to order something, some crucial ingredient Della needed to do her job today? "With what?"

"Hiring me."

Annie gaped at her. "What?"

"I'm not a chef," Della said in a small voice.

"Yes, you are."

Della shook her head. "I'm not."

"You *are* a chef," Annie said firmly. "You are *my* chef."

Della looked down at her feet. "I should have found another job answering phones."

"What are you talking about? You've done this before!"

"But that was for fun," Della protested. "It was never a job. You and Taylor—you're counting on me. What if I let you down? What if the tourists don't like my cooking?"

"They *will* like your cooking, Della. They'll love it. You're an amazing chef."

"What if—?"

"I did *not* make a mistake in hiring you!"

"You didn't?" Della asked tentatively.

"No." Annie stared at the woman who'd hardly left her side over the past two weeks. She'd lost track of the number of times Della had waved her off when she'd told her to go home because she couldn't possibly pay her for all her extra work. Della had already put in more hours than Annie could ever repay her for.

Della had taken on the task of opening this café as it if were her own, as if it meant as much to her as it did to Annie.

Maybe it did.

Annie squeezed her hands. "I have faith in you, Della."

"You do?"

"Yes, but you need to get a grip."

"I know," Della said, letting out a long breath. "I'm sorry. I just don't want anything to go wrong."

"Mom!" Taylor called from the front porch. "They're coming!"

Annie looked back at Della. "Nothing is going to go wrong."

Della sent her a small smile and Annie stepped back, pressing a hand to her suddenly queasy stomach. Their first customers were about to arrive. There was no turning back now.

She checked her reflection in the stove. She'd changed into gray slacks and a white scoop neck sweater, and added a pair of dangly silver earrings.

She was as ready as she'd ever be.

Taking a deep breath, she walked out to join her daughter on the porch as two middle-aged couples strolled up the sidewalk to the café.

A man in a blue windbreaker held up a plastic bag filled with fillets. "Our captain said you were offering to fry up the fish we caught this morning."

"That's right," Annie said, smiling. "We can prepare it any way you like, and we have a full menu of soups and salads if you want something else to go with it."

"Look, Stacey!" a blond woman gushed, nudging her friend and pointing up to the top of the porch. "Look at all the wind chimes!"

Taylor took the bag of fillets from the man and carried them toward the kitchen to deliver to Della as Annie led the two couples inside.

"Oh!" the blond woman exclaimed, pausing in the doorway. "Look at this place! It's adorable!"

Adorable? Annie felt a swell of pride as she led them to a corner table by the window.

The woman laid her arm over her husband's. "Wouldn't it be fun to have a room like this at home for the girls?"

The man muttered an incoherent response as he sat down beside his buddy and started trading fishing stories.

The woman looked up at Annie. "Who's your decorator?"

Annie paused, her hand on the menus stacked up beside the door. "Um...I am."

The woman's eyes widened. "You did all this yourself?"

Annie nodded.

"I'm impressed," she said, lifting her cloth napkin. Her eyes lit up when she saw that everyone's napkin was a different material and every glass and dish on the table was mismatched. "It's all just so cute!"

Annie poured their waters, explained the three rockfish preparations, and left them each with a menu. The word "cute" rang in her ears as she walked back to the kitchen. "Classy," "reserved," "elegant"—those were the words she'd been hoping for when she finally opened her own place.

But she could work with "cute." It was better than "cheap" and "tacky"—the two most common words her mother had used to describe her wind chimes. She'd been worried about how the tourists would react to her homemade decorations, but maybe they could see the same charm in them that Will had seen earlier that morning.

Maybe she was actually going to be able to pull this off.

More footsteps hit the front porch, and Annie turned. Three men and two women were walking up the steps. Another group of men wasn't far behind. She spotted Spencer Townsend with the second group and waved, wondering if he had any news on the resort, but she didn't have a chance to say more than a brief hello because, before long, every table in the café was full.

She spent the next few hours rushing back and forth from the kitchen to the dining room carrying plates of baked rockfish and boiled butter beans. A steady stream of voices and laughter spilled out the front door to the porch, and the wind chimes sang in the cool autumn breezes blowing through the street.

It was close to one o'clock by the time she got her first breather. She was behind the counter, brewing a round of espressos for a table of customers preparing to drive back to the Western Shore when Spencer walked up to the counter.

"Looks like you could use a waitress," he said.

"Tell me about it." Annie smiled, snagging four espresso cups off the rack behind her. She'd posted a few ads about the opening online and bought a small ad in the local newspaper, but Della had assured her that most businesses on the island operated out of word of mouth. In addition to posting signs at the marina,

Della had called every charter boat captain personally last night and told them to send the tourists to the café for lunch. Apparently, when Della called in a favor, people did what they were told. "I had no idea we'd be this busy on opening day."

"Speaking of businesses opening on the island," Spencer said, leaning his elbows on the counter, "I have some news that might interest you."

Annie scanned the dining room to make sure no one needed anything, and then pressed the button on the espresso maker for a single shot. "What's up?"

"Morningstar just upped their offer."

Annie's brows shot up. "They upped their offer?"

Spencer nodded, smiling.

"What did Will say?"

"I haven't been able to reach him. I think he's out on one of his friends' boats."

"He says he won't sell to a resort company."

"He will when he hears what they're offering."

"I don't know." Annie shook her head, pouring the espresso shot into a paper cup. "I'm not sure Will's motivated by money."

"Trust me," Spencer said, chuckling. "No one could turn down this offer. I got a call from the CEO of Hadley Hotels this morning. He wants to close the deal within the next two weeks."

Annie bobbled the cup. "What did you just say?"

"Hadley Hotels," Spencer repeated. "They bought Morningstar last month. I guess they're taking on a pretty heavy hand in the management. Maybe the resort company wasn't doing as well as we thought they were."

Annie stared at Spencer. How could she not have known that the Hadleys owned Morningstar? The day Spencer had told her about Morningstar's interest in building a resort on the island, she'd looked up the company online. She hadn't seen anything about them being a subsidiary of Hadley Hotels.

Spencer straightened, nodding toward the table of men in the corner. "I'm entertaining clients so I better run, but call my cell phone later if you want to talk."

Annie nodded, numb. The Blake Hadley she'd known hadn't wanted anything to do with his family's hotel company. But that was over eight years ago. Things could have changed. *He* could have changed.

She looked back at the kitchen where Taylor sat on a wooden stool inside the doorway, stirring sauces for Della.

She would never have bought this house, or opened this restaurant, if she'd known there was even a chance they would run into Blake.

TEN

*B*lake Hadley strolled into his father's study. "You wanted to see me?"

Lance Hadley didn't bother to look up. He sat behind an imposing hand carved walnut desk, studying a company report, his fingers resting casually around a glass of bourbon. "Have a seat, Blake."

Blake sighed. He knew that tone of voice. His father was disappointed in him.

What else was new?

Crossing the study, he took in the sweeping view of the Mississippi River. It was a beautiful day outside, but instead of enjoying it, his father would most likely spend it inside at his desk, reviewing the company's finances.

The man worked constantly. Blake couldn't remember ever seeing him take a day off.

What was the point in having all that money if you couldn't ever have fun with it?

Sinking into the comfortable leather chair, he hoped this wouldn't last long. He was meeting a few of his former fraternity brothers for drinks in the French Quarter in less than an hour.

"I understand," his father began, turning a page in the report, "that the expansion in Vegas is going well."

"It is," Blake said. "Charles Daley's doing a good job managing the project."

"He is," Lance agreed, lifting his gaze to Blake's. "But I didn't call you in here to talk about Charles Daley."

Here it comes. "What would you like to talk about?"

His father's eyes were sharp, simmering with anger. "I *understand* you spent more time in the casino than at your desk."

"Everybody does a little gambling when they're in Vegas."

"A *little* gambling?" Lance echoed. "I wouldn't call losing a hundred thousand dollars at the blackjack table a *little* gambling."

Blake's eyes narrowed. "You have people spying on me now?"

"This is *my* company, Blake. One *I* built from the ground up." His deep commanding voice boomed through the room. "I have eyes and ears everywhere, even on my own son."

Blake shifted in his chair. He couldn't believe his own father had been spying on him. "I'll win it back."

"You are *not* going to win it back!" Lance slammed his drink down on the table. "I've had it. Your *mother* and I have both had it. We have given you second chances, third chances, fourth chances. We have bailed you out, over and over, waiting for you to grow up, waiting for you to get your act together."

Blake sat back. So it was *this* talk again. Tuning his father out, he gazed at the mahogany shelves filled with books on management and leadership, biographies of presidents and statesmen, historical accounts of Louisiana's role in the Civil War.

His father had made him read all of them.

They were all about as dry as he was.

"We put you through college at Tulane," Lance continued. "We pulled strings to get you into Vanderbilt for your MBA. We offered you a job at the company, assuming you wanted to learn the ropes so you could fill my shoes as CEO one day. But you have never taken this company, or your role in it, seriously."

"You didn't build this company from the ground up," Blake countered, looking back at his father. "You started it with your father's money, *my* grandfather's fortune. Don't act like you were some pauper who started something from nothing."

His father's eyes flashed. "I was fortunate enough to be born into a wealthy family, but I never took my father's fortune for granted. He invested in my idea, but it was *my* idea, *my* company. I doubled my inheritance, Blake. I doubled it so my wife could have everything she wanted, so my children could have everything they wanted, so my grandchildren could have everything they wanted. I'm starting to regret that now."

"What are you talking about?"

His father took a deep breath. "It pains me to do this, Blake. But I am giving you *one* last chance. If you screw up, your mother and I are cutting you off."

Blake shot up, out of his chair. "You can't cut me off! I'm your only son!"

There was pain in his father's eyes now—raw, searing pain—because Blake hadn't always been his only son. Blake's older brother had been just like his father—driven, hardworking, focused. Mark had wanted to take over the company one day. He'd been everything his father had ever wanted in a son, until Blake had killed him in a drunk driving accident.

His father had never forgiven him for it.

"From now on," his father continued quietly, "you'll be working under my supervision." He sat back, studying his youngest son across the desk. "As you know, we recently acquired Morningstar at a steal. Bad management was running that company into the ground, but it has a solid reputation and I intend to rebuild it as the premier luxury resort company in the

South. Part of that plan involves expanding into the Mid-Atlantic. Our team has identified a property on the Eastern Shore of Maryland. It's an easy drive from D.C. and a prime piece of waterfront real estate that would be perfect for one of our resorts. But the current owner is dragging his feet. I want you go to up there and talk him into it."

"Why me?"

"Because despite the fact that you'd rather throw away money than earn it, you can be very persuasive. You have enough charm to convince anyone to do anything you want when you put your mind to it. It's time you put that charm to use for the company, for something other than your own pleasure." He looked away. "Perhaps if we'd had this talk sooner you wouldn't have screwed up your marriage to Emily."

"Emily was a—"

His father held up a hand. "You cheated on Emily, Blake. You cheated on her over and over. She knew it. We knew it. We *hoped* you would grow out of it one day, that maybe you would settle down once she got pregnant."

"It's not *my* fault Emily couldn't get pregnant."

Lance Hadley's voice grew weary. "It's been two years since your divorce. Your mother and I cut you some slack because you got married early. Maybe it wasn't the right match. Maybe you needed to blow off some steam for a while. But it's time to settle down now, Blake. Find a new woman who can make you happy, a good woman who wants to start a family. Maybe having children will give you a purpose in life, make you realize there are other people that matter in this world besides yourself." He lifted his bourbon. The ice clicked against the glass as he took a sip. "Your mother wants a grandchild."

"And if I can't give her one...what?" Blake asked. "You'll cut me off because of that, too?"

"I'm not bailing you out this time," Lance said. "You will earn back every penny of the money you lost gambling. You will earn it back through honest work. My assistant has booked you on a flight to Maryland this week. If you can't close the deal with the owner of this property, consider yourself cut off."

ANNIE CARRIED the last of the dishes into the kitchen, setting them in the sink. She'd sent Della home a little while ago, and Taylor was upstairs watching a movie. Pouring herself a cup of coffee, she walked out to the porch, hoping the fresh air would calm her.

There was no way around it. The Hadleys owned Morningstar.

After Spencer had left, she'd snuck upstairs and pulled up the company's website on her computer. Sure enough, the Hadleys had purchased Morningstar three weeks ago. They'd announced their official ownership a few days after she'd initially researched the company and decided to move here.

Which is why she hadn't seen anything about it on the website before.

Sinking to the top step of the porch, she wrapped her hands around the mug. She hadn't been able to do anything more than shut off the computer and rush back downstairs to continue serving the steady stream of tourists, but she knew now that Blake worked at his father's company.

She hated the fact that seeing his picture on the Internet after all this time could still make her feel small.

Gazing up at the wind chimes strung along the beams of her porch, she watched the shiny silver flutes catch the late afternoon sunlight.

She was only seventeen when Blake came into her life, too young to recognize the hollow promises and practiced manipulations of a charmer. It was the summer after she'd graduated from high school and she'd been working as many shifts as she could to support both herself and her mother, praying things would get better at home.

But her mother's drinking had taken a turn for the worse.

She'd considered leaving. Her mother had made it clear that she didn't care one way or another, but Annie had been afraid of what would happen if she left. How long would it have been before her mother accidentally hurt herself or drank herself to death?

Blake had given her a taste of a different life, one where children didn't have to worry about their parents, where they didn't have to work so hard, where they didn't have to wonder if life would always be a struggle.

She had wanted to believe in the fairy tale.

It wasn't until she'd told him she was pregnant that she'd found out it had all been a lie.

He'd accused her of trying to ruin his life, of trying to force him into marriage, of trying to steal his family's money. He'd blamed her for getting pregnant, as if he hadn't played a part in it, as if none of it had been his fault.

When he'd told her to get rid of it, they'd fought. She'd said she wanted to keep the child, and he'd laughed in her face. *'How are you going to raise a child on a waitress's salary? What are you going to do with it when you have to go to work? Are you going to leave it at home with your mother, who can't even take care of herself?'*

When she'd told him she loved him, he'd taken her hand. She'd thought, for a second, that he'd changed his mind, but he'd only led her through the crowded downtown streets to the nearest ATM and withdrawn a wad of cash. She would never forget his last words as he'd handed her the money. *'Your mother's*

*a drunk and you'll never be anything more than a waitress. Put the
child out of its misery now and get rid of it.'*

That was the last time she'd seen or spoken to him.

A car drove past, kicking up leaves. There was a part of her, a
small part of her now, that hoped Will would reject the Hadleys'
new offer. But she knew the resort coming to this island was the
only way she and Taylor would ever have any stability. The only
reason today had been such a success was because of the influx of
tourists from the fishing tournament. She didn't know if the café
would even make it through the winter.

Besides, even if Will accepted the Hadleys' new offer and the
resort did get built on the island, it wouldn't be a regular Hadley
Hotel. It would be a luxury resort operated by Morningstar. The
chances of Blake being involved in the subsidiary's operations
were small. The chances of him being involved in this particular
acquisition were even smaller.

There was no sense in panicking until she knew they would
cross paths.

Letting out a breath, she watched a woman across the street
decorating her front stoop with gourds and pumpkins. Halloween
was only a few days away and she still needed to get Taylor a
costume. Making a mental note to pick up some candy the next
time she went to the store, she leaned her head against the porch
railing. Her feet throbbed from being on them all day, but she still
had a lot to do. As soon as she finished this cup of coffee...

She heard the dog before she saw it. The frantic scrape of
toenails over the sidewalk gave way to an excited bark. She barely
had time to react before Riley bounded up the steps and all
eighty-five pounds of wet lab landed in her lap. Her coffee
spilled, sloshing over her legs as Riley planted her muddy paws
on her shoulders and showered her face with kisses.

"Riley, down!" Will was at her side an instant later, pulling
the dog off of her and helping her to her feet. "Are you okay?"

"I'm fine," she said, but his hands were all over her, brushing at the mud, making it difficult to concentrate.

"I'm so sorry." His gaze dropped to the coffee stain seeping into the fabric of her gray pants. "I'll buy you another pair."

"Don't worry about it," she said, taking a step back. She was intensely aware of the way her skin warmed under his touch, the way her pulse jumped when his hands skimmed down her arms. She couldn't help recalling how it had felt to kiss him that morning, the desire that had built inside her the moment he'd laid his lips on hers.

His eyes grew concerned. "Your hands are freezing. How long have you been out here?"

"Not that long," she said, trying to ease her hands free. But she paused, remembering what Della had said earlier, that Will had lost his family on 9/11, that he'd joined the SEALs to go after the people who'd killed his mother and sister.

She thought of her own mother, a woman who'd never truly loved her, a woman who'd never even wanted her around most of the time. She thought of Blake, the father of her child, a man who'd offered her five hundred dollars in cash the day she'd told him she was pregnant to get rid of the "thing" inside her.

What would it feel like to be loved so much by someone that he would devote his entire life to going after the people who hurt you?

"Annie?" Will asked. "Are you all right?"

She nodded, taking another shaky step back. "Let me go upstairs and change. I'll tell Taylor that Riley's here."

Will's hands fell back to his sides and Annie turned, walking into the café. Climbing the stairs to her apartment, she saw that Taylor was still curled up on the couch watching her movie. Brushing a hand over her daughter's wispy hair, she went into her bedroom and closed the door.

Leaning against it, she took a deep breath. Even if there was more to Will than he let on, even if what Della had said earlier was true—that he belonged here—it still didn't change the fact that his life and career were in San Diego.

Just because being around him made her feel things she hadn't felt in a long time, didn't mean she needed to act on them. She needed to focus on Taylor, and on making sure the café survived through the winter.

Pushing off the door, she snagged a clean pair of jeans from the pile of laundry on her bed. She slipped them on and walked back out to the living room, checking her reflection in the mirror. "Have you decided what you want to be for Halloween?"

"A butterfly," Taylor answered.

Annie smiled, smoothing out the wrinkles in her sweater. "What kind of butterfly?"

"A monarch," Taylor said. "With orange wings."

They would go shopping for wings tomorrow, Annie decided. In the meantime, there was someone downstairs she knew Taylor would want to see. Just because she didn't know what to do about Will, didn't mean Taylor shouldn't get to spend time with his dog. "Guess who came to see you?"

"Who?"

"Riley."

Taylor's whole face lit up. "Riley's here?"

Annie nodded.

Taylor grabbed her broom off the floor and scrambled off the couch, racing down the stairs to play with the dog.

Annie switched off the TV and followed her down the steps. Dogs and butterflies, she mused. After everything Taylor had been through, dogs and butterflies were what brought the most light back into her daughter's eyes.

She wondered suddenly if that was why Will had asked to "borrow" Riley from his friend while he was here. If he had been in and out of war zones for the past ten years, carrying out some of the most dangerous missions in the military, he had probably seen more death and destruction than anyone should ever see in a lifetime.

Will may be a SEAL, but he was still human. No one could witness that much devastation without reacting to it, without internalizing it and needing to process it in some way.

She watched Taylor run out to the porch. Riley's tail thumped against the floorboards as she rolled onto her back. Taylor dropped down beside the dog, rubbing Riley's belly with both hands.

The pop and splatter of sizzling oil had her turning. The scene of Will behind the stove with a dishtowel thrown over his shoulder, sliding chopped potatoes into a frying pan, caught her completely off guard. "What are you doing?"

"Making you and Taylor dinner," he answered, as if it was the most natural thing in the world.

"Why?"

"Because when I walked up to your porch a few minutes ago, you looked like you were about to fall asleep. You need a break."

She stared at him.

"What?" Will asked. "Surprised I can cook?"

"Well...yes," she admitted, crossing the room to stand awkwardly in the doorway of the kitchen.

"I'm not going to win any competitions, but I can fry up some fish and potatoes."

Annie spied the cooler on the counter beside the stove. Three thick fillets rested on a bed of ice. She'd been serving rockfish all day, but she had yet to taste it. "Is it as good as everyone says?"

"You've never had rockfish?"

She shook her head.

"Best tasting fish in the world."

She watched him dip each fillet into an egg and flour mixture. "Did you enter the tournament?"

"No. Most of the locals leave the competitions to the tourists. I went out for a few hours this afternoon on my friend Ryan's boat. I think you met his twin sister, Grace, the other day."

Annie nodded, reaching for the spatula to stir the potatoes.

He took it from her hand, setting it back in the pan. "You're supposed to be taking a break."

Annie bit her lip. She wasn't used to people helping her, people doing things for her without being asked. Della had been a huge help over the past two weeks, but she was her employee. Even if she had gone above and beyond, at the end of the day, Annie was the one signing her paycheck.

She didn't want Will doing things for her. She didn't want to get used to this, to expect this from him. "You don't have to do this."

"Do what?"

"Cook for us."

"You need to eat, Annie."

"We were planning to eat."

Will smiled and nudged her out of the way as he reached into the cupboard above her for a plate. "Think of it as payback for the chicken tenders."

She opened her mouth, then closed it. She'd completely forgotten about that. She was surprised he'd remembered, and oddly touched that he'd thought to repay the favor.

Will laid the last fillet on the plate and poured the ice down the sink. "So how did it go today?"

"It went well," she admitted. "Really well. Better than I expected."

He smiled. "I'm glad to hear it."

She watched him rummage through the spice rack, completely at ease in her kitchen. "Spencer came in earlier."

"Did he?"

"He said he'd been trying to reach you."

"I might have spoken with him today."

"Will."

"Annie," he said, mocking her serious tone.

She angled her head. "He said they made you a new offer, one you couldn't refuse."

"He was wrong." Will wiped his hands on the dishtowel. "I'm not changing my mind."

"Even if they offer you—"

"Even if they offer me all the money in the world." He turned to face her. "I won't sell the inn to them, Annie. I know you want that resort to come here, but I can't do it. I won't let them tear down my grandparents' home."

At the sound of the door opening, his gaze shifted over her shoulder. His brown eyes warmed as Taylor and Riley walked inside. They wandered into the kitchen and Taylor climbed up onto the wooden stool beside the stove where she'd spent most of the day watching Della. She peered at the pan, inspecting the potatoes, then looked up at Will. "Why didn't you come in for lunch today?"

"I was out fishing with a few friends." Will slipped a piece of raw fish to Riley. "Your teacher, Becca, was one of them."

"I've never been fishing," Taylor said, holding her hands over the steam rising from the potatoes to warm them.

"Never?" Will asked.

Taylor shook her head.

"We're going to have to change that, aren't we?" He pulled his cell phone out of his pocket and flipped through a few screens. "Here, I have pictures."

He handed the phone to Taylor and Annie edged closer while her daughter scrolled through the shots. There were four of them on the boat: Grace, Becca, Will, and another man who she assumed must be Ryan. In every picture, they were laughing.

Will looked so carefree, so happy.

Annie thought back to what Della had said earlier, that she hadn't seen Will happy in a very long time.

'*He belongs here.*' Della's words floated back, and Annie felt a warm shiver dance up her spine as he slipped his arm around her shoulders, leaning close to see the screen.

"This one's my favorite." Will pointed to a picture of Ryan pretending to kiss a fish on the mouth.

"Ewww," Taylor laughed, scrunching up her face. She scrolled to a new picture of Becca holding up an impossibly large fish. "That's Miss Haddaway!"

"It is," Will said, chuckling. "Your teacher caught the biggest fish of the day."

Will squeezed Annie's shoulders, and looked back at Taylor. "Maybe your mom would let me take you both out fishing sometime."

Annie looked down at Taylor, who was gazing up at Will excitedly. "Can we go, mom?"

"We'll see," Annie said.

Will smiled, that slow easy smile that made her stomach flip-flop. He leaned down so his lips were only a breath away from her ear. "We'll see," he whispered, running his hand slowly down her back, "is almost a yes."

ELEVEN

*W*ill didn't get to take Annie and Taylor out fishing that week because the winds picked up and whipped white caps over the Bay for six solid days leading up to Halloween. Gray clouds blanketed the sky on the last day of October as Will walked into the kitchen at the inn, taking two cold beers from the fridge and handing one to Jimmy Faulkner. "How bad is it?"

Jimmy took the beer, twisting the top off and taking a long pull. "I'm not going to lie to you, Will. It's pretty bad."

Will looked out the window, where the branches of the trees bent in the strong gusts blowing across the yard. "How much are we talking about?"

"Eighty grand. Maybe more."

"Shit."

Jimmy strolled over to the sliding doors, running a hand over the curve in the wood at the top. "We could do some cosmetic patchwork, shore up the foundation a few inches. Hope the inspectors don't catch it." He walked out to the porch, lifting a rotted floorboard with his steel-toe boot. "But this entire porch needs to be replaced, and the roof is at least three years overdue to be re-shingled. I'm surprised it hasn't already started leaking."

It had, Will thought. It had started dripping in the attic the night before. He knew because he'd been lying awake in the room directly below when the storm had hit. The rain had only lasted an hour, but the dripping had gone on all night.

"How did the open house go?" Jimmy asked, letting the floorboard fall back into place.

"Not well," Will admitted.

Despite Spencer's protests, Will had hosted an open house for the inn a few days ago. He'd posted signs along the road and ran an ad in the local paper. But only one couple had shown up, and they hadn't been serious about buying.

"I heard you got an offer from a resort company," Jimmy said, strolling back into the kitchen.

Will nodded.

Jimmy leaned against the counter, taking another long sip of his beer. "You should consider taking it."

"You think I should take it?" Will asked, surprised.

"It could mean a lot of work for my crew."

Will set his beer down. "Morningstar wouldn't hire a local crew to do the work. They'd bring in a team from the Western Shore, a big company with a national reputation."

"To do the initial building, sure," Jimmy agreed. "But after that there'd be regular maintenance and repairs, renovations they might want to hire a local contractor to complete."

The wind battered the windows, snatching leaves from the branches of the trees. Will walked slowly over to the sliding glass doors leading out to the porch, dipping his hands in his pockets. Were there others who felt the same way Jimmy did, that the resort would bring jobs and opportunities to the island?

He knew Grace and Ryan were against it; they wanted to preserve the land for the islanders and the wildlife. Becca had been fairly neutral on the subject, and Della had said she'd support him in whatever decision he made.

The only people he knew wanted the resort to come here were Annie, Spencer, and Chase. But maybe there were others who hadn't spoken up because they were afraid to, because they didn't want to upset their friends and neighbors.

Surely, the owners of the shops on Main Street would benefit from an increase in tourism. The charter boat captains would have more people to take out on fishing trips. Even the watermen would benefit from a spike in the number of people who'd want to spend their weekends eating crabs and oysters they purchased straight from the docks.

Right now, there was more money on the table than he'd ever dreamed of making off his grandparents' inn. He didn't really need the money. He made a comfortable salary. His apartment in San Diego was subsidized by the military. He didn't have any debt, and he'd built up a decent savings over the past ten years.

His retirement, if he made it to retirement, would be taken care of by the Navy. When the time came to make room for younger, faster guys on the teams, he'd planned to move into consulting and work for one of the firms who hired former operatives to carry out missions on a contract basis.

But if he took the money the resort company was offering, he wouldn't have to take on contract work after he retired. He could buy a big house on the beach in San Diego and spend his free time surfing and fishing. But what was the point in having a big house if you didn't have anyone to share it with? What was the point in having a yard if you didn't have any kids or at least a dog to play in it?

All he wanted was to sell his grandparents' house to a family who would restore the inn to its glory and care as much about the land and the islanders as their own profit margins. But he only had two weeks left to find a buyer. His time on the island was running out. He knew he couldn't trust Spencer to find the right person after he left. He could hire another agent, but what if it took years for another offer to come along? What if the perfect buyer didn't even exist?

How long was he going to hold onto this place, letting it rot down here at the end of the island, with the salt and the winds eating away at the siding?

Maybe all he had to do was sign on the dotted line and everyone would be better off.

Will looked back out the windows as a cluster of sailboats rounded a red buoy in the distance. Their white sails whipped in the wind as they picked up speed, heading back to one of the country clubs hosting the Friday night races. All he had to do was reach into his pocket, pull out his cell phone and give Spencer the word.

He could go back to San Diego, say goodbye to this house and this place forever.

He should just do it, make the call, get it over with.

A flock of barn swallows wheeled and dipped over the lawn, their high-pitched trills rising over the wind. Why couldn't he bring himself to do it?

"How do they feel?" Annie asked, adjusting Taylor's butterfly wings. "Too tight?"

Taylor flapped her elbows, testing the elastic straps around her arms. "They feel fine."

She could hear the excitement in her daughter's voice. They were downstairs in the café, waiting for Della, who'd insisted on coming with them trick-or-treating tonight. Taylor was wearing all black, with bright orange wings attached to her shoulders. A black headband with black pipe-cleaner antennae held her hair back from her face.

"There," Annie said, putting the finishing touches on her wings as Della rushed in wearing an elaborate witch costume and carrying a broom just like Taylor's.

"Sorry I'm late," Della said, pausing in the doorway when her gaze landed on Annie. "Why aren't you dressed up?"

Annie pulled a pair of cat ears from her back pocket and stuck them on her head. "I almost forgot."

"*That's* your costume?" Della asked, her expression dismayed.

"What?" Annie asked, adjusting the ears and looking down at her black top and dark jeans. "I'm a cat."

"You could have put a little more effort into it."

Annie bit back a smile. When Della had said she was dressing up as a witch earlier, Annie had figured that meant she'd be wearing a pointy black hat over a sweatshirt and jeans, not a costume that looked as if it had taken months to put together.

Annie dug in her purse for a black eyeliner pencil, swiping it across her cheeks to add whiskers. "Better?"

Della huffed out a breath and turned to Taylor, smiling broadly. "Now *that* is a costume!"

Taylor giggled as Della took her hands, twirling her around to admire her wings.

"Where's Joe?" Annie asked, peering out on the porch to look for Della's husband. After hearing that some of the kids were making fun of Taylor at school, he had offered to join them tonight and act as a buffer.

Joe Dozier was six-foot-three and over two hundred pounds of solid muscle. Born and raised on Heron Island, he had spent most of his life hauling his living from the Bay. When he wasn't on the water, he was fighting fires with the volunteer fire department or helping out Jimmy Faulkner on his construction crew.

He had the shoulders of a linebacker, a deep gravelly voice that commanded authority, and he didn't take crap from anyone.

Della batted at a cluster of leaves that blew into the room with her broom. "He overheard a few of the middle-school kids plotting a prank earlier. He's trying to track down Don Thompson to warn him."

"What are they planning to do?" Annie asked. She was used to kids playing pranks on Halloween. In D.C., most of the little kids went trick-or-treating before dark, so they didn't get caught in the teenagers' mischief. Heron Island was such a small community, she'd assumed the parents would keep a tight leash on their kids tonight. She hadn't given the pranksters much thought.

Della swept out the last of the leaves. "Don was storing the leftover fireworks from the Fourth of July celebration in his garage. They're planning to set them off tonight."

Annie's gaze snapped up. "Fireworks?"

Della nodded.

"Did you find Don to warn him?"

"His truck was gone. We think he might have gone into St. Michaels to run an errand. Joe's trying to track down the kids." Della smiled at Taylor, snagging her candy bag off the hook by the door and holding it out to her. "Are you ready?"

Taylor nodded excitedly, picking up her broom.

"Wait," Annie said. She didn't want to keep Taylor from trick-or-treating, but she also didn't want her to mistake the sound of a firework going off for a gunshot. "Do the middle-school kids have the fireworks?"

"Don's garage door was open," Della answered. "There's a pretty good chance they already took them."

Annie looked out at the dark streets. Children dressed in costumes were already starting to wander up and down the sidewalks. "Where will they set them off?"

"They'll probably take one of their father's boats out. Don't worry," she said when she caught Annie's worried expression. "Joe called the Fire Chief. He and a few of the guys are searching the docks now to see if any of the boats are missing. They'll find them soon."

Annie hesitated. She knew she couldn't protect Taylor from every loud noise. She wouldn't be there to hold her hand every time an engine backfired or thunder struck. But Halloween could be a scary holiday. She hadn't given enough thought to the older kids who would be dressed as ghosts and skeletons, the teenagers who would jump out from behind dark corners to scare the younger children.

"Taylor," she said, kneeling down so they were eye-to-eye. "You know the sound a firework makes when it goes off?"

Taylor nodded.

"If you hear that sound tonight, I want you to look up at the sky. I want you to look for the fireworks." If she could get Taylor to focus on the beautiful sparkly display in the sky, instead of on the sounds and the terrible memories they could stir up, they might be able to make it through the night.

Taylor's fingers curled around her broom. "I like fireworks."

"Me too." Annie squeezed her hand. At least, she had, until she'd remembered how much they sounded like gunshots. "Promise me that as soon as you hear them, you'll look up at the sky, that you'll be the first one to spot the fireworks."

"I promise."

Passing out candy to trick-or-treaters wasn't exactly how Will had imagined he'd be spending a Friday night on leave, but nothing was turning out the way he'd expected since returning to Heron Island. Walking up the street to Ryan's house, he kept an eye out for Annie and Taylor as he dodged groups of kids dressed in costumes.

Every house was decorated with pumpkins, gourds, and jack-o-lanterns. White ghosts hung from maple tree branches, and cobwebs cloaked boxwoods and porch rails. The sky was dark, a veil of clouds shrouding the moon. The smell of chimney smoke mingled with the salty air.

He spotted Becca sitting on Ryan's porch steps, and he made his way toward her. She looked up as a group of kids dashed across the lawn to the next house, her smile fading when she saw him. "You look exhausted."

He lowered himself to the step beside her. "I didn't get much sleep last night."

Ryan walked out of the house and handed him a beer.

"Thanks," Will said. He couldn't remember when he'd caught more than an hour or two of sleep at a time. The night-mares were getting worse, and the only way he could fight them was by staying awake.

A loud pop and sizzle had him glancing up. Over the roofs of the houses across the street, an explosion of fireworks went off. Will frowned. "Since when does the island have a fireworks show on Halloween?"

"We don't," Ryan said as another round went off.

Becca set down the bowl of candy. "I heard that some of the eighth-graders were planning to do something stupid tonight." She reached into her purse for her cell phone. "Billy Thompson must have found his dad's leftover stash from the Fourth of July celebration last summer."

Will pushed to his feet, scanning the faces of the children for Taylor. "Was Taylor in school today?"

Becca nodded.

"Do you know what she was dressing up as tonight?"

Becca punched a number into the phone and held it up to her ear. "A butterfly."

A group of teenage girls dressed as black cats raced toward the docks, laughing and carrying sparklers. Will strode into the street, searching for a pair of wings. A cherry bomb exploded by his feet and his muscles clenched, every nerve in his body switching to high alert.

It was Halloween mischief, he thought. Just kids playing pranks. But the memories crept in, chasing him like ghosts. More fireworks popped, lighting up the sky. A cloud of smoke, smelling of sulfur and cordite, floated toward him.

He needed to find Taylor. He needed to make sure she was okay.

Another cherry bomb popped and he spotted two girls wearing costumes with sparkly wings at the house across the street, but neither of them were Taylor. He cut through the neighbor's yard and a boy in a zombie costume streaked past him. Fake blood spurted from a gaping wound in the child's neck.

It's a costume. It's not real.

A cold sweat broke out on Will's forehead as he reached blindly for the side of the house. He leaned against it, his heart pounding as the image of his youngest teammate, Kyle, taking a bullet to the head swam into his vision.

He heard the shots whizzing past him, missing him, as he helped Colin behind the rocks so they could radio for help. He fought to slow the bleeding from his friend's leg, his hands slipping as he tried to keep the sniper alive long enough to make the extraction. His best friend, Dylan, shouted for backup. The sweet hum of rotor blades echoed in the distance.

But it was too late.

He heard Dylan's screams—the screams of a dying man. The same screams that had haunted his dreams for the past six months.

He felt a small hand slip into his, a small *person* lean against him.

Taylor.

She pressed the handle of her broom into his hand.

His fingers curled around it as he lifted his eyes to the woman standing only a few feet away. He held Annie's gaze as the screams faded, as the images slowly subsided, until all that was left was the sound of crickets chirping in the grasses, halyards clanging in the marina, and kids running from house to house yelling, "trick-or-treat!"

"I'm sorry I don't have anything stronger," Annie said, sliding a cup of coffee across the counter at the café to Will. "I'm still waiting on my liquor license."

"This is fine." Will wrapped his big hands around the small cup.

Annie sat across from him, the silence in the room broken only by the sound of the branches scraping against the windows. Things had settled down in the streets, and they'd left Taylor with Della to continue trick-or-treating. She needed to talk to Will alone. "How long has this been going on?"

"The flashbacks started last week."

"How many have you had?"

"This is the second." Will stared at the steam rising from the mug. "During the day, at least. They used to only happen at night."

No wonder he looked so tired, so ragged around the edges. She took in the dark circles under his eyes, the deep lines between his brows, and the tightly coiled bands of muscles along his neck and shoulders. Taylor still had nightmares, but they happened more sporadically now, and she'd never had one sneak up on her during the day. "When was the last time you slept through the night?"

Will lifted the mug, taking a sip of black coffee. "I can't remember."

"Have you thought about talking to someone?" Annie asked gently. "Someone who could help you work through what happened?"

Will shook his head.

"After what happened to Taylor, the school set her up with a grief counselor," Annie said. "She's been a big help."

"It's not that simple." Will set down his mug. "If I make an appointment, it'll be documented. My *symptoms* will be documented."

"But it would be confidential," Annie protested.

"Not in my line of work."

"I don't understand..."

"If I seek treatment, if any part of my health—mental or physical—is not one hundred percent, the military could strip my security clearance. Without it, I wouldn't be able to go on classified missions. I wouldn't be a SEAL."

Annie stared at him. They would take away his job, his *career* because he was suffering through something that happened on a mission they sent him on?

"I know what you're thinking," Will said, "but people depend on me. Lives depend on me, on my ability to make split second decisions. I can't go back out there; I can't lead my team on an op if I can't control my mind."

"But if you don't talk to someone, your symptoms could get worse."

Will rubbed a hand over his eyes. "I just need to find a way to get my head straight. There's got to be a way to outsmart the flashbacks, some kind of mental strategy I can use."

"I don't know if a flashback is something you can outsmart,"

Annie said. "I've done a lot of research on PTSD since the school shooting. What you're going through sounds a lot like PTSD."

Will's gaze drifted to the window as the wind snatched at the leaves clinging to the knobby oak branches.

"What happened, Will?" Annie asked.

Will tipped the coffee mug, letting the black liquid run around the rim. He didn't talk about what happened. Ever. But maybe just this once, he could tell someone. He could try to get some of it out. "Do you follow the news?"

"I haven't kept up with it much since we moved, but I used to watch the headlines on the evening news."

"Do you remember a story last spring, about Governor Foley's son?"

Annie nodded slowly. Everyone in the Beltway area had heard about what happened to Colin Foley. The governor of Maryland's son was a Navy SEAL, or at least he had been until he'd lost a leg on a mission in Afghanistan that had gone terribly wrong. Two other SEALs had died, and only one of them had come back unharmed.

"That was my team," Will said quietly. "I was in charge of those guys. I went out with three teammates, and I only brought one back. The two men who died, they had families—wives, children, mothers, fathers. They had people at home who depended on them. Even Colin had a fiancée. Not that she stuck around for long when he came back without one of his legs."

Annie felt a deep well of anger form toward that woman, whoever she was.

Will rolled the cup around on the counter, watching the dark liquid threaten to spill over the edges. "I'm the only one who could have died and it wouldn't have mattered."

"Will," Annie said, her heart going out to him as she reached across the table and laid her hand on his. "You can't think that way."

A dark cloud of grief passed over his eyes. "I can't stop replaying that day in my mind. I keep thinking about what I could have done differently. Why I'm the only one who came back in one piece."

Annie squeezed his hand. "Do you know how many times Taylor has asked me why she was the only one who survived the school shooting?"

Will shook his head.

"Countless," Annie said. "And I don't have an answer for her. All I know is that her life was spared. She was given a second chance. And so were you."

Will looked down at their joined hands.

"Will," Annie said softly. "Della told me why you joined the SEALs."

His eyes lifted back to hers.

"I understand why you needed to get back at the people who hurt your family, but is this really what you want?"

"It's who I am, Annie."

She slowly withdrew her hand from his. "It's not going to bring them back."

"Maybe not," Will said, "but as long as there are people out there who hate us, who want to destroy everything we stand for— as long as there is a war on terror, I want to be fighting in it."

He stood abruptly, pushing back from the counter. Shoving his hands in his pockets, he started to pace. "The nightmares will go away eventually. I just need to find a way to control the flashbacks."

Annie rose slowly, wanting to go to him, wanting to wrap her arms around him like she did with Taylor at night. But she knew there was nothing she could say or do to convince him that he needed help. "No matter how hard you fight to force them back, the memories will always be there."

He stopped pacing, looking back at her. "I need more time."

"It's been six months, Will." Annie rounded the edge of the counter, walking toward him. "If Taylor was experiencing what you're experiencing now, six months after the fact, I would be very worried."

"But Taylor's doing fine," Will argued. "You saw her tonight. She wasn't even fazed by the fireworks. It just takes some people longer than others to work through it."

"The only reason Taylor wasn't afraid of the loud noises tonight was because Della warned us it might happen. She'd overheard some of the middle-school kids talking earlier. Taylor made it through the night because we talked about it beforehand. She knew what to expect. But there will be times when she won't. And we'll deal with them, the best way we can, when they happen."

Laughter drifted in from the street, where a trio of girls dressed as fairy tale princesses searched for the last few houses with candy. Annie walked to where Will stood in the middle of the dining room watching the children. She held out her hand. "I want to show you something."

He looked down at her outstretched hand.

She remembered what Della had said about Will, that when he put his mind to something he wouldn't stop until he got it. Will wouldn't have made it into the SEALs if he was a quitter. It would go against everything inside him to admit he had a problem, that there was something wrong with him he couldn't fix.

But she needed to show him, to help him understand that this wasn't something he was going to be able to push through in the two weeks he had left on Heron Island. It was going to take a lot longer than that.

She took his hand, leading him up the stairs to her apartment. Walking with him to Taylor's room, she paused in the doorway, waiting for him to take in the hideouts, the tent draped over her bed, the homemade wind chimes and dream catchers hanging from the ceiling. Dozens of hand-painted brooms adorned the walls, and several more were propped in the corners.

"Taylor thinks brooms mean safety," Annie explained. "I don't know how long it'll be until she moves on from that. But it if helps her cope, I'll buy every broom I can find and decorate her room with them."

Will reached up, running a hand over a crooked-stemmed broom on the wall. It was painted purple and the bristles were covered in pink streamers from the handles of an old bike.

"She's healing, Will, but it's going to take a long time. I've been reading books and articles, everything I can get my hands on about PTSD. It's not something that goes away. It's something you learn to deal with, to live with." She looked up at him—at this man who'd been to some of the darkest, most dangerous places in this world, but who had been brought to his knees tonight because of a flashback. "All we can do is start in one corner, together, and slowly begin sweeping out the memories."

TWELVE

*P*TSD.

Will sat in an Adirondack chair at the end of the dock, mulling over the four letters Annie had dropped like a bomb in his lap last night.

What the hell was he going to do if he had PTSD?

A cold wind whipped over the Bay. A few fishing boats bobbed in the distance. He couldn't imagine life outside the teams. Being a SEAL wasn't a job; it was a way of life.

But his ability to control his emotions was what set him apart from other men, was what had drawn him to Spec Ops in the first place.

He had no intention of ringing the bell on his career now, not after everything he'd gone through. Not after his teammates had made the ultimate sacrifice and *he* had come back in one piece, still able to serve.

He would be a SEAL until his body broke down and forced him into retirement, or he died in action.

Quitting wasn't an option.

He glanced down at the phone in his hand, scrolling through his contacts for his former teammate, Colin Foley.

Colin answered on the second ring. "Well, if it isn't my favorite Lieutenant Commander."

"You know you don't have to call me that anymore," Will said, watching an osprey dive into the shallow water.

"As long as you keep calling every Friday to check up on my progress, I'll keep calling you that," Colin shot back.

Will smiled as the osprey lifted a wiggling perch out of the Bay. "How's the leg?"

"Not bad," Colin said.

Not bad. It was the same answer Will got every time he asked. "Are you still training for the 5K in January?" Will asked. "The one in Baltimore?"

"Yes," Colin answered. "Why? You want to sign up?"

Will knew he was joking. The charity run was barely over three miles, and before the grenade had blown off his friend's leg six months ago, they'd both been able to run that distance without breaking a sweat. But Colin was still getting used to the pros-thesis that had taken the place of his leg, and still working on restoring the muscles that had gone dormant after the amputa-tion. It was going to take him a long time to get back to the point where he could run three miles. "No, but I could help you train."

There was a long pause at the other end. "What? Over the phone?"

"No." Will watched a powerboat cut through the water. "I'm still in Maryland."

"At your grandparents' house?"

"Yeah."

"I thought you were selling that place?"

"I am. It's complicated. Listen." Will leaned forward, resting his elbows on his knees. "Why don't I come up to Annapolis one

day this week? We can go through some of the drills your physical therapist recommended."

"I don't need your help, Will."

Will winced.

"That's not what I meant," Colin said, backpedaling, but his
voice had grown weary.

Will gazed down at the thin cracks snaking through the
wooden planks. He knew what Colin meant. He didn't want
Will calling every week to check on him. He didn't want to be
treated like a charity case.

SEALs didn't ask for help. They were the ones who *gave*
help, the ones who answered the call of duty when no one else
could.

But the ability to answer that call had been taken away from
Colin—because Will hadn't been able to protect him.

"I have to go up to Walter Reed on Monday for an adjustment," Colin said. "I won't be able to run for a few days after that
anyway."

Walter Reed.

Will still regretted not being able to visit his former teammate
at the military hospital when Colin had been bedridden for
several weeks earlier this year. But Will had remained in
Afghanistan to finish out his deployment after Colin had been
medevac'd out, and his other two teammates had gone home in
body bags.

"What time is your appointment?" Will asked.

"One-thirty," Colin answered. "Why?"

Colin might not be lying in a hospital bed at Walter Reed
anymore, but there were plenty of other service men and women
who were. The medical center in Bethesda was less than two
hours away from Heron Island. He should have thought to make
the trip sooner.

Even if all he could do was offer moral support, it was better than nothing. "I'll see you at Walter Reed on Monday."

PATIENCE, Annie thought, was not one of her strong suits. Over the past week, business at the café had slowed to a trickle. Her first loan payment was due in ten days, and at this rate, she wasn't going to make it.

She needed to make that payment.

Flipping the sign on the door from *OPEN* to *CLOSED*, she walked back to the kitchen to help Della pack up the leftover desserts. "We need more customers."

Della draped a layer of plastic wrap over the coffee cake. "Business will pick up. Give it time."

"We don't have time."

"The Waterfowl Festival is two weeks away," Della said. "We'll get a surge of tourists then."

But what about *after* the festival? The Waterfowl Festival was the last local event that would bring tourists to the island before the winter lull set in. If the café was going to make it through the winter, they needed to find a way to reach out to the islanders. They needed to offer more than good food and a charming atmosphere; they needed to find a way to integrate the café into the local community.

She and Della had been tossing ideas around all week: offering to host the monthly waterman's association meeting, providing a discount to teachers and firemen on the last Saturday of the month, catering fundraisers for local charities, starting a monthly book club with a themed menu based on the chosen story.

All good ideas, but none of them would spike sales overnight. She needed to find a way to get people in here *this* week.

Picking up a tin of peanut butter cookies, she searched for the matching top as Taylor walked into the kitchen holding up a paper butterfly. "Mom, look!"

Annie softened as she took in the orange wings with black spots, the long strand of purple yarn threaded through them. "It's beautiful."

Taylor beamed.

"Do you want me to help you hang it?" Annie offered.

Taylor shook her head, gravitating toward the cookies. "I made it for Will."

Annie froze. Ever since her conversation with him last night, she'd felt an endless range of conflicting emotions—concern, sympathy, frustration, begrudging respect.

She didn't want to respect him. She didn't want to worry about him. She wanted him to sell the inn to the resort company.

Or, at least, she *had* until she'd found out the Hadleys owned Morningstar. Now she didn't know what she wanted.

Taylor snagged a cookie from the tin. "He said the monarchs are almost all gone, so I made him one to remember them by."

Annie's heart constricted. Taylor had disappeared over an hour ago saying she had something "important" to do upstairs. *This* was what she'd been doing? Making a butterfly for Will?

She stole a glance at Della. The other woman's gaze was glued to the butterfly.

"Taylor," Annie suggested lightly, "why don't you grab a sweater from upstairs and we'll walk down to the marina to watch the sunset?"

"But what about the butterfly?" Taylor protested. "We need to take it to Will."

Annie struggled to come up with an excuse.

Della caught Taylor's hand, drawing her back to stand beside her. "You know," she said, tucking Taylor's hand through her arm, "the best spot on this island to watch the sunset is at the inn."

"It is?" Taylor asked hopefully.

Della nodded and Annie heard a faint clanging of copper wind chimes out on the porch—the same ones she'd heard last night as she'd lain awake thinking about what Will had told her, about how he blamed himself for his teammates' deaths, about how he couldn't seek help for the flashbacks and the nightmares because it could cost him his career.

Della gestured to the tin of cookies Annie was holding. "I was going to take those leftover cookies by the inn tonight, but why don't you and your mother take them instead? I'm sure Will would much rather see you than me."

Taylor looked up at Annie. "Can we go see Riley, mom? Please?"

Riley.

Annie let out a breath. Of course. Maybe Taylor had only made the butterfly as an excuse to see Riley. Maybe it didn't have anything to do with Will.

She looked down at the butterfly, suspended from the strand of yarn from her daughter's hand.

Maybe the only way to find out was to go to the inn, watch Taylor give Will his present and see for herself.

The moment she sensed even a hint of attachment on Taylor's part, their friendship with Will would be over. Done. She'd end it so fast Will wouldn't know what hit him.

Because Taylor was her priority—her *number one* priority. She would not let her get caught in this. She would not let her get hurt.

"We can go," Annie said slowly, "but we'll only stay for a little while. I still have a lot to do tonight."

Taylor grinned, unwinding herself from Della's arm and darting out of the kitchen to grab her sweater.

Della and Annie stood in the small kitchen for several long moments, watching each other. Annie finally broke the silence. "I

don't want you getting the wrong idea about Will and me." She
held up the cookies. "Or trying to play matchmaker."

"Taylor made him a present," Della said quietly.

"It doesn't mean anything."

"Doesn't it?"

"No." Annie caught the tiny flicker of hope in the other
woman's eyes, remembering what Della had said last week, that
the only way Will would ever get over the loss of his mother and
sister was by starting a family of his own.

She couldn't possibly think that Annie and Taylor...?

No, Annie thought. That was crazy.

She wasn't the kind of woman men turned their lives upside
down for. She wasn't the kind of woman men put down roots
with. She was the kind of woman men left, the kind of woman
men dated briefly and forgot about just as fast.

At the sound of Taylor's footsteps on the stairs, she turned
and walked out to the dining room. "Ready?"

Taylor nodded.

Annie followed her out to the porch and down the steps to
where her car was parked on the street. They drove down the
long flat road leading to the inn, taking in the late afternoon
sunlight slanting over the marshes. Taylor chatted away happily,
stealing a cookie from the tin whenever she thought Annie wasn't
looking.

By the time they pulled into Will's driveway, the butterfly
had crumbs all over it, and a new worry had sprouted wings
inside her. What if Will had company? What if he had asked
someone else over to watch the sunset? What if she and Taylor
were interrupting?

Her hand hovered over the gearshift. She should have called
first, at least to tell him that they were coming.

A dog barked and Riley bounded around the side of the
house to greet them. Taylor opened her door and the yellow lab

jumped inside and gave her a big sloppy kiss. Taylor squealed when Riley grabbed her broom and darted away with it. She scrambled out of the car, her paper butterfly flopping behind her as she raced after the dog.

There was nothing Annie could do but turn off the car and follow her. Climbing out of the driver's seat with the cookies, she heard music playing from a muffled stereo in the back yard. She followed the sound around the side of the house to where a rusted ladder led up to the roof and rotted shingles were scattered over the lawn.

She glanced up, catching the expression on Will's face as he watched Taylor chase Riley across the yard. He was smiling and his eyes were filled with warmth. The relief that he didn't already have company, that he was actually glad to see Taylor, was replaced instantly by a deeper emotion as he stood and made his way across the roof.

He'd taken his shirt off, and when he swung down to the ladder, the sleek muscles of his back and shoulders gleamed in the fading sunlight. A pair of ripped jeans hung low across his narrow hips, and she could see the outline of his hard thighs through the worn denim.

A muted clang rang through the air as his work boots tapped the metal rungs of the ladder. He jumped easily down to the ground and then turned, spotting her. All Annie could do was stare as a rush of heat shot straight through her.

He started toward her and she lifted the tin, desperate to put something physical between them. "Della sent cookies."

Will's lips curved. "Cookies?"

She nodded, gripping the metal tin as sparks threatened to shoot from her fingertips.

He paused when he was standing directly in front of her, when he was close enough that she could smell the salt and soap on his skin. "What kind?"

"Peanut butter."

"My favorite," he murmured.

Annie's knees almost gave out when his hands covered hers so they were both holding the tin instead of taking it from her. "Taylor might have eaten half of them on the way over."

He laughed, a deep rich sound that rolled all they way through her. "Is that why you came here? To bring me cookies?"

Annie shook her head. "Taylor has something for you. She made you something."

"She made me something?"

Annie nodded.

He held her gaze for a long moment, and she caught the shift deep in his eyes, the silent question that swam into them. Slowly easing the tin from her hands, every brush of his calloused fingers sending jolts of electricity crackling through her, he turned. "Taylor," he called, his deep voice echoing over the yard to where she was playing tug-of-war with Riley for her broom.

Taylor finally managed to snatch the broom back from Riley. Lifting it up over her head, she ran across the yard with the dog on her heels. By the time she got to them, she was out of breath, her cheeks were flushed, and her eyes were shining with pure joy.

Will smiled down at her. "Your mom said you made me something."

Taylor lifted the paper butterfly. "It's a monarch."

Will gazed down at the butterfly. The wind snatched at the orange paper, causing the wings to flutter and flap. "You made this?"

Taylor nodded, suddenly shy. "So you won't miss them when they're gone."

Will knelt slowly, taking the butterfly from Taylor. It looked so small, so fragile in his big hands. "Thank you," he said when they were eye-to-eye. "I'll treasure it."

Taylor took a tentative step forward, lifting her arms and wrapping them around his neck.

No, Annie thought helplessly. Taylor wasn't supposed to hug him. She was supposed to give him the butterfly and run away to play with Riley again.

But she wasn't running away. And now Will was hugging her back.

Annie's throat felt tight. Her daughter hadn't come here to see Riley. She'd come here to see Will.

Will pulled back, standing. "I know just the place for it," he said, taking Taylor's hand and leading her toward the house.

"Wait," Annie said.

Will turned.

"We have to go."

"What?" Taylor asked.

"You just got here," Will protested.

"And now we're leaving," Annie said, struggling to keep the emotion out of her voice. If she cut off their friendship now, it wouldn't hurt as much later. "Say goodbye to Riley, Taylor."

"But we need to help Will hang the butterfly," Taylor said, refusing to let go of his hand.

"Annie?" Will asked, his expression confused.

"I have a lot to do tonight," she said simply. "I told Taylor this would only be a short visit."

"We'll be quick, mom. I promise," Taylor said. "We just need to help him hang the butterfly."

Annie fought back the urge to grab Taylor and race back to the car before this went any further.

"If you're that busy," Will said, keeping his tone light, "why don't you head back to the café and I'll bring Taylor over in a little while."

That was the last thing she wanted.

"Mom," Taylor said, "don't you want to see inside the house?"

No, Annie thought. She didn't want to see inside the house. She didn't want to know what it looked like. She didn't want another reason to feel closer to this man.

But she didn't want to leave Taylor alone with him either.

Taking a deep breath, she looked up at Will. "We'll come in to hang the butterfly and then we're leaving."

He smiled. Turning, he led Taylor across the yard and up the rotted porch steps, pointing out where to place her feet so she wouldn't fall through. Dodging the loose floorboards, he opened the door and guided Taylor inside, holding it open for Annie.

Annie crossed the threshold, and the feeling of home swept over her so fast it stole her breath. A big, family-style kitchen opened up to a cheerfully cluttered living area filled with two oversized couches, cozy armchairs, and a wide brick fireplace. Built-in floor-to-ceiling shelves held paperbacks, board games, and videos.

There were pictures everywhere—pictures of the Dozier family, of guests eating dinner on the patio in the summer, of men holding up enormous rockfish on the dock, of Will in his dress uniform decorated with medals.

Releasing Taylor's hand, Will walked over to a casual wooden dining table nestled into a breakfast nook. Lifting the butterfly, he looped the strand of yarn around an antique country chandelier that hung from the ceiling.

"What do you think?" he asked, stepping back.

Taylor climbed up on the chair beside him, readjusting the yarn so that the wings were even. "It's perfect," she said, beaming.

The sun sank lower on the horizon, painting their profiles in a soft orange glow. Taylor's gaze shifted to a string of sparkly bottle caps dangling from one of the arms of the chandelier.

She reached up, touching one of the bottle caps. "Who made this?"

"My sister."

"She makes wind chimes, too?"

"She used to," Will said. "She passed away a long time ago."

Taylor watched the bottle caps spin. "Do you miss her?"

"I do."

"I miss my friends," Taylor said quietly.

Annie started toward her. She didn't want Taylor bringing Will into this. She didn't want her turning to him to seek any kind of comfort.

It was way past time for them to go.

She reached up to take Taylor's hand and lead her down from the stool, but Will's hand closed over hers first. She opened her mouth to protest, but he drew her back gently to stand beside him.

"Sometimes," he said to Taylor, "we have to say goodbye to people we're not ready to say goodbye to. But we can still remember them. We can still think about how they used to make us laugh or smile, how we used to feel when they were around. After a while, the memories get easier and new people come into our lives." He threaded his fingers through Annie's. "Usually, when we least expect it."

Taylor looked back at the string of bottle caps and her paper butterfly swinging from the arms of the chandelier. "I made a new friend last night."

"You did?" Will asked. "Who?"

"Jess Casper."

"Casper?" Will glanced down at Annie. "John and Ellen Casper's daughter? The one who lives next door to Della?"

Annie nodded. Della had taken Taylor over to visit with Jess the night before, after they'd finished trick-or-treating and Annie and Will had gone back to the café to talk.

"Jess is a year younger than me," Taylor continued, "but she's really nice. Her mom and dad just got her a puppy. She said I could come over and play with him whenever I wanted."

"What about Riley?" Will asked, poking her in the side playfully.

Taylor giggled. "Riley's still my favorite."

"Good." Will dug a handful of dog biscuits from his pocket. "And you'll be her favorite if you run out and give her these."

Taylor took the biscuits and grabbed her broom, climbing back down from the chair. Annie watched as she dashed across the porch and down the steps to the yard where Riley was chewing on a new stick.

It was time to say goodbye, Annie thought. She should tell him it was over, that this was the last time they were going to see each other. But when she looked up at him, she couldn't form the words.

He took her hand, leading her into the kitchen and grabbing them both a beer from the fridge. "How about a tour?"

She hesitated, but he was already nudging her toward the stairs. He led her through the house, showing her every room, telling her funny stories about the guests who had stayed in them. A strange sense of peace settled over her as she thought about all the people who would have come and gone over the years, the steady stream of people who would have filled the rooms when the inn was open for business—laughing, chattering, happy people on vacation, or taking a weekend away from a stressful job in the city.

What would it be like to live in this big house constantly filled with people? To know you were bringing so much joy to everyone who visited?

By the time they walked back downstairs, she couldn't bear the thought of a resort company sending in a corporate decorating team to strip away the character of this house. They would streamline the colors and furniture to match the latest trends. They would turn this place into something it was never meant to be.

This house belonged here. Just the way it was. And Will belonged here with it.

When she spotted the box of wind chimes on the ottoman in the living room, she let go of his hand and walked over to it, peering down at the strings of seashells, pop tops, and sparkly ribbons. "Are these the chimes your sister made?"

Will nodded. "I brought them down from the attic after I saw what you'd done with the café."

She looked back at him, where he stood in the doorway watching her. "What are you going to do with them?"

"I don't know yet."

Annie reached into the box, lifting out one of the chimes. "Will you take them with you when you leave?"

The words hung between them.

She heard Taylor's laughter out in the yard where she was laying in the grass with Riley, catching the leaves as they spun down from the trees.

Will took one step into the room and Annie's fingers curled around the chime.

"Annie," he said quietly.

She crossed the room to where he stood, walking into his arms.

When his mouth came down on hers, she kissed him back.

And for the first time in her life, she wished more than anything that she had the power to make a man stay.

THIRTEEN

On Monday, Will made his way across the Walter Reed National Military Medical Center campus in Bethesda. He'd spent most of the past weekend with Annie and Taylor. He wasn't surprised that the more he got to know Annie the more he liked her, but he hadn't expected to enjoy hanging out with her eight-year-old daughter so much.

Taylor was different than most kids her age. After everything she'd been through this year, they could understand each other.

He'd asked Annie what had happened to Taylor's father. She'd said they'd both been really young when she got pregnant, and he hadn't been ready to be a father. But Will had a feeling there was more to the story than that.

He'd decided not to press it. For now.

Walking into the Prosthetic Care Center, he signed in at the front desk. The receptionist pointed him down a hallway and he followed the sound of voices to the fitness center, where a dozen injured veterans and active duty service members were lifting weights inside a large room filled with exercise equipment. Physical therapists and prosthetic technicians were tracking their progress, and a few family members were on hand for moral support.

Scanning the room for Colin, he spotted the former SEAL on a treadmill in the far corner. Six months ago, when Colin had been medevac'd out of Afghanistan, Will hadn't known if he would survive. He should have known better.

Colin was a fighter.

Will stepped into the gym and several people glanced up, including Colin.

His former teammate's face broke into a smile as he paused the belt and stepped off the machine, walking with a slight limp on the prosthesis. "Long time no see," he said, holding out his hand.

Will took it, not at all surprised that from the waist up, Colin could have still passed for a SEAL. His upper body hadn't lost an ounce of its active duty bulk. "You look good, man."

"Thanks."

So did most of the people in this room, Will realized. It didn't matter that they'd lost legs or arms. They were working hard to restore their bodies back to the shape they were in before they got hurt.

He would be doing the same thing if he were in their shoes.

Will drew his hand back, looking down at the prosthesis attached to the lower half of Colin's left leg. "How does it feel?"

"Not bad," Colin said. "It takes a little getting used to when they make an adjustment, but I can't complain."

No, Will thought, Colin wouldn't complain. Several years ago, they had spent forty-eight hours in a 115-degree Somali desert to gather intelligence on a high-ranking Al Qaeda terrorist. They had lain perfectly still in the scorching sand for two days while flies chewed on their faces.

Colin hadn't complained once.

They wove through the exercise equipment to where a young

black man, about nineteen or twenty years old, was doing resistance training on the mats. He wore prostheses on both legs. "Sergeant," Colin said, helping him to his feet. "I'd like you to meet my former teammate, Lieutenant Commander Will Dozier."

The young man held out his hand. "Vince Morgan, sir. It's an honor to meet you."

"Call me Will," Will said as several more pairs of eyes in the room swung toward him. "Are you the same Vince who talked Colin into signing up for the run in Baltimore?"

He stood up straighter. "I am, sir."

"How many miles are you up to now?"

"Only one. But I'll get there." Vince squared his shoulders. "We'll all get there."

Colin smiled. "He's got eleven of us signed up now."

"Eleven?" Will looked back and forth between the two men. "I'm impressed."

"I'm aiming for twenty-five," Vince said.

Colin looked back at Will, his voice sobering. "Everyone's committed to raising a thousand dollars to go toward a handicap-accessible home for one of the guys in his unit. His friend was paralyzed from the waist down. He'll be in a wheelchair for the rest of his life."

"How old is your friend?" Will asked Vince.

"Twenty-three."

Will shook his head. Twenty-three was way too young to be paralyzed. He gestured to the metal contraptions that had taken the place of both Vince's legs. "Did this happen at the same time?"

Vince nodded. "Our convoy ran over an IED in Kandahar. I was one of the lucky ones."

One of the lucky ones. Will glanced back at Colin. For the past six months, he'd lost sleep over severing his friend's career as a SEAL, for killing his marriage before it even happened. But did

Colin feel the same way Vince did? That he was one of the lucky ones—lucky to be alive?

"If we can raise $25,000 for the run," Vince continued, "my friend will have enough for the down payment of the house and a live-in nurse for the first few months."

Will looked at Vince's dark, determined eyes. Twenty-five grand wouldn't set up the disabled vet for the rest of his life, but it was a start. The government was only going to do so much for these guys. Who else was going to step up and help them if not their fellow service members?

"Come on," Colin said, nodding toward the rest of the room, "I'll introduce you around."

Over the next hour, Will talked to every wounded warrior in the room. He heard their stories, their struggles, and their triumphs. He listened to their fears about their future. A few of them were planning to stay in the service, but the ones who'd been injured too badly to serve were worried about the transition to civilian life.

He didn't blame them. He'd heard enough disturbing accounts of vets who couldn't adjust, who couldn't find work, who slowly withdrew until they became completely isolated, even from their friends and family.

By the time he and Colin left the Prosthetic Care Center, he was beginning to wonder how many more former service members were out there struggling, too proud to ask for help?

"Are you still planning to work on your father's reelection campaign through the fall?" Will asked as they crossed the lawn to the parking garage. He could hear the traffic on Rockville Pike zooming by in the distance.

"I am," Colin said, shouldering his gym bag.

Will noted the resigned tone in his friend's voice. "You don't sound too happy about it."

Colin shook his head. "I want to support my father. He's

done a lot of good things for the state. But I don't want to be a prop."

"What do you mean?"

"He wants me to come to his speeches, stand on the stage, show off my leg. Look at my son, look what he sacrificed for the country, look how patriotic we are."

"To help get the military vote?" Will asked.

Colin nodded.

"Why don't you just say no?"

"I could, but I haven't come up with a better plan yet. To be honest, I spend most of my free time here. Some of the patients, especially the ones in the beds," he said, nodding toward the main hospital, "don't get as many visitors. I come here a few times a week to hang out with people, see if they need anything. A lot of them just want to talk. But I wish I could do more, figure out how to help them get back on their feet."

Will let that sink in as they walked into the garage and rode the elevator up to the floor where they were both parked. They stepped out onto the top level, navigating through the rows of cars. "When does your father's campaign get rolling?"

"Not for a couple of weeks."

Will paused when they reached his SUV, a plan slowly beginning to form. "Didn't you used to have an uncle who was a carpenter?"

Colin nodded. "I spent all my summers in high school and college working with him."

"Feel like swinging a hammer for the next few days?"

Colin lifted a brow. "What did you have in mind?"

"I could use some help fixing up my grandparents' place."

"The one you're trying to sell?"

"Yeah." Will unlocked the SUV, wondering why that question suddenly left such a bad taste in his mouth. "The one I'm trying to sell."

"Tell me something," Colin said, studying him. "Does the *complication* you mentioned over the phone a few days ago have anything to do with a woman?"

Will leaned against the vehicle, looking back at his former teammate—a man who he'd been on countless missions with, who he'd graduated BUD/S with, who he'd learned how to dive with, jump out of helicopters with, fire a sniper rifle with. A man who he'd trained with and fought with for over ten years. "Have you ever known me to let a woman complicate things?"

"No."

Will smiled. "Then, no."

"But there is a woman, isn't there?"

"There are a several women on the island."

Colin smiled back. "Then count me in."

ANNIE RUMMAGED THROUGH HER CLOSET, searching for something to wear. Behind her, Della sat on her bed, sipping a wine cooler and flipping through a *Southern Living* magazine.

"How'd we do today?" Della asked.

"Good." Annie pulled a black wrap dress off a hanger and tossed it onto the bed. "Better than I expected."

"Good enough to keep the bank off our backs for another week?"

Annie nodded, glancing over her shoulder. "I might even be able to cut you a paycheck on Friday."

Della beamed. "I told you we'd be back on track in no time."

Annie turned back to the closet, passing over a gray jacket and two more black cocktail dresses. "The only reason we're back on track is because you called every person on this island and begged them to come in and have lunch this week."

Della flipped the page in the magazine. "There's nothing wrong with calling in a favor now and then."

"But that's the second time you've called in a favor for me." Annie slipped a black pencil skirt off the hanger and laid it on the bed. "What are they going to expect in return?"

"These things have a way of working themselves out." Della picked up the skirt, shaking her head. "This looks like something you'd wear to work at an office."

Annie tossed it back in the closet. "But what if no one comes back next week? What if they only came in because they were doing us a favor?"

Della smiled. "They'll be back."

"How can you be so sure?"

"You need to have a little faith."

Annie's fingers closed around the sleeve of a blue wrap dress. "I should stay in tonight. I have too much to do."

Della set down the magazine. "You are *not* staying in tonight."

"The Waterfowl Festival is less than two weeks away. I need to update the website, start building some buzz on social media."

"You can work on the website tomorrow."

"We still need to come up with a special menu."

"Leave that to me."

Annie's fingers worried over a button coming loose at the hem of her shirt. "I should look into how much it would cost to run an ad on the radio."

"You've already put an ad in the local paper and in three different magazines." Della swung her legs over the side of the bed and walked over to Annie's closet. She pulled out the blue wrap dress and a green sweater dress. "Here," she said, handing them to Annie. "Wear one of these."

Annie took them from her, the hangers clinking together as

she hugged her arms around the dresses. "What if Taylor calls? What if she can't reach me?"

Della strolled back over to the bed, picking up her wine cooler. "Did you give Jess's mother your cell phone number?"

"Yes."

"Then she'll be able to reach you."

Annie sank to the edge of the bed. The elementary school was closed for parent-teacher conferences tomorrow. There was no reason why Taylor shouldn't be allowed to spend the night at a friend's house. But what if something happened? What if she had a nightmare? "We haven't spent a night apart since..."

"I know," Della said gently. "But she's going to be fine." The mattress shifted as she sat back down on the bed, picking up the magazine and setting it in her lap. "When was the last time you had a night to yourself, Annie?"

Annie looked back down at the dresses in her hands. She couldn't remember. But she knew who she wanted to spend it with. Ever since Halloween, she hadn't been able to get Will out of her mind.

She'd tried to ignore the attraction between them. She'd tried to tell herself it wasn't worth getting involved with someone who was leaving and probably never coming back. But the more time she spent with him, the more she wanted him.

"I shouldn't be talking to you about this," Annie said. "He's your nephew."

"Who else are you going to talk to about it?" Della smiled, flipping to a new page in the magazine. "It's not like you've had time to make many friends on the island. You need to get out more."

Annie lifted the green dress and a tiny voice whispered, *'Don't do it. He's leaving. You're going to get hurt.'*

But if she *knew* he was leaving, if she knew exactly what she was getting into, couldn't she steal herself against the pain of saying goodbye?

People had flings all the time. They fell into each other, had a good time, and fell apart. She was an adult. She could do this. There was no need to be dramatic about the fact that he was leaving.

Maybe it was time *both* she and Taylor took a step forward in their lives.

Just because she hadn't been with a lot of men since Taylor was born, didn't mean she hadn't wanted to accept the occasional invitation to go out on a date. It didn't mean she hadn't wanted to have sex.

Who better than a gorgeous Navy SEAL to help her get back in the game?

Pushing to her feet, she walked into the bathroom and shimmied into the green sweater dress. She let her hair down, added a touch of mascara, and a dab of perfume. She checked her reflection and swiped a bit of color over her lips.

She walked back into the bedroom, pulled on a pair of high heel black boots, added a pair of dangly earrings, and turned to face Della. "What do you think?"

Della pretended to wipe a tear from under her eye. "I'm so proud."

Annie rolled her eyes, grabbing her purse and heading for the stairs before she could change her mind. "Don't wait up."

IT WAS STRANGE, Will thought, the feeling of home that swept over him as he crossed the drawbridge back to Heron Island. Even after all the years away, there was still something about this place that pulled at him, that made him wonder what his life would have been like if he'd never left.

Beside him, in the passenger seat, Colin cracked the window. A gust of cool, salty air flowed into the SUV. "I can't believe I grew up in Maryland and I've never been down here."

"Most people don't make it past St. Michaels. Not much to attract the tourists besides peace and quiet."

"It's nice, though," Colin said, gazing up at a flock of geese flying in a V-shape over the marina. Their calls filled the sky as they searched for a quiet cove to rest for the night. "Not that Annapolis is that big of a city, but it still seems like everyone's in such a hurry all the time. It feels good to get away."

Will cruised down the sleepy street as the setting sun tinted the clouds orange. He felt the same way. It was hard to imagine returning to the crush of traffic in San Diego, the five lane interstates, the miles of endless sprawl.

He could breathe on this island, in a way that he hadn't been able to for a long time.

A thin flash of refracted light drew his gaze to the porch of the white house with purple shutters at the end of the cluster of shops. The chimes shivered and swayed, catching the last rays of sunlight slanting over the island.

When the door opened and a woman stepped out of the café, it took Will several seconds to process that it was Annie. She wore a tight green dress scooped low at the neck, and cut high across the legs. Black heeled boots lifted her up several inches, making her legs seem impossibly long. Her thick red hair hung in loose waves around her shoulders, teasing the lush curves that he had been dreaming of getting his hands on for weeks now.

His mouth went dry when she bent down to fix a crooked planter on the porch step, oblivious to the vehicle that had slowed in the street.

"Damn," Colin murmured, rolling the window all the way down. "Who's *that*?"

Apparently satisfied with the adjustment to the cheerful

cluster of chrysanthemums on the steps, Annie straightened and headed down the sidewalk to where her car was parked on the street. Will could only stare as her hips swayed with every click of her boots on the cement.

Colin leaned his arm out the window to get a better look.

"Stop looking at her ass," Will growled.

"What?" Colin's brows shot up as his gaze swung back to Will's. "Look who's talking?"

"Show some respect," he said, his voice deep and dark as he jerked the wheel and slid into a parking spot a few cars behind her rusted Honda.

The look of shock on Colin's face slowly morphed into a knowing smile. He looked back at Annie. "So that's her."

"What are you talking about?" Will snapped distractedly, already climbing out of the driver's seat.

"The woman who's complicating things for you," Colin answered.

Will glanced back, just for an instant, before slamming the door and stalking down the street to where she was fitting the key into her car door. Complicated didn't even come close to explaining the conflicting emotions that were pumping through him with every step closer to the woman who'd *said* she wouldn't date until things settled down for her and Taylor on the island.

But where the hell else would she be going dressed like that?

"Hot date tonight?" he asked, his voice calm and controlled, not betraying a hint of the jealousy burning inside him.

Annie dropped the keys, startled. Her hand flew to her heart. "Will," she said, whipping around to face him. "I didn't even see you there."

He leaned down, picking up her keys.

Nerves simmered just beneath the surface of her skin, flushing her neck and chest with color. "I didn't realize you weren't home," she said, glancing uncertainly at the man in the passenger seat of his car. "I was just on my way to the inn."

To the inn? He looked down at her outfit, drinking her in with his eyes. "Dressed like that?"

She blushed, running a hand through her hair. The smell of vanilla drifted toward him, driving him crazy. "Yes."

"Why?"

She looked up at him, confused. "To see you."

"Where's Taylor?"

"At a friend's house."

"For the night?"

Annie nodded.

Will's heart began a slow dull thud. She wasn't going out on a date with another man. She'd been on her way to see him, to spend the night with him. His hand felt heavy as he reached for her. He drew her close, until her soft curves molded with the hard length of his body.

A gull cawed, circling above them in the fiery sky. He dipped his fingers into her hair as his mouth claimed hers. Her full lips parted, melting under his. He drank in the taste of her, riding that sweet wave of longing until he caught the sharp sultry edge of her perfume and thought he'd go mad.

"Will," Annie breathed, pulling back slightly.

He held her close, unable to let her go. He was aware of a few people on the sidewalk passing by and staring. Let them, he thought, his fingers twisting into the silky strands of her hair.

He wanted to take her home, strip her out of that dress and have her naked and under him for the rest of the night. But he'd invited Colin to the island. He couldn't ditch out on his friend. "How do you feel about oysters?"

"Oysters?" she asked breathlessly.

"For dinner."

"That sounds good."

"I invited a friend to the island for a few days." His thumb stroked the soft curve in her throat where her pulse jumped. He wanted to kiss her there. He wanted to spend the rest of the night discovering all the places that would drive her crazy. He wanted to take his time exploring every inch of her body. "We were on our way to meet Becca and Ryan at Rusty's. Will you join us?"

She nodded, her green eyes still filled with desire for him, her lips still slightly swollen from his kiss. "Let me go upstairs and change first. I'll meet you there."

"You look perfect." *You are perfect.*

"I can't go to Rusty's dressed like this."

"Yes, you can." He wasn't letting her go. He wasn't going to give her the chance to change her mind.

"People will talk."

"Let them." His hand closed over hers, and he led her back to the sidewalk, over the carpet of leaves to the SUV.

Colin opened the passenger side door, stepping out to give Annie his seat.

"Annie," Will said, "this is my friend, Colin Foley. Colin, this is Annie Malone."

Annie hesitated, just for a moment, and Will caught the flash of recognition deep in her eyes.

They were both full of surprises tonight.

"It's nice to meet you, Colin," Annie said, offering her hand.

Colin's eyes danced with laughter as he took her hand and lifted it. "Annie," he said gallantly, brushing his lips over her knuckles. "The pleasure is *all* mine."

FOURTEEN

*W*ill slipped his arm around Annie's waist as they walked through the doors, in a casually possessive gesture that had her head spinning. The restaurant was packed, a long line stretching out from the buffet where serving dishes held fried oysters, oyster fritters, oysters Rockefeller, oysters Chesapeake, steamed oysters, bacon wrapped oysters and oyster stew.

A man in a white apron stood behind a serving station, shucking raw oysters and setting them in the half shell on a bed of ice. Will leaned down, his lips grazing her ear. "Have I mentioned how much I like that dress?"

"I think you might have," Annie said as several women at the bar turned to stare. She spotted Becca in the buffet line and waved, trying to act normal, trying to act like her whole body wasn't still on fire from the way Will had kissed her out in the street. They made their way through the crowd and Will introduced Colin to his friends.

Becca's face flushed a warm shade of pink when Colin took her hand. Annie didn't blame her. At six-foot-four, Colin towered over most of the men in the room. He had the same hard body as

Will, but he'd let his midnight black hair grow out an inch or two longer. Add a pair of cool blue eyes, a strong jaw and a full mouth, and it was a pretty irresistible combination.

Well, Annie thought as Will slipped both arms around her from behind and drew her back against his warm solid chest, irresistible to *most* women.

Becca released Colin's hand and glanced over at Annie. She gave Annie's outfit a once over and wiggled her eyebrows. "*Hot,*" she mouthed before stepping back into line between Ryan and Colin and snagging a plate from the buffet table.

Annie turned her face up to Will's, lowering her voice. "Why didn't you mention Colin was coming to visit?"

"I didn't know he was." Will grabbed two plates from the table and handed her one. "It was a spur of the moment decision." They moved forward a few steps in line and the smells of lemon and butter wafted up from the steaming seafood trays. Will nudged her toward a tray of baked oysters covered in spinach, crabmeat and Parmesan cheese. "These'll go fast, so grab a few while you can."

She snagged two for each of them, and glanced back up at him. "Did you drive all the way to Annapolis to pick him up?"

Will added a generous slice of cornbread to each of their plates. "I met him at Walter Reed this afternoon."

Walter Reed? The military hospital in Bethesda?

No wonder he hadn't told her where he was going. He'd dodged all her attempts to raise the topic of PTSD since Halloween night, but maybe this was his way of reaching out. Going to Walter Reed, inviting his former teammate back to the island for a few days. Maybe if he could spend some time with other people who understood what he was going through, it would help him heal.

"He had a physical therapy appointment," Will said, as if that explained it. He picked up a fried oyster, setting it on her plate. "I wanted to see how things were going."

"And how are they going?"

"Good," he said, nudging her toward the fritters. "Colin's mastered the use of the prosthesis. He only has to go back now and then for an adjustment. We spent most of the afternoon talking to guys with injuries a lot worse than Colin's." His gaze darkened, dropping to Colin's left leg where his friend's prosthesis was hidden beneath a pair of jeans. "I wish I'd gone sooner."

Annie followed his gaze. If it weren't for the subtle protrusion of metal through his jeans when he walked, she wouldn't even know Colin's real leg wasn't underneath. She thought about Will, and the burden he carried deep inside him. How many service men and women were back here, living among them, carrying these hidden scars?

"Though I admit," Will murmured, his voice growing husky as he leaned down, "I may have regretted my decision to invite him down to the island when I saw you wearing that dress tonight."

Amazing, Annie thought, that he could switch gears so quickly. He put his hand on the small of her back, leading her back to the table.

As soon as they were settled at a booth by the window with a round of drinks, Becca turned to Colin. "How long have you known Will?"

Colin reached for his beer. "We were in the same training class in Coronado, got placed on the same team afterwards." He looked over at Will. "About ten years, I guess."

Will nodded.

"Is the training as hard as they say?" Becca asked.

"It's brutal," Colin said. "But worth it."

"What was Will like?" Becca asked, unable to hide her curiosity. "When you first met him?"

Colin smiled. "Will's reputation in BUD/S is legendary."

"They don't want to hear this," Will cut in.

"Yes, we do," Becca argued.

Colin popped a fritter into his mouth, lowering his voice. "They called him the Escape Artist."

"Colin," Will warned.

"Come on, Will." Becca laughed. "You've never told us anything about that time in your life."

"He's just being humble." Colin leaned toward Becca. "When we were in training, Will had a knack for finding a way out of every trap, knot, or bind the instructors put us in."

Will remained perfectly still, his hands wrapped loosely around his bottle of beer, but Annie could feel the tension simmering off him. He wasn't proud of this, she realized. Why did it make him so uncomfortable?

"We had to do this one exercise called drown-proofing," Colin explained as Becca hung on his every word. "Everyone dreads it. You basically have to jump into a pool with your hands and feet tied together with ropes and do a series of drills without drowning."

Becca reached for the cocktail sauce. "That sounds awful."

"It is." Colin chuckled. "If you panic and someone has to rescue you, you fail. If the ropes come untied, you fail. If you can't complete the drills, you fail. The only way to pass the test *without* completing all the drills is to physically break free of the ropes." Colin grinned at Will. "Only two SEALs have ever succeeded at breaking the ropes. Will's one of them."

Will took a long pull from his bottle. When he set it back down on the table, he lowered his hands to the bench. Annie could see the tightly coiled muscles of his forearms, the tense rigidity of his fingers as he curled and uncurled them under the table.

"It drove the instructors nuts." Colin laughed. "But Will always found a way to escape the worst situations they put us in, even when everyone else got trapped." Taking a bite of cornbread, Colin launched into another story about a training exercise that had Becca and Ryan in stitches.

Annie stole a glance at Will. She knew now why he wasn't proud of that story. He didn't want to be the one who always escaped. He didn't want to be the only one who'd come back from that terrible mission in Afghanistan in one piece. He'd told her himself he wished he'd been the one who'd died.

She thought about Taylor, and the guilt she still felt for being the sole survivor of the school shooting.

The noise from the bar and the voices in the dining room grew, drowning out the rest of Colin's story as Annie looked down at where Will's hand rested on the bench seat beside her.

She inched her hand toward him, until her smallest finger brushed against his.

Without a word, he looked down, and hooked his fingers around hers, holding onto her as if she was his rope now, and if he let go, everything would begin to unravel.

WILL TOSSED his car keys to Colin as they strode out of Rusty's later that evening. "Keep driving until the road ends. You can't miss it."

"Any particular room you want me to sleep in?"

"Pick whichever one you want," Will said. "There's beer in the fridge, a TV in the room off the kitchen, and DVDs on the shelves. If you decide to go out to the dock, watch the floorboards on the back porch. A few of them are rotted."

Colin sent him a mock salute and nodded goodnight to Annie. Will's hand closed over hers, and they crossed the parking lot to the quiet neighborhood street leading back to the café. Becca and Ryan had decided to stay for another drink at the bar, which meant...she and Will were alone.

Heading back to her place for the night.

She was the one who'd started this. She was the one who'd decided to take this step. But was she really ready? Was she really going to do this? Risk her heart like this?

It was only one night, right?

Then why did it feel like so much more?

"Annie."

"Yes?"

"Look at me."

She lifted her gaze to his. In the moonlight, his eyes seemed impossibly dark. Dark and deep and full of secrets. She couldn't stop thinking about what Colin had said at the table, that Will could get out of any trap, any bind, any knot.

Did he see her as a trap? As someone who would tie him down, make his life complicated?

He could get out of any knot, but she was just learning how to tie them. All she wanted was to root herself to this island with as many knots as she could.

"You're nervous," he said.

She nodded.

He stopped walking, pulling her close under the shivering boughs of an ash tree. His hand came up, cupping her cheek. "You have nothing to be nervous about."

But didn't she? Didn't she know exactly what she was getting into? There was no way she would have decided to spend the night with him if she wasn't already halfway in love with him. And if she was already halfway in love with him, there was no way he could leave now without breaking her heart.

He ran his thumb gently over her bottom lip before his mouth lowered, brushing over hers.

Butterflies, low in her belly, began to stir. They floated up, fluttering tentatively, then flapping their wings faster, until an orange glow fanned out around her heart.

Stay.

The word pulsed inside her, a reckless hope that built with every beat of the wings.

He tugged gently at her bottom lip with his teeth and eased back. Her breath released on a sigh. "Are you still nervous?"

She shook her head.

"Good." He smiled and slipped his arm around her waist.

They started back down the path and she focused on putting one foot in front of the other, trying to hide the fact that her legs were wobbling not from nerves now but need. They were still a few blocks away from the café, and the only sounds were the crickets chirping in the grasses and the gentle swish of falling leaves.

She stole a glance back up at his profile, wanting to hear the sound of his voice again. "Tell me something else about your day."

He looked down at her. "What do you want to know?"

"You said you wished you'd gone to Walter Reed sooner. Why?"

He told her about his day at the hospital, about how it had affected him. He told her about Vince, and how he and Colin and a bunch of other vets were training for a run to raise money for an injured Marine so he could go home.

Crossing the street, they climbed the steps to the café. Moonlight illuminated the silver chimes swaying in the wind. "I wish I could be there," he said, turning to face her. "I wish I could see those twenty-five guys cross the finish line. I wish I could see Vince present his friend with that check."

"Could you come back for it?" Annie asked.

Will was quiet for a long time as he gazed down at her. "I don't think I'll be stateside in January."

Of course, Annie thought. She knew that. She'd just thought maybe...

"Annie," he said softly. "I wish I could tell you I was coming back, but I can't."

"I know." She looked down at their joined hands. He'd made it clear this was all he had to offer. He'd been straightforward and honest from the very beginning. All he wanted was a night to wash away his pain.

She could still back out. She could still tell him she'd changed her mind. But when she looked back up at him, all she wanted was to wrap her arms around him and help him forget. Even if it was just for one night, she wanted to see the light come back into his eyes.

Taking a step toward him, she pressed her keys into his hand.

"Will," she whispered, drawing his mouth down to hers. "Take me to bed."

WILL's mouth never left hers as he fit the key into the lock. Pushing the door open, he guided her into the café. The scent of coffee and pie crusts clung to the air, mingling with the sultry spice of her perfume.

Every touch of her fingers had his muscles tightening, had a flood of warmth building inside him. Her lips tasted of sherry, her skin like spun sugar. He dropped the keys on a table, shoving the door closed with his foot.

He had waited so long for this, so long for her.

A soft sigh escaped from somewhere deep in her throat when he pulled her to him, fitting her body to his. His hands roamed over her curves, imprinting every inch of them into his memory. She shuddered when his palm closed over her breast, when his thumb skimmed over the sensitive tip through her dress.

Had he ever wanted—needed—anything as much as this woman?

Outside, the leaves shivered. The branches tapped against the windows. The restless chant of the chimes drifted over the wind.

She kept her hips locked to his as he backed her slowly, step by step, to the stairs. He fought the urge to lift her up in one fluid motion, to hook her legs around his waist and take her hard and fast against the wall.

Instead, he edged her away from him, backing her up the steps until they were eye-to-eye. When she reached for him, he took both her hands, placing one on the banister, the other on the opposite wall.

She watched him uncertainly at first, but when his fingers curled around the back of her knee, coaxing it to bend, desire swam into her eyes. He unzipped one boot, then the other, letting them drop to the tiles until she was barefoot.

"Will," she breathed, pulling him up to where she stood.

She kissed him hungrily, desperately, as if she needed him as much as he needed her. He followed her up the stairs to the apartment. A single lamp burned in the corner, illuminating the streaks of gold in her hair.

He ached to see her, to watch that warm glow slide over her bare skin.

He reached for her, peeling her dress off, letting it fall to the floor.

She stood before him in ivory lace, her full breasts rising over the thin fabric that barely held them in place.

"Annie," he breathed, dipping his mouth back to hers.

Heat raced like fire through his veins as he eased the straps down her shoulders, as he unhooked the clasp holding the delicate fabric together.

Her breasts spilled into his hands, and the need to bury himself inside her grew painful. But if he only had one night with her, he wanted to savor it. He wanted to remember every moment.

He lowered his mouth to her breasts, one after the other, taking his time. Annie's head fell back, her fingers curling around his shoulders as his hands moved down to her hips, his thumbs dancing under the scrap of ivory-colored lace.

Her skin sparked, heating under his touch. He heard a soft sound, like the hiss of wet wood burning, right before she came apart.

ANNIE DIDN'T KNOW what she'd expected, but it hadn't been this. The few men she'd been with in the past had all been in such a rush. They'd seldom cared about pleasing her; they'd only been concerned with the satisfaction of their own release.

Her heart fluttered when Will scooped her up, carrying her into the bedroom. She lowered her mouth to his neck, loving the taste of him, the feel of his salty skin on her lips. She wanted to make him feel the way he'd made her feel—weightless, like a leaf spinning away in the wind.

When he laid her down on the mattress, she reached for his shirt, dragging it over his head. A restless ache built inside her as she traced the hard ridges of his chest, the broad planes of his shoulders, the long lean muscles of his upper arms.

How had she lived for so long without this, without *him*?

Moonlight spilled through the window as he lifted her mouth back to his for another searing kiss. His hands skimmed down her hips, over her thighs, up the inside of each of them until she shuddered, arching up to meet him, desperate for his touch.

When his fingers slid over her, into her again, his name escaped from somewhere deep in her throat, a desperate, pleading voice she didn't recognize as her own.

Will.

She needed to see him, to touch him, to make all his pain go away. She fumbled with the top button of his jeans. He helped her slide the denim down, stepping out of his jeans and covering himself with protection. She barely had time to glimpse that hard warrior's body when the mattress shifted and he was on top of her again.

Her hand trembled as she lifted it, touching his face—the slightest brush of her fingers over his cheek. The force of the emotions in his eyes, the need in them, nearly stole her breath. She felt dizzy, like she was spinning out of control. "Will, I..."

He slid inside her.

A flash of colors—monarch wings, autumn leaves, marsh grasses at sunset—danced into her vision.

She gasped as he began to move, as the lines between what she wanted and what she could have began to blur. Her palms fanned out, over his chest, memorizing every angle, every edge, every scar he had taken in this war, both inside and out.

When his mouth found hers, she rose up to meet him, matching him beat for beat, breath for breath, stroke for stroke as he pushed them both toward the edge of pleasure.

The air grew thick, filled with fire-colored wings, like a thousand monarchs breaking free of their chrysalises, and realizing for the first time they could fly.

FIFTEEN

*W*ill lay in Annie's bed, his arms wrapped tightly around her. He could tell from the whisper of light along the horizon that it was nearly dawn. He listened to the sound of her slow steady breathing, the faint rustling of her curtains in the wind.

For the first time in months, he felt calm, rested, relaxed.

Maybe this was all he had needed, maybe *she* was all he had needed. He inhaled the sweet scent of her hair as it tickled his bare chest. His arm curled around the underside of her breasts, tucking her small body closer to his.

If she was anyone else, he would be gone by now. He would have come up with an excuse sometime in the middle of the night and left with a promise to call the next day.

A promise he probably wouldn't have kept.

But this was Annie—a woman who already knew more about him than most of his friends, a woman who decorated her daughter's bedroom in dream catchers and brooms so she wouldn't be afraid of the dark.

Gazing around her room while she slept, he took in the bare

walls and stack of unpacked boxes beside the closet. With a stab of guilt, he realized that she hadn't had time to unpack her own things.

If he hadn't put off selling the inn, she might have been well into the renovations for her French bistro. She might have been interviewing potential staff instead of working as a waitress, barista, and manager at a café she'd thrown together in a matter of weeks.

If he hadn't put off selling the inn, she wouldn't have had to put everything else in her life on hold to get the café up and running just to keep the bank off her back.

She stirred, and he felt a strange tightening in his chest when her eyes fluttered open. She blinked, like she was surprised to find him there. His hand felt heavy as he lifted it, brushing a strand of hair out of her eyes.

From the moment he'd set foot on this island, he'd made her life complicated and difficult. And yet, somehow, despite that, she'd given herself completely to him last night. He'd never imagined how much more of her he would want afterwards.

He kissed her slowly, savoring the taste of her soft lips, the feel of her warm body pressed against his. When she reached for him under the covers, wrapping her legs around his waist, his body responded instantly.

A soft sigh escaped her lips as he slid inside her. He rose up over her, covering her body with his, moving slowly in and out of her. Would he ever be able to get enough of her?

Her fingers tangled in his hair. He felt the pressure build, the desperate need for release. She kissed him back urgently, as if he'd disappear if she let go. When her breath caught and her head fell back, her body arching like a bow, he buried himself all the way inside her.

They lay for a long time afterwards, tangled up in each other. He wanted to stay here all day, bringing them both back to that place where they could let the rest of the world fall away. But Taylor would be home soon.

He eased back, stroking a hand up and down her bare arm. "What are the chances Della left any sweet rolls downstairs?"

She opened one eye, looking him up and down. "You're not going downstairs like that."

"I'll put pants on."

"And a shirt."

"And a shirt," he conceded, smiling.

She closed her eyes, turning her face back into the pillow and muttering something incoherent.

"What was that?" he asked.

"Coffee," she mumbled.

"How do you take it?"

"With sugar."

"How much?"

She sat up, rubbing her eyes. "I should help you."

He shook his head. "You're not leaving this bed yet."

"Why not?"

Because I don't know when I'm going to get you alone again and I haven't had enough of you yet. He rolled away from her, grabbing his jeans off the floor. "When do you think Taylor will be home?"

"She said she'd call when she woke up."

"Good." He stood, stepping into his jeans and pulling them up over his hips. He turned, bending down and dropping a light kiss on her lips. "I'll be right back."

When she leaned back, her red hair splayed over the pillow, her green eyes watching him curiously over the rumpled sheets, he felt his heart skip a beat.

Two weeks isn't going to be enough.

He dragged his shirt over his head.

Shit. It had to be enough.

It was all he had to offer.

THREE HOURS LATER, Annie was still floating. Sugarcoated butterflies had taken over her body, had nested in her hair. Everywhere she looked, there was a dusting of sugar. It coated her bare feet as she walked down the steps to the café, clung to the windows like snowflakes, gathered in the corners like sparkling snowdrifts. She ran her fingers over the gleaming silver counter top; they came back covered in sugar.

She would never think of sweet rolls the same way again.

Will had left a little while ago, giving her just enough time to tidy up the apartment and take a shower before Taylor got home. Spotting her brown boots behind the counter, she pulled them on over her stretchy jeans and glanced up at the sound of footsteps on her porch.

She straightened and blinked. Once. Twice. "Della?"

"Hmm?"

Annie stared at the crowd gathering outside the café. "Della," she hissed, ducking into the kitchen. "What's going on?"

"What do you mean?" Della asked innocently.

"Did you do this?" Annie pointed to the growing group of islanders talking and laughing on her porch, waiting for the café to open. "Did you get all these people to show up?"

Della smiled, her eyes twinkling as she stirred a simmering pot of cream of crab soup. The mouthwatering aromas of melted butter, Old Bay seasoning and sherry floated into the air. "No, Annie, this time it was all you."

"Me?" Annie twisted her damp hair into a knot, shoving a pen through it to hold it in place. "But I didn't do anything. I mean, nothing's changed since yesterday." She adjusted the chunky brown belt she'd fastened around the waist of her cream-colored sweater earlier. "We haven't changed the menu. We're not offering any specials. It's not even a weekend."

Della added a pinch of cayenne pepper to the soup. "Nothing's changed since yesterday?"

Annie's hands stilled on her belt.

Della smiled and grasped the handle of the oven, the hinges squeaking as she inched it open to scrutinize a loaf of cheese bread.

Annie's whole body filled with heat as the memory of Will licking icing off her fingers in bed that morning swam back. "But...that doesn't have anything to do with this."

Della laughed, closing the oven. "Honey, this is an island." She added a dash of tarragon to the bowl of chicken salad sitting on the counter beside the stove. "What you do outside of work is going to get a lot more attention than putting an ad in the paper. Your personal life is the best marketing tool you have."

Annie stole a glance back out at the islanders. A few of them had broken off from the crowd and were peering in the windows. "They're all here because of what I did with Will?"

"Will hasn't been back to the island in ten years, Annie." Della tasted the chicken salad and nodded, satisfied. Covering the bowl with plastic wrap, she set it in the fridge. "He came back after all this time, and instead of selling his grandparents' house and leaving right away, he stayed. Now he's involved with someone—a woman who lives on the island, a woman who's new here, and who very few people know." Della nodded toward the porch. "Every single person out there wants to know who you are now."

Annie's palms started to sweat. She and Will weren't involved. It was only one night. "Della—"

Della smiled and gave her a gentle nudge toward the door. "I think you better greet your customers."

Annie's breathing grew shallow as she made her way toward

the door. What was she going to do? Will had made it perfectly clear again last night that he wasn't interested in anything long-term. He was leaving in less than two weeks and she would probably never see him again.

But what was she supposed to tell the islanders? That there was nothing going on between them? That it was a meaningless fling?

She was a mother, for God's sake. She didn't make a habit of sleeping with men she'd only known for a few weeks.

But if she didn't tell them the truth, they would draw their own conclusions and assume she and Will were together.

Her fingers grasped the cool metal handle of the door. This could be her only chance to make an impression on the locals who hadn't bothered to set foot in the café yet.

She wasn't going to blow it.

Pasting a smile on her face, she opened the door. The temperature had dropped several degrees overnight and a gust of cold air swept into the room. "I hope you're hungry," she said brightly. "Della just whipped up a fresh batch of cream of crab soup and it smells amazing."

"That sounds wonderful," an elderly woman gushed, slipping inside.

"Cream of crab soup on a cold day sounds perfect," another said, hanging her coat on the rack inside the door.

"I love your sweater," a woman in her early-thirties said as she maneuvered an oversized baby stroller inside.

"Thank you," Annie said, leading her and her two rambunctious twin boys to a corner table by the window.

"Did you get it around here?"

"I got it in D.C."

"D.C." The woman's voice was wistful as she wrestled a toy out of her son's mouth. "I can't remember the last time I was in the city."

Annie handed her a menu and offered to bring a box of crayons and construction paper over for the kids.

The woman sent her a grateful smile, and Annie turned, almost colliding with an elderly man strolling up to the counter.

He tipped his hat, leaning on a wooden cane. "I hear you make the best cup of hot chocolate on the island."

She smiled and took his arm, helping him onto one of the stools. "Would you like whipped cream? It's homemade."

The man took his time unfolding his newspaper, laying it out on the counter. "Sure, why not? I'll take a slice of apple pie, too."

"Coming right up," she said as several more islanders filed into the café.

She spotted Eddie Valiant, Heron Island's Fire Chief, who always came in right when they opened.

"The usual?" she asked him.

He nodded, strolling up to the counter while she poured coffee into a to-go cup and wrapped up a sweet roll.

Normally, he went into the kitchen to visit with Della while Annie filled his order. Today, he stood by the register, grinning down at her. When she handed him his coffee and pastry, he passed her a crumpled bill and winked. "Keep the change."

Annie's head spun as she passed out menus, jotted down orders, refilled coffee cups, and dodged questions about her and Will for the next several hours. By the time the last customer left, she had a shooting pain in her right eye and a dull ache throbbing in each temple.

Part of her was grateful for the business, but the other part—the part that knew the only reason everyone had come in today was because they were dying to know if she and Will were together—was afraid this was all going to blow up in her face.

Emptying the coffee grounds from the espresso machine, she watched Taylor refill the saltshakers on the café tables. Thankfully, her daughter had spent most of the morning upstairs making wind chimes out of the box of buttons Jess's mom had given her. When she'd come downstairs at lunchtime, Della had fixed her a sandwich and put her to work icing sugar cookies.

Annie didn't expect anyone to purposefully blurt out the fact that she'd slept with Will in front of her eight-year-old daughter. But what if Taylor overheard a conversation in passing? What if one of the kids in her class had seen them kissing in the street last night? It wouldn't take long to put two and two together.

The *last* thing she wanted was for Taylor to get her hopes up that she and Will might have some kind of future together. Taylor was already so fond of Will. If she spent any more time with him, it would break her heart when he left.

She knew what it was like to get close to a man her mother was dating, to start looking up to him like a father figure. Most of all, she knew how much it hurt to say goodbye.

Pushing back from the espresso machine, she opened the register and pulled out a pile of receipts. She could hear Della singing along with a country song in the kitchen, pots and pans clanging around as she put everything away for the night. Making two piles, one for cash, one for credit cards, Annie stole a glance back up at Taylor and caught her daughter staring out the window. "What are you looking at, sweetie?"

"Nothing," Taylor said quickly, grabbing a saltshaker from the closest table.

Annie watched her refill it and twist the top back on. When she moved on to a new table, Annie went back to tallying up the day's receipts. A few minutes later, she glanced back up and found Taylor staring out the window again. "Taylor."

Taylor looked up guiltily.

Annie set down the receipts. "What is it?"

"I thought Will might bring Riley over."

Annie's heart constricted. This was exactly what she'd been

afraid of. "I don't think Will's coming over tonight," she said gently.

"Why not?"

"Because he has a friend in town."

"Maybe we could go to the inn?" Taylor asked hopefully.

Annie stepped out from behind the counter and crossed the room to her daughter. She took both of Taylor's hands in hers. "You know Will's leaving soon, right?"

Taylor looked down at their joined hands and nodded.

"You can still visit with Riley after he leaves," Annie said, squeezing her hands. "She's not going anywhere."

"I know." Taylor lifted her big green eyes back up to Annie's. "But won't he miss her?"

"I'm sure he will."

"Do you think he'll come back and visit?"

Annie took a deep breath. "I don't know. But if he does, it won't be for a really long time."

Taylor looked back out the window, at where the leaves were drying and crinkling in the streets. "I wish he wasn't leaving."

Me too, Annie thought. But wishing and hoping weren't going to get them anywhere. She pushed to her feet. "Why don't you show me the new wind chimes you made today?"

Taylor took one last look out the window. "They're upstairs."

"Come on," Annie said cheerfully, tucking her daughter's arm through hers. "Let's find a place to hang them."

They were almost to the steps when a dog barked in the front yard.

Taylor whirled. "Riley!"

Annie turned slowly as Taylor ran for the door. Taylor dropped her broom with a clatter on the tiles as she raced out onto the porch and dashed down the steps to throw her arms around the wiggling dog.

Will and Colin turned up the walkway a moment later.

Annie took one look at Will and her palms grew damp. What was he doing here? Shouldn't he be keeping his distance, letting things cool down between them after what happened last night?

He paused at the bottom of the steps to talk to Taylor. When he finally lifted his gaze, and caught her eyes through the screen door, the heat that sizzled between them could have set the café on fire.

There was nothing cool or distant about that.

Della walked out of the kitchen, drying her hands on a dishtowel. "Well, well, well," she murmured, pausing beside Annie. "Look who finally decided to make an appearance?"

"What?" Annie asked distractedly, her mouth going dry as Will slowly climbed the steps to her porch. His T-shirt was covered in dirt and sawdust. A pair of ripped jeans hung from his narrow hips. His strong forearms were tan and glistening with sweat.

Colin walked in behind him, scuffing his work boots on the doormat and gazing around the café appreciatively as they stepped inside. "Nice place."

"Thank you," Annie managed.

Colin turned his attention to Della. "You must be the famous chef Will's told me so much about."

Della beamed. "I don't know about that, but you look like you could use a slice of pumpkin pie."

Colin grinned at her. "You read my mind."

He followed her into the kitchen, leaving Annie and Will alone.

Annie's pulse quickened. He shouldn't be here. She wasn't ready to see him yet.

She needed a few days to catch her breath, to regain her balance. Last night had been...more than she'd expected. But it was time to take a step back, to start putting some distance between them.

It would be easier that way when he left.

Stepping behind the counter, she busied her hands with the receipts, pretending not to notice the flash of confusion that clouded Will's eyes when she moved away from him instead of toward him.

He strolled up to the counter, his gaze dropping to the receipts. "Are all those from today?"

She nodded.

"I'm impressed."

"It was a good day." *Thanks to you.* She continued to sort the receipts, her hands methodically separating them into the two piles. It was easier when she had a task to focus on, when she didn't have to look at him.

She froze when he reached across the counter and adjusted the pen she'd stuck haphazardly in her hair that morning.

"I like this," he murmured, his fingers lingering in her messy hair.

Her neck tingled, her skin flushing with heat. "I didn't have time to do much else with it this morning."

His chocolate eyes warmed as he drew his hand back. "You should wear it like that more often."

She opened her mouth, closed it. He was *not* making this easy for her. Twisting a rubber band around the cash pile, she nudged it aside and turned her attention to the credit card receipts. "Did you and Colin get a lot of work done on the inn today?"

He nodded. "It helps to have an extra set of hands."

"I can imagine."

"Annie."

Her gaze flickered back up to his.

He took her hand, prying the receipts from her fingers. "Ryan invited us out on his boat to watch the sunset. Can you come?"

"Ryan's boat?" she asked, struggling to concentrate when he brushed his thumb gently over her knuckles.

He nodded. "It might be the last time we can get out before winter sets in. Ryan wants to show us a few of the projects he's been working on. Taylor will love it."

Annie drew her hand back, catching the surprise and disappointment in his eyes. "I wish I could say yes, but I can't."

"Why not?"

"I have a meeting with Shelley Needham, the principal at Taylor's school, in an hour."

Disappointment shifted quickly to concern. "Is something wrong?"

"No, it's just a standard meeting. We agreed to check in once a week, talk about how things are going."

"But everything's okay?" he pressed.

"Yes. Everything's fine. Shelley just wants to stay on top of the situation. Becca fills her in on everything that happens in class and we discuss Taylor's overall progress both at school and at home." She took a deep breath, looking away. "In case..."

"In case *what?*"

"In case anything like this ever happens again."

Will's jaw hardened. She caught the flash of anger, the cold fury that swam into his eyes. He had spent the last ten years of his life hunting down the people who'd murdered his mother and sister. The thought that something so cold-blooded would happen at home, in a school, to innocent children, wasn't easy to swallow.

"It makes me angry, too," she said quietly. "But it helps to talk about it. These weekly meetings with Shelley are the one chance I get to discuss Taylor's progress with someone face-to-face, someone who cares about getting it right as much as I do."

"Taylor doesn't go with you to the meetings?"

"She does sometimes," Annie admitted. "Della offered to watch her for me last week, but she's got a church meeting tonight, so I'll probably take her."

"I could watch Taylor for you tonight."

"Thanks," Annie said, reaching for the receipts, "but I've got it covered. Shelley downloaded a bunch of games on her laptop. Taylor has no problem popping in a pair of earplugs and tuning us out."

"You'd rather she play computer games than come out for a ride on Ryan's boat with me?"

Annie looked up at him. "She's not going out on the water without me."

"Why not?"

"Because..." Why was Will doing this? He'd made it clear he didn't want anything permanent. She was trying really hard to keep things light and simple between them. He wasn't helping by asking to hang out with Taylor without her. "Because I don't feel comfortable."

"It's just a boat ride, Annie. If she's going to grow up on this island, she needs to get out on the water. She needs to start learning about the Bay."

"And we'll get out on the water, *together*, another time."

"You don't trust me."

Annie took a deep breath. "It's not that I don't trust you."

Will walked around the counter and took her shoulders in his hands, turning her to face him. "I won't let anything happen to her."

"It's not that I don't trust you to keep her safe."

"Then, what is it?"

How could she tell him she didn't want her daughter hanging out with him because she was afraid Taylor would get too attached and start looking up to him as some sort of father figure?

"Becca will be there," Will said. "Ryan, Colin, and I will be there. Both of Ryan's dogs will be there. You know how much she loves spending time with those dogs."

Annie looked out at the porch, where Taylor was sprawled out on the floorboards laughing while Riley chewed on her hair.

"Trust me," Will said gently.

Annie looked down at her hands. "She's not a strong swimmer. I'm going to sign her up for lessons at the YMCA soon. I know she needs to learn. We just haven't had time yet."

"Nothing's going to happen."

Colin walked out of the kitchen, catching the tail end of their conversation. "I can vouch for Will's swimming skills, if that's what you're worried about."

Will smiled.

Annie felt herself cave. She knew Taylor would love to go out on the boat. It wasn't fair to make her stay inside and play computer games when she could be out on the water, watching the sunset. "You'll bring her back as soon as the boat ride is over?"

Will nodded.

"And you'll make sure she's wearing a life jacket."

"Of course."

"And you won't leave her side."

"I won't leave her side." He took her hand, leading her out from behind the counter.

"Hey, kiddo," he said to Taylor when they got to the porch. "Want to go for a boat ride?"

Taylor sat up, her eyes widening. "A boat ride?"

He nodded. "We might even put a few lines in the water, see if we can get a fish to bite."

Taylor looked up at Annie expectantly. "Mom?"

Annie slipped her daughter's jacket off the coat rack by the door. "You can go, but you have to promise you'll be careful."

"I promise!" Taylor scrambled to her feet, grabbing her jacket. She stuffed her hands into the arms, looking up at Will. "Can Riley come?"

"Of course."

Riley jumped up, wagging her tail. Taylor followed Colin down the steps, heading toward the marina with the dog on her heels.

Annie's gaze fell to Taylor's broom, lying on the floor, forgotten.

Will squeezed her hand. He bent down to pick it up, and dropped a light kiss on her lips before heading down the steps. When he caught up with Taylor and Colin, Taylor glanced over and noticed her broom in his hand.

Annie waited for her to reach for it, to take it from him and drag it along the sidewalk through the leaves. Instead, she reached for Will's hand.

"Isn't that a sight?" Della murmured.

"He's leaving," Annie breathed. "In two weeks."

Della was silent for a long time as she watched them walk down the street toward the marina. "You're sure about that?"

Annie looked over at Della. "His career is in San Diego."

"Lots of people change careers," Della said lightly.

Not Navy SEALs, Annie thought, looking back at her daughter and Will holding hands. Especially not one who'd dedicated his life to going after the people who'd killed his family.

"Besides," Annie said. "I need him to leave. I need him to sell the inn to Morningstar so I can open my French restaurant."

"Is that really still what you want?" Della asked, her voice sad.

"Yes." Annie nodded. Of course, it was. Wasn't it? "You knew this was only temporary."

The wind picked up, the chimes singing in the salty autumn breezes.

"I know," Della said quietly. "I just keep hoping you'll change your mind."

SIXTEEN

*W*ill kept Taylor's small hand in his as they motored out of the marina. The setting sun painted the marsh grasses a fiery copper. Fingers of water snaked in and out of the meandering shoreline. Flocks of Canada geese flew overhead, their calls filling the sky.

Taylor's face was turned up to the pink clouds, her wispy red hair flying out in the wind. Her broom was lying at their feet. She hadn't reached for it since they'd left the café. He wished Annie could see her. He wished she could see how relaxed and happy she was.

Whenever he thought about what had happened to Taylor at that school in D.C., a hard knot of anger formed in the pit of his stomach. He had joined the SEALs to protect this country, to prevent another attack like 9/11 from happening, to make sure that no one else lost their mother and sister to terrorism. But Taylor had been through her own personal war here at home.

Who was here to protect her?

Becca walked over, leaning against the railing on the other side of Taylor. "Ryan's telling Colin the story about the time you guys went crabbing in your grandfather's canoe and tipped it over."

Will looked back at where Colin and Ryan stood at the helm laughing. "There are *two* versions of that story."

Becca smiled and lifted the top of the cooler, fishing out a soda for Taylor. "You might want to set the record straight."

Taylor let go of his hand to take the soda, and Will caught the beer Becca tossed to him. Twisting the cap off, he strolled back to the helm.

"We'd been out on the water for a few hours," Ryan was saying, "catching maybe five or six crabs at a time."

Will leaned a shoulder against the center console.

"We had this old bushel basket sitting between us," Ryan said. "It was wet and kind of soggy at the bottom, but neither of us paid much attention to it. It held the crabs; that's all that mattered."

Will took a sip of his beer, remembering all the carefree days he and Ryan had spent out on the water, fishing and crabbing and chasing after girls on sailboats.

Ryan lifted his hand, waving to three fishermen in a yellow boat heading back to the marina. "We'd filled the bushel about halfway, and Will was leaning over the side of the canoe pulling up the trot line, when a tiny crab, probably half the size of my hand—"

"It was at least three times that size," Will cut in.

Ryan looked back at Colin. "This *tiny* crab pinched Will's toe and he let out this huge shout and started kicking his leg to try to get it off. I tried to help—"

"You did not try to help."

"He was flailing around—"

"I did not flail," Will corrected. "I have *never* flailed."

Ryan's shoulders shook with laughter. "He knocked the

bushel over and the bottom fell out. At least three dozen live crabs escaped into the canoe."

Colin laughed. "Who jumped out first?"

"Will," Ryan said at the same time Will said, "Ryan."

Will shook his head while Colin laughed louder and Ryan launched into another story about their childhood. To this day, neither one of them would admit to being the first who'd bailed.

When the canoe had tipped, they'd lost the crabs, both paddles, and Will's grandfather's favorite fishing rod.

His grandfather had not been happy when he'd found out.

Especially since Will and Ryan had both been grounded the day before and shouldn't have even been out in the canoe. He couldn't remember what they'd been grounded for now, but it was probably something stupid like putting a toad fish in Grace's backpack or a bag of bloodworms in Becca's locker.

Looking out at the water, Will took another pull from his beer. He'd forgotten how simple life could be, how easy it was to grow up on this island. Before he'd come back here, that time in his life had felt like a million years ago. Now, out on the Bay with two of his childhood friends, it didn't seem so far away anymore.

He thought about Becca who hadn't left the island except to get her teaching degree, and Ryan who'd left and come back. They had both chosen this life, and even though Becca said she was marrying Tommy and moving to D.C. next year, Will had his doubts.

She was happy here. And so was Ryan.

A sudden overwhelming desire to stay, to become a part of this place again, swept through him. He thought he'd changed too much to come back here. He hadn't considered how easy it would be to fall back into a rhythm with the friends he'd left behind.

"We used to spend hours catching bait fish off Will's dock," Ryan said, his hand resting on the wheel as they motored toward the open Bay. "We'd fill big buckets of water with perch and leave them overnight to take out fishing the next day, but Will's sister would go down at sunset and feed them little bits of bread. She'd take her dolls with her and let them play with the fish. By the time we were ready to take the fish away the next morning she'd grown so attached to them, she'd make us throw them all back."

Colin laughed and Will turned, looking back at the island. He was so used to blocking the memories, he almost didn't let himself go back there. But this time he wanted to remember. Just this once, he wanted to let the memories in.

He could see his grandparents' inn coming into view through the branches of the pines. The setting sun warmed the pale yellow siding of the house, making it glow. Maples and oaks reflected on the shallow water, their leaves painting the surface amber.

Autumn had been Bethany's favorite time of year. She'd loved the way the sunsets had shimmered over the water, the way the colors had bounced off the railing of the sailboat in the evenings, the sheen on the scales of the fish that he and his grandfather had caught and thrown back.

He heard a child's giggle behind him and it sounded so much like his sister, he turned, almost expecting to see her. But it was only Taylor, trying to free her broom from Riley's mouth. He watched her for a long time, remembering how nice it had felt when she'd reached for his hand on the street earlier.

"Miss Haddaway?" Taylor pointed at something on the shoreline. "What's that?"

Will followed her gaze to a small wooden structure on the edge of the marshes covered with straw, cornhusks and grass.

"It's a duck blind," Becca answered slowly.

"What's a duck blind?" Taylor asked.

Becca exchanged a look with Will. "It's for hunters."

"Oh." Taylor's fingers curled around her broom. "My mom

told me about them."

Will walked back to stand beside Taylor. "A lot of people around here hunt for sport. A duck blind is a place where they can hide out to wait for the ducks and geese to fly over."

"They use guns, don't they?"

"They do," Will said. "There's a festival coming up soon. Did your mom tell you about it? The Waterfowl Festival?"

Taylor nodded. "She said there might be a lot of people here...hunting. That I might hear guns." She hugged her arms around her orange life jacket. "I don't like guns."

"I don't blame you."

She looked up at him. "Will you be hunting?"

"No."

"You don't like guns either?"

Will looked back out at the duck blind. That was a good question. He liked *his* guns, the ones he used to protect his teammates and his country, and he didn't have a problem with the ones his friends used to hunt deer and waterfowl. But he did not like the guns that a mentally deranged teenager had used on a room full of second-graders.

Becca put her hand on Taylor's shoulder, pointing toward a nest on top of a red channel marker. "You see that nest?"

Taylor nodded.

"That's an osprey nest," Becca explained. "Remember when I told you about how the ospreys were endangered several years ago?"

Taylor nodded. "Because they couldn't find any safe places to build their nests."

"Exactly," Becca said. "This is one of the ways we were able to bring them back, by building platforms on top of channel markers for them to make nests on. We had to give them back what they'd lost."

Taylor looked up at Becca. "Will the monarchs come back if

we grow more milkweed?"

"Maybe," Becca said. "Every species is different, but since our way of life has destroyed so many of their natural habitats, we have to do what we can to bring them back."

The boat rounded the tip of the island and the duck blind disappeared from sight. Will let out a long breath.

Becca took Taylor's hand, leading her back to the helm. "Ryan's going to tell us about a project he's been working on to give the oysters back *their* home."

Ryan cut the engine and they drifted in the quiet waters as he pointed to a tributary on the north side of the island. "In a few weeks, a barge is going to dump a ton of fossilized shells into that river to create a man-made oyster reef. Right now, the bottom of the Bay is so silted, the oysters have nothing to grab onto. They need a hard surface to attach to so they can grow."

"What's so special about oysters?" Taylor asked.

"A single adult oyster can filter between twenty and fifty gallons of water a day," Ryan explained. "Restoring the oyster populations in the Bay would improve the water quality and help bring back other fisheries, like crabs, clams, and rockfish."

Will gazed out at the water. It wasn't just oysters, ospreys and monarchs. Hundreds of species depended on this fragile ecosystem for survival. His eyes followed the path of a blue heron as it glided over the marshes to land on the trunk of a fallen oak.

His grandfather had treated these wetlands like a sanctuary, as if they belonged to the wildlife rather than to them.

Wasn't it his responsibility to do the same?

Colin grabbed two more beers from the cooler, passing one to Ryan. "What do you work on in the winter when you can't get out on the water?"

"I'm trying to get funding for a few projects I'm hoping to launch next spring," Ryan answered. "Aside from that, some of the islanders have offered to donate boats and engines to the cause, but they're old and rusted and need a lot of work. I've got five workboats sitting under tarps at the marina right now and I haven't even had a chance to get started on them yet."

Colin popped the top off his bottle. "Do you need help?"

Ryan nodded. "I can use all the help I can get. The projects I have in mind for next year are going to require a lot of volunteers. To be honest, I'm not sure where I'm going to get them all yet."

Colin glanced at Will. "I know some people who are out of the military and looking for work. I bet they wouldn't mind lending a hand now and then. I could make some calls, see who's around."

"That would be great," Ryan said. "I'd like to get these boats ready to use by next spring."

Next spring. Will looked back at the inn as the sun sank into the horizon. He wouldn't be here next spring.

But what if he couldn't find a buyer who would protect the land, who would respect it and take care of it the way his grandparents had? Shouldn't he hold onto it until the right person came along, even if that was months from now?

And if that perfect person never came along?

Maybe he could find a way to keep it. Maybe he would never have to let it go.

ANNIE GLANCED up at the jingle of Riley's collar on the sidewalk. It was dark, but she could see the silhouette of a tall figure turning up the path to the café. Closing her laptop, she stepped out from behind the counter.

Will had dropped Taylor off a few hours ago, but he hadn't stayed long and he'd seemed distracted. Surprised to see him back again so soon, she crossed the dining room and opened the door.

He paused on the top step, studying her in the dim porch

light. There were emotions in his eyes she couldn't read. "Is Taylor asleep?"

Annie nodded, walking outside and closing the door behind her. "Is everything all right?"

He crossed the porch to where she stood, and simply drew her into his arms.

It felt so natural, so right, to tilt her face up to meet his kiss. But there was nothing simple about the way his mouth claimed hers. There was nothing simple about the way his arms came around her, fitting her body to his like it belonged there, like it had *always* belonged there.

"Will," she breathed, pressing her palms to his chest. The wind rushed through the street, whistling through the branches, snatching at the leaves. "Wait."

He pulled back reluctantly.

She looked up, her heart skipping a beat when she caught the need in his eyes. "You can't come in."

"I know," he said, without letting her go. "I wanted to see you."

A warm feeling swept through her, but she stole herself against it. He shouldn't be saying that. He shouldn't even be here.

She needed a minute to focus, to breathe.

Stepping out of his arms, she picked up a wool blanket draped over a chair and wrapped it around her shoulders. "We need to talk."

His gaze held hers, dark and intense.

"Last night was...unexpected. It was more than I could have imagined." Annie began. "But don't you think we should take a step back?"

"Why?"

"Because you're leaving."

He studied her for a long time. "I don't want to take a step back."

"Will." Her breath came out in a rush. "I don't know if Taylor's going to spend the night at a friend's house again before you leave. We might not have another night to ourselves. Shouldn't we stop this now, before someone gets hurt?"

"I'm not going to hurt you."

Maybe not on purpose, Annie thought as he closed the distance between them again, taking her face in his hands.

"Do you want me to go?" he asked, brushing a thumb over her cheek.

"No," she whispered.

"Good," he murmured, lowering his mouth back to hers.

By the time he pulled back, the only thing she knew for sure was that she didn't want him to leave. Not tonight. Not in two weeks. Not ever.

He took her hand and led her over to the steps, pulling her down to sit beside him. "Did Taylor have a good time on the boat tonight?"

Annie nodded, tucking the blanket tighter around her shoulders. She didn't trust herself to speak yet. Across the street, the last of the lights went off in the houses. Riley curled up a few feet away, closing her eyes and letting out a long sigh.

Will leaned back against the railing and pulled her into his arms. They sat for a long time like that, with her back resting against his chest, watching the town fall asleep and the stars come out.

"Did Taylor show you what Ryan gave her?" Will asked.

"She did." Annie lifted her gaze to the chimes spinning and swaying in the wind. Ryan had given her daughter a plastic bag filled with tiny silver fishing weights, blue fishing line, sparkly lures, and plastic worms. He'd removed all the hooks so she could make a wind chime out of them.

Annie had been touched by the gesture, but more than that, she'd been surprised at the islanders' overall reaction to her homemade decorations. Several people who'd stopped by the café for the first time today had told her how much they loved her chimes. And it wasn't just the islanders. The tourists had gone crazy over them, too. On opening day, one woman from Annapolis had asked if she would consider taking on commissions; she'd wanted to order a special set for her daughter's graduation with memories from high school.

Too stunned to give her an answer, Annie had taken her number and said she would call.

Relaxing into Will's arms, she listened to the soothing melody mingling with the sound of the geese chattering on the cove and Riley's quiet snoring.

"Tell me about making one of them." Will said, his voice warm and rich in her ear.

"One of the wind chimes?" Annie asked, surprised.

He nodded.

"Which one?"

He pointed at a chime made of red clay rings and turquoise stones.

She was quiet for a long time, watching the rings and stones spin in the moonlight. *Of all the chimes for him to pick.* "I made that one in Santa Fe."

"Did you live there long?"

"Almost three years." It was the longest she'd lived anywhere before moving to D.C. It was the only place, before moving to this island, that she'd ever really considered home.

"How old were you?"

"I was nine when we got there."

"A little older than Taylor is now."

She nodded. "We moved there for the art scene, but a few weeks after we got there my mother met a man named Jeff Alvaro. He'd lost his wife to cancer the year before and my mother was the first woman he'd dated since."

They had fallen in love in a matter of weeks. Her mother had always fallen in love with men hard and fast. But as soon as the initial excitement of the relationship had worn off, she'd been the first to bail. *'Don't give them a chance to leave you first, Annie,'* her mother had told her when she was still a little girl. *'Don't ever give a man the satisfaction of seeing that he's hurt you, that he has that power over you. The only way you can ensure you always have the upper hand is to be the first one to walk out the door.'*

Annie picked at a string dangling off the corner of the blanket. "A few months after they started dating, he asked us to move in with him. He had a small house with a chili pepper garden in a neighborhood close to downtown. There were lots of kids my age on the street. He taught me how to ride a bike, helped me with my homework at night, even cleared out a place in his shop so I could make wind chimes while he worked on restoring a vintage truck his grandfather had left him."

"Why did you leave?"

"My mother decided it was time." Annie twisted the string around her finger. "She'd heard that some of her friends were opening a studio in San Francisco and she wanted to join them."

"Did he try to stop her?"

Annie shook her head. "We left one night when he was asleep, like we always did. Without saying goodbye."

Will was quiet for a long time, letting that soak in. "Were there a lot of different men in your mother's life when you were growing up?"

Annie nodded. "None of the others ever wanted anything to do with me. Jeff was the first man my mother fell for who was really nice, who was really good to *both* of us. It was hard not to get attached to him." Annie looked back up at the wind chime of red clay rings and turquoise stones. "Jeff was the closest I ever got to having a father."

"Have you ever thought about looking him up?"

Annie shook her head, unwinding the string from around her finger. "I'm sure he's moved on by now. He's probably found a new family." She lifted a shoulder. "He doesn't need me walking back into his life and reopening that old wound. My mother broke his heart that night. I know she did, because she broke mine, too."

Will turned her around slowly to face him. "Is that why you didn't want me to take Taylor out on the boat earlier? Because you're afraid she's going to get attached to me?"

"Yes."

He studied her face for a long time, like he wanted to say something. But what could he say? They both knew he was leaving in less than two weeks. Even if he came back to the island from time to time to visit, she wouldn't put Taylor through the confusing situation of never really knowing if Will was going to be there for them or not.

Easing out of his arms, she took a deep breath. "I should probably head in. I still have a few things to do on the computer before I can call it a night."

Will nodded, but she could see he was struggling again, like he wanted to say something but didn't know how to get the words out. He stood slowly, helping her to her feet. "Annie," he began when they were standing. "I..."

He looked down at her, those dark eyes swimming with emotions as he brushed the hair back from her face and leaned down, touching his warm lips to hers again.

When he pulled back, she waited for him to say something.

Instead, he patted his leg to wake Riley and turned, walking down the steps with the dog on his heels.

Annie stood on the porch, watching him and Riley walk away until they were only shadows in the night. Until there was nothing but darkness and the whisper of falling leaves hitting the sidewalk.

SEVENTEEN

"If I didn't know better," Colin shouted over the whirr of the power saw, "I'd say you were looking to settle down with this woman."

Will pulled up a moldy floorboard from the back porch, tossing it into the yard. "I'm not looking to settle down."

Colin guided the two-by-four into the blade. Sawdust sprayed onto the grass. "Crazier things have happened."

Not to him, Will thought, working a rusted nail free with the sharp edge of a hammer. Besides, Annie had made it clear the night before that she wanted to let things cool down between them. He understood now why she was so protective of Taylor where he was concerned. It wasn't because she didn't trust him; it was because she was afraid of her daughter getting attached to him.

The last thing he wanted was to hurt Annie or Taylor when he left. He couldn't stand the thought of not being able to see them, of not being able to spend time with them during the rest of his stay on the island, but he respected that Annie was only trying to do what was best for her daughter.

Taylor had been through enough this year.

"What does she have to say about it?" Colin asked.

"About what?"

"About you being a SEAL, jackass."

"I haven't asked her."

"Why not?"

Will tore a broken porch rail off the banister and threw it into the pile. "Because it doesn't matter. We're just having fun until I head back to San Diego."

Colin powered down the saw. "Fun?"

"That's right."

"You practically bit my head off when I tried to talk to her that first night at Rusty's."

"That's because I know you," Will countered. "You can't be trusted."

Colin smiled. "All I'm saying is that for someone who's planning to cut things off soon, you're acting pretty possessive."

Will fished out a tennis ball hidden beneath the porch steps. He tossed it across the yard for Riley, who was lolling in the grass beside a juniper bush.

Colin dug a tape measure out of his pocket and walked over to the porch. "You're not going to be able to keep other men away from her after you leave."

Will ripped up another rotted floorboard. "She'll be free to do whatever she wants once I'm gone."

"But she's not free to do whatever she wants now?"

"No."

"Does she know that?"

Will glanced up. "I'm starting to regret my decision to invite you down here."

Colin smiled again as he stretched the tape across the steps, measuring the width of the boards. "Take it from someone who's not on the teams anymore. There's more to life than being a SEAL. If you like this woman, don't screw it up."

If you like this woman? Will looked out at the yard, where Riley was chewing on the tennis ball he'd thrown for her. *Like* didn't even begin to describe how he felt about Annie now. Hell, he'd spent most of last night lying awake, wondering if he could transfer to the base in Virginia Beach so he could be closer to her.

But would it be fair to ask her to wait for him? It could be six months to a year before he could see her again. And what if something happened to him when he was overseas? What if he never came back at all? He knew what it was like to lose the people he loved most in the world. He wouldn't do that to Annie, or to Taylor.

No, he wouldn't ask her to wait for him. But he would come back the next time he was on leave. Ryan had said he could always use more volunteers, and he wanted to get involved with some of the work Colin was doing at Walter Reed.

If Annie *happened* to still be single when he came back from time to time...

What was he thinking? Annie wasn't going to stay single. As soon as he left, men would be lining up to ask her out. She'd said she wouldn't date until things settled down for her and Taylor on the island. But Taylor was starting to make friends. Business at the café was starting to pick up. Soon, there'd be no reason why she shouldn't accept a few casual invitations to dinner.

Yanking up another floorboard, he threw the splintered wood into the yard. When the phone in the house started to ring, he ignored it and picked up the hammer to pry out a row of rusted nails.

Colin jotted down the measurements of the steps, walking back to the power saw. He glanced up when the phone continued to ring. "Aren't you going to get that?"

"No."

"It's been ringing all morning."

"I know."

"Don't you want to know who it is?"

"I know who it is," Will said. "It's the guy from the resort company. He's left over a dozen messages."

Colin picked up another two-by-four, laying it across the sawhorse. "Maybe you should pick up the phone and hear him out."

Will shook his head. "I'm not giving up on finding another buyer yet."

Colin paused, his hand on the power switch. "I think the only reason you're putting off selling this house is to have more time with Annie."

Will turned to face him. "I'm not selling this house because I don't want to turn my family home over to a corporation who cares more about its bottom line than this island."

Colin studied him from across the yard. "What are you going to do if you can't find another buyer?"

"I'll find one." Will turned back around, and the power saw roared to life. Taking out his frustration on a band of rusted nails, he pried each one up with the hammer and dropped them into a pile at his feet.

He had to find another buyer. There was no way he was going to sell out to Morningstar now, not after hearing about all the projects Ryan was working on to save the Bay. These waters were being threatened by years of neglect and bad decisions by the people who lived on its shores. This land was his responsibility. He owed it to his friends and the rest of the islanders to preserve it. He would find a buyer who agreed to maintain the land around the inn as a sanctuary, or he wouldn't let the place go.

Ripping out the last of the nails, he caught a movement in the yard out of the corner of his eye. Lowering the hammer, he turned to face the man rounding the side of the house and heading toward him.

He had blond hair, a lanky build, and the confident stride of a man who was used to walking into situations where he hadn't been invited. He wore a charcoal suit and a blue tie, and when he took off his sunglasses, there was something vaguely familiar about his face.

"Mr. Dozier?"

Will stepped over the pile of rotted boards as Colin powered down the saw. "Can I help you?"

The man held out his hand, his smooth, cultured voice carrying a hint of a Southern accent. "I'm Blake Hadley. You didn't return any of my calls, so I thought I'd drop by."

Will made no move to shake his hand. "I didn't return your calls because we have nothing to talk about."

Undeterred, Blake dropped his hand back to his side and wandered over to the porch, eyeing the gaping hole where the steps used to be. "I understand from your realtor that you have some concerns."

"That's right."

"I'd like to address them."

TEN YEARS of working in special operations had sharpened Will's instincts to a razor's edge. When something didn't feel right, there was usually a reason for it. And something definitely didn't feel right about this situation.

Sitting across from Blake at the kitchen table, Will took the binder the other man handed him, opening it skeptically. "You want to turn this place into an eco-resort?"

Blake nodded. "One of the main reasons we acquired Morningstar was to move into the eco-resort business. Morningstar has built a solid reputation as a luxury resort company, but we want to rebrand them as the premier eco-friendly resort company in the country."

Will flipped through the pages in the binder. The pictures of the eco-resorts Blake had included as models looked like small-scale, family-run inns. They didn't look anything like the massive hotels surrounded by manicured gardens and golf courses that he'd seen on Morningstar's website.

"The natural environment is the main draw," Blake explained, sitting back. "We've seen a significant increase in environmentally conscious travelers over the past few years. There's a growing trend to get back to nature, especially among the baby boomers—basically hippies who have a lot of money now." Blake laughed. "They want to stay in a nice place, but they want to learn about local conservation efforts and give back while they're there."

Will thought about all the projects Ryan was going to need help with in the future. Would these guests be the kind of people who'd want to volunteer? Who'd want to spend a few days on the Bay lending a hand for a good cause?

"What about all the land around the inn?" Will asked. "Would you develop it, or leave it as a wildlife sanctuary?"

Blake nodded. "We have no interest in developing that land. It's ideal for nature walks, bird watching, kayaking tours, interactive classes for the kids—you get the idea."

"What about the house?"

"The house needs some work," Blake admitted. "We'd want to put in solar panels and skylights, replace the heating and cooling systems to make them more energy efficient." He glanced over at the kitchen. "We'd want to update most of the appliances in the kitchen and laundry room, but I don't see any reason why we couldn't retain the original structure."

Will looked back down at the pictures of the eco-resorts. If what Blake was saying was true, he would be able to sell the inn with a clean conscience, knowing the company who bought it was committed to protecting the land and restoring the house he grew up in. It would create dozens of new jobs for the islanders— guides, outreach coordinators, not to mention the service related jobs. Annie would be able to open her fancy French bistro, and Ryan would have a steady stream of volunteers and potential donators.

It was a win every way he looked at it.

But something definitely felt off...

Closing the binder, Will sat back. "If this was the plan all along, why didn't you mention something about it sooner?"

Blake smiled. "I would have if you'd ever answered the phone."

Will continued to study the man across the table, wondering again why that smile seemed so familiar. "Why didn't you have Spencer tell me?"

Blake leaned his arms on the table. "I didn't share this information with Spencer. My father and I don't want our competition to know we're getting into the eco-resort business. Right now, we're focused on acquiring properties. We want to secure several prime spots before we make a public announcement."

That was a perfectly reasonable explanation, Will thought, glancing out the window at where Colin was cutting a new piece of wood to replace the porch steps. But it all seemed just a little too good to be true. Sliding the binder across the table, he stood. "I'll think about it."

"Keep it." Blake pushed to his feet. "Look up a few of the resorts online, read the reviews, and see for yourself." He handed Will his card. "I'll be around for a few days, if you have any questions."

Will took the card. "You're staying in the area?"

Blake nodded. "I want to talk with some of the locals, get a better feel for the place. If you decide to sell, this will be our first eco-resort. I want to make sure we get it right."

BLAKE SMILED as he drove away from the inn. He had no intention of opening an eco-resort on the island. It was Spencer who'd initially planted the seed—unknowingly, as the small town realtor probably couldn't close a seven-figure deal if his life depended on it. But after speaking with him several times over the phone during the past week, Blake had gotten a pretty clear picture of why Will was dragging his feet.

It wasn't just an emotional attachment to the house as his father had led him to believe; it was that he felt a social responsibility to do what was best for the island. According to Spencer, most of the islanders were opposed to the idea of a resort, including one of Will's closest childhood friends who'd recently moved back to start an environmental nonprofit on the island.

As soon as he'd heard that, Blake knew he'd found his angle.

An eco-resort.

It was brilliant.

Cruising down the deserted road leading back into town, he took in the soybean fields and pine forests, the rambling marshes and overgrown stretches of grass, weeds and wildflowers. In a few years, this land would be transformed into a gated community of private residences, swimming pools, tennis courts, and a nine-hole golf course.

Morningstar's management would work closely with the developer to ensure the community met specific standards. In exchange, the residents would gain exclusive access to resort activities, spa services, and weekly discounts to the five-star restaurant.

What was the point in having all that land if you weren't going to do anything with it?

Blake tapped the brakes as he neared the elementary school. It was three o'clock and school was just letting out for the day. Children were streaming out the front doors, laughing and squealing. The parking lot was filled with parents waiting to pick them up.

A pair of young girls dashed across the street, their colorful backpacks bouncing up and down. The last thing Blake wanted was a kid. But his mother was itching for a grandchild. Even if he closed this deal with the inn today, and his father dropped the threat of cutting him off, his mother would be pushing for him to find a nice girl and get married again as soon as he got home.

He had about as much interest in marriage as he did in having children.

He knew what it was like to be married, to have a clingy wife pestering him about coming home in time for dinner, nagging him about hanging out with his friends at night instead of her, begging for another ten grand for the fertility shots that were *supposed* to help her get pregnant.

His parents blamed him for screwing up the marriage, but Emily was the one who'd pushed him away with her calendar of ovulation cycles and detailed spreadsheets dictating when they should and should not have sex.

Was it any wonder he'd sought pleasure in the arms of other women—ones who still enjoyed having sex rather than turning it into a chore?

He angled the rental car into an open spot on the side of the road lined by a pitiful scattering of shops. He'd booked a room for the night at a hotel in St. Michaels, but there was no point in driving all the way over there just to turn around and come right back. It would only take Will twenty or thirty minutes to check out a few of the companies online to confirm Blake's story.

As soon as he did, he'd be calling him on his cell, ready to move forward.

Stepping out of the car, Blake crossed the street to the island café, taking in the tacky display of wind chimes on the porch. He might as well grab a cup of coffee while he waited. If he could close this deal within the hour, he could cancel his reservation in St. Michaels and get on the road, heading back toward civilization before dark.

ANNIE BARELY GLANCED up as the door to the café swung open. "Grab a seat wherever you can find one," she said, waving the new customer inside and turning back to the table she was serving.

For the second day in a row, the café had been packed since the moment she'd opened the doors. Jess's mom had dropped by earlier and offered to pick up both girls after school and watch Taylor until Annie could come get her. Grateful for the reprieve, Annie had accepted and promised to bring her a pint of cream of crab soup and a loaf of cheese bread for dinner, but she didn't want to make a habit of not picking Taylor up from school.

If this pace kept up through the weekend, she would need to start thinking about hiring a waitress.

Tucking her pen and notebook into her apron, she dropped off a few checks and scooped up two empty coffee mugs before heading to the kitchen to pick up more plates from Della. Out of the corner of her eye, she noticed the man in the suit still standing in the doorway. "There's a seat here, if you want it," she said, pointing to an open stool at the counter.

"Annie?"

She froze, almost dropping the mugs. That voice—she would

know it anywhere. Turning, slowly, she looked at the man's face for the first time and the room began to spin.

"It *is* you," the man said, taking a step toward her.

"Blake," she managed, vaguely aware that the rest of her customers had gone quiet, that every eye in the room was now focused on the two of them. "What are you doing here?"

"I'm here on business." He took another step toward her. "What are *you* doing here?"

Business. Annie's heart stuttered. He must have come to the island to talk to Will about selling the inn. "I live here."

"You live here?"

She nodded, her gaze darting to the window when she caught the sound of Taylor's laughter out in the street.

A cold knot of dread formed in the pit of her stomach when she spotted Taylor and Jess climbing the steps to the porch.

What were they doing here?

The screen door opened, the hinges creaking through the silence. Taylor paused in the doorway with Jess peering over her shoulder. "Mom?"

"Hi, sweetie," Annie said, forcing the words out.

Taylor looked around the crowded room, then back at Annie. "Why's everybody so quiet?"

Annie spotted Jess's mom turning up the path to the café. "I thought you were going to Jess's house after school."

"We are," Taylor said, glancing up at Blake. "I wanted to show them the wind chimes I made from the buttons Mrs. Casper gave me."

Annie's hands shook as she set the mugs down on the counter. Crossing the room to where they'd hung a set of chimes from the ceiling at the foot of the stairwell, she slipped the delicate cluster of strings and buttons off the hook. "Here," she said, carrying them over to Taylor. "Why don't you take these with you and I'll bring the rest over later when I pick you up."

"Okay," Taylor said, frowning as she looked back and forth between Annie and Blake.

Helen Casper climbed the steps to the porch and sent Annie an apologetic smile. "I've been trying to catch up with them since they took off outside the school." She placed her hands on Jess's shoulders. "Why don't we head home and see if Grandma's made any more chocolate chip cookies?"

Jess grabbed Taylor's hand and tugged her back toward the steps, but Taylor hesitated, taking one last look at Annie and Blake. "Mom?"

"Everything's fine, sweetie," Annie said, smoothing her daughter's hair back from her face. "I'll come get you in an hour."

Taylor didn't look convinced, but she turned and followed her friend. Annie stood in the doorway, her blood rushing in her ears as Blake walked up behind her. She felt his hand on her elbow, guiding her out the door, away from the room full of customers.

"*That's* your daughter?"

"Yes."

Blake paused on the top step, staring out at the girl in the street. "How old is she?"

"It's not what you think..."

"How *old* is she, Annie?"

Annie swallowed. "She's eight."

His shocked blue eyes met hers. "Is she *mine*?"

"Yes."

EIGHTEEN

*A*nnie stood on the porch, watching the yellow leaves scatter like secrets escaping with the wind. That was the problem with secrets—once they were exposed, there was no turning back. There was nothing you could do but try to manage the fallout.

Easing her elbow free from Blake's grip, she fought back the urge to run across the street, scoop Taylor up, and take her somewhere far away from here. She didn't want her getting hurt. She didn't want her getting caught in the middle of this.

"You had our *daughter*?" Blake stammered. "And you didn't tell me?"

Annie lowered her voice. "I did tell you."

"You told me you were pregnant," Blake said, stunned. "You didn't tell me you decided to keep the child."

Annie held his gaze. "There was never a question of whether or not I was going to keep her."

Blake cursed, dragging a hand through his hair. "I didn't even know it was a *her* until today."

Annie watched his golden blond locks fall back into place.

He still had the same classically handsome features, the same ocean blue eyes, the same lanky physique. She remembered how when they had first started dating, she had lit up inside whenever he'd reached for her hand.

Now, she felt nothing.

Looking back at the street, she watched Taylor turn the corner to Jess's house. Over the years, when she'd imagined this moment, she'd pictured herself as a successful businesswoman. She'd pictured herself as the owner of an elegant French restaurant that had been written up in several popular food magazines.

Blake would have come in for dinner one night, and she would have acted like she barely remembered him as she'd told him there weren't any tables available, as she'd turned him away. She would have finally been able to throw his words back in his face: '*You'll never be anything more than a waitress.*'

But as she looked back up at him now, she felt a spark of anger—not at him—at herself.

There was nothing wrong with being a waitress. There was nothing wrong with the path she'd chosen. Why had she wasted so much time trying to fit into his world? Trying to prove she was worthy?

"We were kids, Annie," Blake said as a truck drove by and the driver gunned his engine. "What did you expect me to do?"

"I didn't expect you to do anything," Annie said calmly. "I didn't ask you to do anything."

Blake stared at her. "You didn't have the decency to tell me? To let me know you'd decided to go through with it?"

No, Annie thought. She had never even considered telling Blake the truth. The day he'd given her the cash, she'd bought a bus ticket to D.C. She'd used the rest of the money to put down a security deposit on an apartment in Adams Morgan.

Blake had been right about one thing—she couldn't bring a baby up in the same apartment with her mother and she couldn't afford to take care of them both. The owners of the restaurant where she'd been working in New Orleans had recently opened a sister restaurant in D.C. and she'd applied for a job.

A few weeks later, she'd been serving overpriced martinis to senators and congressmen on Pennsylvania Avenue and raking in enough tips to save up for childcare so she could keep working after Taylor was born. She had never once looked back. "I did what I thought was best for my child."

"Don't you mean, *our* child?" Blake countered.

Annie shook her head as a gust of wind blew through the street, sending the chimes into a frantic spin. "We were never married. You have no legal claim on her."

Blake's brows shot up. "I'm not sure the law would see it that way."

Annie felt a sharp prick of fear, but she stood her ground. "You said you didn't want her."

"It never occurred to you that I might have changed?"

"No."

"That I might *want* to be a part of her life?"

"No." Annie's hands curled into fists. Taylor was *hers*. As far as she was concerned, Blake had lost any claim on their daughter the day he'd left her alone beside the ATM. She wasn't going to let him waltz back into their lives after all these years, like nothing had happened.

She would not let him hurt Taylor. She would not let him hurt either of them ever again.

"You made your choice," Annie said, turning. "Now, if you'll excuse me, I have to get back to work."

Blake caught her wrist, stopping her. "If you think I'm going to walk away from this, you're wrong."

Annie turned slowly back around to face him. "I have nothing else to say to you."

Blake's disapproving gaze combed down the front of her, over the coffee stains on her white sweater to the apron tied around her waist. "This conversation is not over. I'll let you get back to work, but you and I are going to have a nice long chat later tonight."

"And if I say no?"

"Then you'll be hearing from my lawyer first thing in the morning."

THE SUNSET PAINTED the clouds crimson as Will drove into town. The café had closed fifteen minutes ago, but Della had promised to set aside two orders of chicken and dumplings for him to take back to the inn. Colin had laughed when Will had told him where he was going.

They both knew the only reason he was headed to the café was to see Annie.

He'd spent most of the day denying there was anything serious going on between them, but the truth was, he'd never felt this way about a woman before. For the first time since joining the SEALs, he was beginning to question the lifestyle he'd chosen.

Blake Hadley had offered him an easy way out, a clean ticket back to his former life. But did he even want that anymore?

He had no doubt that a lot of people on this island would benefit from an eco-resort. So far, everything Blake had said that afternoon had checked out online. But something still felt off. He couldn't put his finger on it, but he wasn't ready to jump on board yet. At least, not until he'd talked to Annie.

She may have moved here initially because of the resort, but was it possible she felt differently now? Was it possible the café was beginning to grow on her? He needed to know if her dream of opening a fine dining restaurant was still as important to her now as it was when they'd first met.

If it was, then any thoughts he was harboring about keeping the inn would only stand in the way of her happiness.

The last thing he wanted was to stand in the way of her happiness.

Pulling into the parking lot of The Tackle Box, he cut the engine and stepped out of the SUV. A cold wind carried the first biting hints of winter. He looked up at the red sky, watching an osprey wheel and dip in the currents.

He had one quick errand to run before heading to the café.

Nodding to Don Fluharty, who was sitting outside on one of the benches drinking a beer and patching a hole in a nylon fishing net, he walked into the store and made his way to the wall of fishing rods.

When he'd taken Taylor out on Ryan's boat the night before, he'd given her a crash course in casting. But all the rods had been too heavy for her. If she was going to learn how to fish, she needed her own rod.

He picked out a purple children's rod and walked up to the register. He wasn't sure how Annie would react to him giving Taylor a present, but he figured he'd take his chances. He wanted to give Taylor something to focus on, a new skill to distract her when the bad memories crept in after he left.

Scanning the headlines of the newspaper while he waited for Don to make his way inside to ring him up, he couldn't help overhearing the conversation between two women in the next aisle.

"Did you get a good look at his face?" the first woman asked.

"I did," the second said. "You can definitely see the resemblance."

"I heard he wants to build a resort here. A resort! Can you imagine?"

Will glanced up from the newspaper. They were talking

about Blake. But how did they even know who he was? And who did they think he resembled?

Turning, he tried to see who was talking, but both women's backs were to him and their heads barely cleared the top of the aisle.

Hadn't he thought there was something familiar about Blake's face when he saw him for the first time earlier today?

"Do you think he chose this island because his daughter lives here?" the second woman asked. "So he could spend more time with her?"

Will frowned. Blake had a daughter who lived on the island? Why hadn't he mentioned he had family here?

"I don't know," the first woman said. "But it must have been hard for Taylor to grow up without her father."

By THE TIME Annie pushed the last customer out the door, it was close to four-thirty. She'd managed to keep it together through the rest of the shift, but all she could think about was picking up Taylor and bringing her home before she overheard someone talking.

She knew how fast gossip could spread on this island.

"Leave the dishes, Della." Annie untied her apron and dropped it on the counter. "I'll deal with them later."

"Now, wait just a minute," Della said, marching out of the kitchen. "Before you go, we need to talk."

"I can't." Annie grabbed her coat off the hook by the door, slipping her arms through the sleeves. Della had already asked her a dozen questions since Blake had left and she'd answered all of them as truthfully as she could. But she didn't have time to fill in the rest of the blanks now. "I need to tell Taylor that Blake's here before she finds out from someone else."

"I understand that." Della crossed the room to stand in front of the door. "But no one's going to say anything to her while she's at Jess's house. You need to take a few minutes to think about what you're doing."

"What's there to think about?"

"You said Blake wanted to talk later. Why don't you hear him out first? He might only be reacting from the shock of finding out he's a father. He might not even want to meet Taylor or get to know her at all once he's had time to process it. There's no point in bringing her into this if he's just going to walk away again."

Annie shook her head, reaching for the doorknob. "He's not going to let this go."

Della stepped back from the door, but her face was troubled. "Why don't you let me keep her tonight? Joe and I will watch her while you deal with Blake. Once you find out exactly what he wants, we can take it from there."

Annie was touched Della wanted to help, but she needed to deal with this herself. She wasn't naïve. Blake's family was rich and powerful. People with that much money could do whatever they wanted. "He's already threatened to call his lawyer, Della."

"Annie." Della took her hands. "No one is going to let him take Taylor away from you."

A cold wind rushed into the room when the door swung open. Annie took one look at the expression on Will's face and a wave of uneasiness swept through her. His eyes were so dark; they were almost black. His muscles were coiled, his jaw clenched. He stepped into the room and slammed the door. "Is this some kind of joke?"

"Will." Annie took a step back. He must have heard what had happened. Someone must have told him about Blake. "Let me explain."

His voice cut through the empty dining room. "Blake Hadley is Taylor's father."

It wasn't a question. It was an accusation. And there was nothing she could do to deny it. "Yes."

"Blake Hadley," Will repeated, a muscle in his jaw starting to tick. "The man who wants to buy my inn and turn it into a resort?"

When he put it that way, it didn't sound good. It didn't sound good at all. "Yes."

"Is that why you moved here?"

"What?" Annie stammered.

He took another step toward her. "Is that why you moved here? To *this* island?"

"Will," Della warned, but he didn't even look at her. His eyes never left Annie's face.

"No." Annie shook her head. "Of course, not. I didn't even know the Hadleys had bought Morningstar until a couple of weeks ago."

"But you *did* know?"

He was so close now she could feel the anger vibrating off him in waves. She had never seen him like this before. "Yes, but—"

"Is this how you two play it?" he cut in, his words like ice. "You move here first, get to know the locals, butter up the owner, maybe even sleep with him so he agrees to sell. Then Blake comes in when you can't close the deal?"

Annie jaw dropped. "Excuse me?"

"I can't believe I fell for it."

"How dare you?" Annie breathed as shock gave way to anger. "How dare you accuse me of trying to seduce you? I didn't ask for this! I never even wanted this! Whatever this"—she waved her hand between them—"even is!"

Will's eyes were cold. "A lapse in judgment, on my part."

Annie staggered back, as if he'd punched her in the stomach. She could only stare as he turned, his long strides eating up the checkerboard tiles. "You're not even going to give me a chance to explain?"

He paused, his hand on the door. "Why should I? You'll only tell me half the story anyway."

Annie watched him leave, watched him walk down the steps as the screen door slapped shut. How could he think so little of her? After everything they'd shared, how could he believe she would do this?

A voice inside her screamed not to go after him, but this wasn't just about her anymore.

"Will, wait." She walked out to the porch, her hands gripping the railing as he crossed the street to his car. "Don't do this. Taylor won't understand."

Will turned, his gaze hard and unforgiving in the fading twilight. "I'm sure Taylor would rather spend time with her father."

BLAKE STOOD at the window of his hotel room overlooking the St. Michaels Marina. Sailboats bobbed in the quiet waters. Historic homes lined the quaint neighborhood streets stretching away from the shoreline. A few tourists strolled the grounds of the Maritime Museum, snapping pictures of the lighthouse at dusk.

After the initial shock had worn off, it hadn't taken him long to realize that Annie Malone could be the answer to all of his problems. Not only was she still single—he'd noted from the lack of a ring on her finger but she was the mother of his child.

He could hardly believe his luck.

It would take some explaining, some serious finessing on his part, to convince both his parents and Annie that it had all been a terrible misunderstanding, that he would never have let her go if he'd known she was planning to keep their child. But he'd find a way to spin it.

He always found a way to spin it.

Rocking back on his heels, he gazed across the marina at the weathered crab deck where a few hearty diners were huddled around a picnic table, picking the last steamed crabs of the season. Surely Annie didn't want to work as a waitress for the rest of her life. And she couldn't possibly have *chosen* to live on that island.

As soon as things were smoothed out between them, he would talk her into coming back to New Orleans with him. He would set her and their daughter up a beautiful home in the Garden District. His mother would come by daily to dote on her grandchild, and his father would have no choice but to give him his job back and forgive all his debts.

Everyone would get what they wanted.

Turning away from the window, he walked to the desk and picked up the phone. If, for any reason, Annie refused, he could always threaten her with a custody battle. He had a feeling she would do anything to keep her child, even if it meant marrying a man who she thought had never loved her.

Dialing the front desk, he waited for the receptionist to answer. All he had to do now was convince her that he had.

"Good evening, Mr. Hadley. How can I help you?"

"I need a reservation for two at seven o'clock at the nicest restaurant in town, and the phone number for the Wind Chime Café on Heron Island."

NINETEEN

*W*hat the hell happened to you?" Colin asked when Will walked into the inn three hours later.

Will dropped a bag of takeout from Wendy's on the kitchen counter. "I went for a drive."

Riley came up and sniffed his hand, wagging her tail. He fed her a French fry on his way to the fridge to grab a beer.

"Will."

He stiffened at the female voice, but it was only Becca. She was sitting on the couch in the living room with Ryan, a pile of food spread out on the table in front of them.

"I had to call in reinforcements since you left me here without a car." Colin took the beer from his hand and popped the cap off with an opener. He handed it back, eyeing the Wendy's bag. "I thought you were picking up dinner from the café?"

"I was." Will took a long sip. From the expression on Becca and Ryan's faces, he could tell that they knew. Della had probably called them and asked them to check up on him since he wouldn't pick up any of her calls. But they must not have said anything to Colin.

Good. He didn't want to discuss it with Colin. He'd already made up his mind anyway. It had taken almost three hours behind the wheel to calm down, but for the first time since coming back to the island over a month ago, he was finally beginning to think clearly.

Getting involved with Annie had been a mistake.

Walking across the living room to the chair beside the sofa, he sank into the worn leather. Ryan's chocolate lab, Zoey, was curled up on the rug waiting for someone to drop a piece of food on the floor. He tossed her a fry and glanced over at the TV. "Who's winning?"

"The Red Sox are up by two," Ryan said, handing him a basket of clam strips.

"Who's pitching?"

"Lackey."

Will sat back, focusing on the game. If tonight was going to be his last night in this house, he might as well try to enjoy it.

Colin continued to watch him from across the room. When Will didn't say anything else about where he'd been or why he hadn't picked up dinner from the café, Colin wandered over to sit in the chair on the other side of the sofa. "I told Ryan about the eco-resort."

Will popped a clam strip into his mouth, glancing over at Ryan. "What do you think?"

"I've never stayed at one," Ryan said, "but I've heard good things."

"Do you think you'd be able to work with them on some of your projects—the ones you need volunteers for?"

"Sure." Ryan nodded. "I imagine most of the people who stay at a resort like that aren't afraid of getting their hands dirty. They might be interested in helping out, or at least learning about what's going on in the area to preserve the environment. A place like that could bring all kinds of potential donors to the island."

He broke off a piece of fried fish, dipping it into a bowl of tartar sauce. "I'm not going to lie. I'm intrigued. Are you considering it?"

"I'm signing the papers tomorrow."

"What?" Becca sat up. "Why?"

Will slipped Riley a clam strip. "I came back to sell this house. I got a good offer. I'm taking it."

Becca set her plate down, turning to face him. "You don't have to do this, Will. You don't have to sell this house if you're not ready. There are other options you might not have even considered."

"Yeah," Colin added, looking just as surprised as Becca. "One option is that *you* could stay here and run this place."

"Just because I grew up in an inn, doesn't mean I know how to run one." Will stood, gathering the empty bottles and carrying them over to the sink. "Besides, my life is in San Diego."

"But it doesn't have to be forever," Becca argued. "This is your home, Will. You need a place to come back to when—"

Will dumped the bottles into the sink, drowning out the sound of her voice. No. He didn't need to come back here. He should never have stayed on the island as long as he had. It was time to go back to California, to refocus his mind on the teams, to shed all the complications that were only holding him back from moving on.

Colin twisted around to face him. "What about all the time you spent fixing up this place? Don't you want to keep looking for another buyer until you have to leave?"

Will shook his head. "The resort will bring jobs to the island. It'll bring tourists. It'll raise awareness for Ryan's projects."

"Don't sell the inn on my account," Ryan said. "I'd much rather know that you still had a tie to this island. That you might come back here one day."

Becca nodded. "If you don't want to run it, hire someone else to do it. But don't sell it to Blake Hadley."

"Why not?" Will asked. "Because he wouldn't do a good job?"

"No," Colin said, frustrated. "Because you love this house and you love that woman, and you're going to lose them both if you walk away."

Out of the corner of his eye, Will caught the flutter of orange wings over the kitchen table. Taylor's paper butterfly hung from the chandelier, spinning in slow circles beside his sister's chime. Taylor had given him the butterfly so he would remember the monarchs after they'd gone. But what was the point in holding onto the memories, when it was so much easier to let them go? "I've made up my mind."

Annie stepped out of her car in downtown St. Michaels, ducking her head against the winds. Street lamps illuminated the picturesque shops lining the street, many of them already decorated for Christmas. Maryland flags waved from porches and balconies as she made her way over the uneven brick sidewalk to the restaurant where Blake was waiting.

He'd sounded reasonably calm over the phone when he'd invited her to dinner. Maybe Della had been right; once the shock of finding out he was a father had worn off, he'd realized they could sit down and discuss this as adults.

But if that was the case, why did she feel like she was walking into a trap?

Handing the hostess her jacket, she took in the white table-cloths and iron sconces hanging from the exposed brick walls. There were only five tables in the dining room and a cozy fire crackled in the hearth. A waiter in a starched white shirt and black tie poured her a glass of wine as she sat down across from Blake.

Blake studied her in the flickering candlelight. "I thought, perhaps, we could start over."

She nodded, unfolding her napkin, but something about the tone of his voice set her on edge. It was too smooth, too civilized. She'd only agreed to let Della look after Taylor for the next couple of hours so she could find out exactly what Blake wanted.

So she could be ready to fight if she needed to.

"Why don't you start by telling me a little about our daughter?" Blake suggested.

"Taylor," Annie said, bristling at the word, 'our.' "Her name's Taylor."

Blake picked up a roll, breaking it in half. "If she's eight, that would put her in second grade, right?"

"Yes."

"She goes to school on the island?"

Annie nodded.

"Does she like it?"

"Yes."

Blake sighed. "We're not going to get very far if you only give me one word answers."

Annie reached for her water glass. "If you think I'm going to share intimate details about Taylor's life with you, you're wrong."

Undeterred, Blake took a bite of his roll. "We have to start somewhere."

"Why don't we start by getting straight to the point. Why did you invite me here, Blake?"

He looked down at the menu. "Should we order a couple of appetizers? What do you think of the grilled quail?"

"I didn't come here to sample the appetizers."

Blake signaled for the waiter and Annie gritted her teeth as he ordered the quail and a cheese plate for the table. She was here for Taylor. She needed to stay calm so she could find out what he wanted. If he was going to play games, she could deal with it for one evening.

He looked back at her, smiling as the waiter scurried away. "I'm sorry. Where were we?"

"We were discussing—"

"Right." His smile deepened. "I remember." Reaching across the table, he took her hand. "We were about to talk about you."

She stared down at their joined hands. "What are you doing?"

"Changing the subject," he said smoothly. "If you're uncomfortable talking about Taylor, maybe we should talk about you instead."

Slipping her hand free, she picked up her wine glass. What the hell was he up to? "What do you want to know?"

"How do you like living on an island?"

"I like it."

"What about the café? Do you enjoy working there?"

"I do." She took a sip of her wine. "It would be a shame if I didn't, since I own it."

Blake paused in the act of buttering the second half of his roll. "You *own* it?"

"Yes." She wasn't surprised he hadn't made the connection between her and the name, Wind Chime Café. Like her mother, Blake had never taken her wind chimes seriously. She had made him one once, out of black sea glass. She'd found it a week later, smashed on the floor of his car among the crumpled fast food wrappers and dirty gym clothes.

Blake sat back, regarding her in a new light. "I'm impressed."

"I'm so relieved," she said sarcastically.

He smiled, raising his glass in a silent cheer. "Since we'll both be business owners on the island soon, we should discuss strategies. I'm working on a deal to purchase a piece of real estate for my father's company so we can build a resort there."

"I know." Sipping at the buttery chardonnay, which had probably cost more than her car payment, she could hear the click and scrape of every fork against every plate in the room. The low murmur of hushed conversations mingling with the hiss and pop of the fire made her want to whisper.

She was surprised how much she longed for the chaotic atmosphere of the café—Della's pots and pans clanging around in the kitchen, the islanders laughing and gossiping in the dining room, the clap and clatter of her wind chimes out on the porch.

It was hard to believe she'd spent almost a decade of her life working in this type of environment. It had become such an obsession to be the most charming waitress, to provide the most impeccable service, to ingratiate herself to a clientele who couldn't care less about her; she'd never taken the time to consider if this was what she really wanted.

Had she actually moved to Heron Island to open a restaurant like this? One where every patron was quietly sizing each other up? Where the waiters walked on eggshells and only a very small portion of the population could even afford the menu?

She set down her wine, taking a deep breath. "Did you have any luck convincing Will to sell?"

Blake nodded. "I'm expecting a call back from him tonight."

"You think he's going to say yes?"

"It's only a matter of time," Blake said confidently. "Is he a friend of yours?"

Annie smoothed her hand over the cloth napkin in her lap. There was no way Will would agree to sell the inn to Blake now, not when he knew Blake was Taylor's father. At least that was one less thing she had to worry about. "It's a small island, Blake. Everyone knows everyone else's business."

"But you won't tell me yours?"

"No."

"Because you don't trust me?"

Annie sighed. "Because Taylor's been through a lot this year and she doesn't need you walking back into her life and upsetting things right now. I know this will be hard for you to swallow, but this isn't only about you."

"What could possibly happen on an island that small?"

Annie hesitated. "Nothing. I only meant..." She trailed off. Blake didn't know what had happened to Taylor at Mount Pleasant. Even if he'd seen the reports on the news, he wouldn't have recognized Taylor's name or her picture.

Blake set down his wine. "What are you not telling me?"

"Nothing," she lied. "Taylor's overly sensitive right now. She doesn't need any more stress in her life."

"She's eight," Blake countered. "What could she possibly be stressed about?"

Annie reached for the bread basket, forcing herself to stay calm. "Life's harder for kids nowadays."

Blake narrowed his eyes. "Why did you move to Heron Island?"

Annie chose a roll from the basket, setting it on her plate. "To open a restaurant. Like I said."

"But why would you pick an island, in the middle of nowhere?"

"Because the price was right." She added a pad of herbed butter to her plate. "Does it matter?"

"It matters that you're hiding something about our daughter. Did something happen to upset her? Is that why you moved here?"

Annie's hand stilled on the butter knife. If Blake came back to the island tomorrow, and spent any amount of time in the village, he could overhear someone talking about Taylor. If he decided to type in her name to a search engine on the Internet later, he would get dozens of hits.

It wouldn't take him long to find out the truth.

Wouldn't it be better if she told him now, if she handled it face-to-face, instead of dealing with a potential confrontation in front of Taylor later?

Annie set down the knife. "We moved here six weeks ago because of something that happened at Taylor's school in D.C."

"At her school?" Blake's brows furrowed. "You said she was in second grade, right? What could possibly...?" His face went pale. "You don't mean...?"

Annie looked back at him, unable to hide the truth from her eyes.

"She went to Mount Pleasant?"

Annie nodded.

"The girl that survived...that was Taylor?"

"Yes."

Annie watched the familiar range of emotions sweep over his eyes: horror, shock, anger, sadness.

When he was finally able to speak again, his voice was low and shaky. "I can't believe I didn't know this."

"You had no right to know it," Annie said quietly.

Blake stared at her, stunned.

"We're doing fine, Blake. Taylor has her setbacks, but we're doing fine."

He reached across the table for her hand again. "I'm so sorry you had to go through this alone."

I wasn't alone. Annie eased her hand free. She had no desire to be comforted by him. *I had Della. I had Shelley. I had Becca. I had Will.*

The waiter came out of the kitchen with their appetizers and

Blake waved him away. "Let me make it up to you. To both of you."

"We don't need your help," Annie said. "Taylor needs stability. She doesn't need a father who may or may not decide he wants to stick around."

"I'm not going anywhere," Blake said firmly. "Tomorrow, I'll look for a house to rent in the area. I was already planning to spend more time on the island working on the resort. Now that I know you and Taylor live here, I'll make sure I'm the one overseeing the project."

Annie's fingers curled around the stem of her wine glass. That was the last thing she wanted. "How's Emily going to feel about that?"

"Emily and I are divorced." He held up his hand, showing off his bare ring finger. "Going on two years."

Of course he was divorced, Annie thought. She wasn't even surprised.

"Annie," Blake said quietly. "I invited you here tonight to talk about our daughter. But I also wanted to talk about us."

She tensed. "There is no us."

"I made a mistake."

"A *mistake?*"

"I was young and foolish." Blake lowered his voice. "I've changed."

Annie shook her head. It was going to take a lot more than dinner at a fancy restaurant to convince her that he'd changed.

"I married Emily because my parents expected me to," Blake said. "I wasn't in love with her. I was in love with you."

Annie gaped at him.

"I don't expect you to forgive me overnight," Blake said. "But at least give me a chance. Let me spend some time with Taylor. Let me get to know her in my own way."

"Taylor's not ready for this." *And neither am I.*

"I promise that I won't mess up this time." Blake took her hand. "All I ask is that you give me a chance."

WHAT CHOICE DID SHE HAVE? Annie sat on Taylor's bed an hour later, waiting for her daughter to process the news that her father was in town and wanted to meet her. If Blake was going to look for a house to rent on the island, he wasn't leaving. There was no way she could keep Taylor from him.

She didn't believe for a second that he'd changed, but by agreeing to cooperate she could at least maintain control of the situation. He wouldn't go near Taylor without her permission. She would supervise every meeting, every conversation. If Taylor was at all uncomfortable around him, then that would be it. No more meetings.

"I don't understand," Taylor said, hugging her stuffed animal to her chest. "Why is he here?"

"He wants to buy Will's house."

Taylor huddled deeper into her mountain of pillows. "Why?"

"Blake's family owns a big hotel company. They're hoping to open a resort—sort of a fancy hotel—on the island."

"But where will Will live?"

"Will's home is in California," Annie said gently. "He's going back there soon. You knew that."

Taylor's gaze dropped to the broom lying on top of her yellow comforter. "Where will he stay when he visits us?"

"I don't know if he *is* going to visit us, Taylor."

Taylor was quiet for a long time, and Annie wished she knew what to say. But what could she say? She was the one who'd allowed Taylor to spend time with Will. She was the one who'd allowed her daughter to get too attached.

When Will left, Taylor would be heartbroken.

And it was all Annie's fault.

Gazing up at the wind chimes and dream catchers that hung from the ceiling, Annie watched them catch the soft lamplight as they spun overhead. She'd agreed to introduce Blake to Taylor first thing in the morning. Most of the islanders probably knew he was on the island by now. This way, they could stay ahead of the gossip and no one could say anything to upset Taylor at school.

But if Taylor wasn't ready, they could postpone it. She would be happy to postpone it as long as possible. "If you don't want to meet Blake yet, you don't have to. It's completely up to you."

Taylor picked at a feather coming loose on the edge of her comforter. "I thought he didn't want us."

Annie's heart constricted as she reached for her daughter's hand. "He didn't want *me*, sweetie. You had nothing to do with it."

"Did he change his mind?"

That was a good question, Annie thought. She didn't know what Blake was up to. As far as she was concerned, there was nothing he could say or do to convince her to give him a second chance. But she would try to be civil, for Taylor's sake. "I don't know what Blake wants, other than a chance to get to know you." She squeezed Taylor's hand. "But no matter who comes into our lives, it won't change anything between us. You are, and always will be, the most important person in *my* world."

Taylor's troubled eyes lifted to hers. "Did you love him?"

"It was a long time ago, but, yes, I did love him."

"But you don't anymore?"

"No."

"Do you think you'll get back together?"

"No."

"Because of Will?"

Annie shook her head slowly. "No. Not because of Will."

"But I thought you were in love with him."

Annie felt a slow roll in the pit of her stomach. "Even if I was in love with Will, it wouldn't change anything. His life is in San Diego, and ours is here."

Taylor looked down. "I thought..."

"What?" Annie pressed. "What did you think?"

"I thought Will was going to be my dad."

TWENTY

*I*t was official, Annie thought, walking down the stairs the next morning. She was the worst mother in the world. Tying her damp hair back in a ponytail, she crossed the dining room to answer the door. Blake was standing on the porch, dressed in a gray suit and looking far too put together for six in the morning.

"You're early," she said.

He smiled. "It's nice to see you, too."

She eyed the package tucked under his arm. "What's that?"

"A present for Taylor." He looked past her, into the café. "Where is she?"

"Upstairs." Annie stepped back so he could walk inside. She didn't like the idea of him bringing Taylor gifts, especially not so soon. His dress shoes clicked over the tiles, echoing through the empty room. Closing the door, she headed back to the foot of the stairs leading up to the apartment. The sooner they could get this over with, the better.

"Taylor," she called out. "Blake's here."

Blake continued to circle the room, taking in the photographs of watermen and workboats, the seashells woven into the netting strung across the wall, the rustic chalkboard listing the day's specials. He said nothing, but she could feel his disapproval stretching out in the silence between them.

She glanced up when Taylor started down the steps. She'd warned Blake about Taylor's broom the night before, but seeing her with it now only reminded her how vulnerable her daughter still was. No matter what happened, she would not let Blake hurt her.

Taylor paused at the bottom of the stairs, looking uncertainly at Blake.

Blake smiled. "You must be Taylor."

She nodded, leaning against Annie.

Annie put her arm around Taylor's shoulders.

Blake walked across the room to where she stood, holding out his hand.

Taylor took it awkwardly.

"I'm so glad your mom agreed to let us meet."

Taylor pulled her hand free, looking back up at Annie.

Annie squeezed her shoulder. "Are you hungry?"

She nodded.

"I'll see if we have any bagels left." Annie guided her toward the closest bar stool, helping her climb up onto the seat. "What kind do you want?"

"Blueberry," Taylor said, keeping a close eye on Blake as he slid onto the stool beside her.

"So," Blake said, reaching for the cream cheese after Annie had spread everything out on the counter. "We have a lot of catching up to do, don't we?"

Taylor picked at her bagel, putting a small piece in her mouth.

Unfazed by her guardedness, Blake slathered cream cheese

over both halves of his bagel. "It must be nice to live above a café. Do you get to sample the desserts?"

Taylor shrugged. "Sometimes."

He nodded toward the chalkboard, which listed Della's sweets along with the rest of her specials. "Which one's your favorite?"

"It's not on there."

"Why not?"

"Because Della doesn't make it."

"Who makes it?"

Taylor looked at Annie.

Blake lifted an eyebrow. "I'm intrigued."

Annie added a spoonful of sugar to her coffee. "Turns out, I have a knack for making hot chocolate."

"Hot chocolate?" Blake's lips curved. "That's my favorite, too."

Taylor's gaze flickered up. He'd finally caught her attention. "It is?"

Unbelievable, Annie thought. Taylor could have said anything and Blake would have said it was his favorite, too. Had he always been this see-through? Probably. She'd just been too young to realize it before.

Blake leaned toward Taylor conspiratorially. "What do you think my chances are of getting your mom to make me a cup of hot chocolate?"

"Zero." Annie slid a mug of black coffee across the counter to him. "This is as close as you're going to get."

Blake picked up the coffee, winking at her.

Annie sent him a withering look. She'd underestimated how thick he would lay on the charm this morning. She should have done more to prepare Taylor so she wouldn't get caught up in it.

Blake turned back to Taylor. "Would you like to open your present now?"

Taylor paused, her bagel halfway to her mouth. "You brought me a present?"

Blake nodded, handing her the package.

Taylor set her bagel down and reached for the gift.

"Open it," he urged.

She peeled off the wrapping and stared at the object inside.

Blake waited a few beats. "Do you like it?"

"It's a doll," Taylor said.

"That's right."

Taylor lifted the plastic box with the doll inside and set it on the counter.

Annie bit back a smile. The doll was wearing a green velvet gown and a tiara. She had long red hair and carried a sparkly wand.

"I thought it looked like your mom," Blake ventured.

Taylor continued to stare at the doll for several long minutes. "It doesn't look like my mom."

"They have the same color hair," Blake said.

Taylor looked up at Annie, then back at the doll. Frowning, she started to open the box.

"Wait," Blake said.

Taylor paused. "What?"

"It's a Collector's Edition."

She blinked up at him. "What does that mean?"

"It means it'll be worth more later, if you don't open it."

"You gave me a doll I can't play with?"

Blake looked helplessly at Annie, then back at Taylor. "I guess you can open it."

Taylor tore into the box, pulling the doll out. She studied her from several different angles, then carefully pried the tiara off her head. She slid the wand out of her hand and pushed both objects across the counter to Annie. "We could make a wind chime with these."

Blake gaped at Taylor when she laid the doll back in the box and pushed it aside. "I don't understand."

"I don't like dolls," Taylor said simply.

"But I thought all girls played with dolls."

Taylor shook her head, climbing down from the stool. "Mom, can we go watch the sunrise at the marina?"

"Sure, sweetie."

Taylor walked over to the hook by the door to get her coat.

Annie smiled at Blake. "I think that went well."

WILL DIDN'T USUALLY DO goodbyes, but he wanted to catch Della before she headed to the café for the day. She'd left over a dozen messages on his voicemail asking him to give Annie a chance to explain. He knew his aunt meant well, but there was nothing she could say to change his mind now.

He'd said goodbye to Becca and Ryan last night. He'd asked Ryan to pass on a message to Grace—that he would try harder to stay in touch this time. But he honestly didn't know if that was true. It might be easier to cut them all off again. Start fresh. Put the past few weeks behind him.

The first hints of sunrise broke over the horizon as he passed the marina, where a few watermen were preparing their boats to head out for the day. In the passenger seat, Riley pressed her nose to the glass, whimpering. He tried not to think about the fact that this would be their last drive together. Glancing out the window to see what had caught her attention, he swallowed, hard, when he saw Annie and Taylor turning the corner to the marina.

What were they doing up so early?

Riley craned her neck to keep her eyes on them as Will drove past. In his rear view mirror, he caught a glimpse of Blake crossing the street to catch up with them. His muscles clenched, his grip tightening on the steering wheel as he turned onto Della's road. If there'd been even a shred of doubt left in his mind that Annie had planned this, it was gone now.

The first woman he'd let himself fall for in over ten years, and she'd played him. He shook his head, pulling to the curb outside his aunt's house. Screw it. In twelve hours he'd be at the airport, boarding a flight back to San Diego. He wouldn't have to see her or think about her ever again.

Cutting the engine, he stepped out of the SUV and held the door open for Riley to jump out. Her paws had barely grazed the pavement when the first gunshot went off. It tore through the quiet morning, echoing over the water. Geese honked frantically, beating their wings against the surface as they took off, flying away from the sound.

A block away, he heard Annie yell, "Taylor, wait! Stop!"

A second shot rang out, followed by an explosion of rapid fire and Will slammed the door. "Riley," he called as he took off, cutting through Della's yard to the marina. The dog ran ahead of him, racing over the fallen leaves and crushed oyster shells.

The shots were behind him now, coming from the mainland. He rounded the neighbor's shed, getting a clear view of the marina across the parking lot of Rusty's where Taylor was struggling with Blake.

Blake had one hand on her broom, the other fisted in her jacket, trying to stop her from running away. Taylor jerked free, hesitating for only a split second when she realized he wasn't going to let go of her broom.

Another shot went off and Taylor released her hold on the handle, sprinting toward the marshes.

Will cursed when she slipped through a small tear in a metal fence one of the local conservation groups had put up to protect the wetlands.

"Taylor!" Annie shouted, already climbing the fence to go after her.

Blake stood frozen in the parking lot, holding onto Taylor's broom.

Will ran past him, catching Annie's hand and pulling her back to the ground. "Find Joe and tell him to go to the Fosters' farm and get the hunters to stop. There's a blind on the south side of the property. He'll know where it is."

Annie's gaze darted back to where Taylor had vanished into the tall grasses.

"Annie," he ordered as Riley scrambled through the hole in the fence after Taylor. "Go find Joe. Now."

With one last look at the wetlands, she took off across the parking lot to Della and Joe's house.

Will climbed the fence, landing easily on the other side. Tim Foster wasn't going to be happy when Joe told him to stop shooting, but Will would deal with the hunters later. He could hear Riley barking in the distance as he tracked Taylor's footprints across the soggy stretch of land.

The first rays of sunlight streaked over the water, lighting the marshes on fire. The sky was filled with the call of geese and the rattle of gunfire. When he spotted an old wooden rowboat with a tarp thrown over it, he slowed.

"Good girl," he murmured to Riley who was sniffing at the edge of the tarp. His boots sank into the shallow water as he made his way to the side of the boat.

"Taylor," he said softly. "It's Will."

He could hear a small sound—a child's strangled breathing coming from inside the boat. He kept his voice low and soothing as he reached for the edge of the tarp. "I'm going to pull the cover back slowly to make sure you're okay. Riley's with me. There's nothing to be afraid of."

The sight that greeted his eyes when he lifted the corner of the tarp had his heart twisting painfully. Taylor was cowered at the bow, her whole body trembling as she clung to the rotted bench seat.

He resisted the urge to reach for her, to simply haul her out of the boat and into his arms. He didn't want to frighten her. She needed to come out of this on her own. "Taylor, it's me," he said gently. "It's Will."

She turned her head away from him, her eyes squeezed shut as her body shook from both fear and cold.

Riley crept closer to the boat, whimpering.

On a hunch, Will lifted the dog up, setting her inside the boat. "Look," he said. "Look who came to see you."

Riley bowed her head, her ears flattened in submission.

Another round of gunshots rumbled over the water and Taylor shrank back. Riley inched toward her, until she was leaning against her, her entire body curled around Taylor protectively.

Taylor lifted her hand slowly, twisting her fingers into Riley's fur.

"That's it," Will whispered brokenly. "You're safe now."

Taylor lifted her other arm, wrapping it around Riley's neck.

"The shots you hear—they're from the hunters," Will explained. "The ones we talked about when we were out on Ryan's boat. Remember?"

"Make them stop," Taylor whispered.

Her shattered voice sliced all the way through him and he reached for her. Pulling her into his arms, he cradled her against his chest. "Remember when the fireworks went off on Halloween and you found me? You brought me back, Taylor. Let me bring you back this time."

They were still in the same position—Will kneeling in the frigid water, Taylor clinging to him—when Annie and Della found them a few minutes later. He slowly untangled Taylor's arms from around his neck, nudging her toward her mom.

Annie held onto her daughter for a long time, unable to speak. When she finally eased back, she spent the next several minutes checking every inch of Taylor's body to make sure she wasn't hurt. Will rose, walking over to where his aunt was standing. Della was still trying to catch her breath from the sprint.

"Are you okay?" he asked.

She nodded. "Joe should be at Tim's by now."

Will looked back out at the water. The gunshots had stopped a few minutes ago. The only sound now was the wind whistling through the marsh grasses and the occasional cry of a hawk overhead.

Finally satisfied that Taylor was still in one piece, Annie stood and walked slowly over to them. Her clothes were covered in mud. The front of her jeans were wet from where she'd been kneeling in the wetlands. He could tell she was fighting back tears.

The need to pull her into his arms was so strong, he had to curl his hands into fists to keep from reaching for her. But when Taylor's small fingers brushed against his, he didn't think twice. He lifted her up, settling her against his chest. "Come on," he said as she buried her face in his shirt. "Let's get you home."

NUMB, Annie walked down the stairs to the café an hour later. She'd given Taylor a bath, thrown all their dirty clothes in the laundry, and scrubbed the mud off Riley—who refused to leave Taylor's side now. The two of them were curled up on the sofa in the living room, watching a movie.

Blake had driven back to his hotel in St. Michaels after

making up some excuse about having an important business call at seven o'clock. He hadn't been able to get away fast enough.

Not that she was sad to see him go.

Crossing the dining room to the kitchen, where Della had insisted she would be in case Annie or Taylor needed her, Annie wasn't surprised to find Will in there, too. Despite how he felt about her now, he wouldn't leave until he knew Taylor was okay.

That was the difference between a man of honor and one who didn't care about anyone but himself.

"How is she?" Will asked as soon as he saw her.

"She's better. I think..." Annie trailed off when Della turned her face away, wiping her eyes with a tissue. "Della?"

"I'm sorry," Della whispered, pushing out the back door.

"What's going on?" Annie asked, alarmed.

"She'll be fine." Will walked over to the stove to turn off the burner beneath the soup pot. "Does Taylor need anything?"

Annie shook her head, but a wave of uneasiness swept through her as she watched Della walk down to the dock. "I'm going to keep her home from school today so I'll be with her if she does."

Will turned to face her. "How are you?"

"I'm fine," she lied. She was about as far away from fine as a person could be, but she knew he was only being polite. He hadn't hung around for the past hour to check on her. He'd stayed to check on Taylor.

Now that he knew she was okay, he'd probably want to be on his way.

"I couldn't get Riley to come downstairs with me," Annie said. "Is it okay if I bring her back later?"

"Don't worry about it." Will dipped his hands in his pockets. "I'll tell Ryan she's here."

Annie nodded, wishing she knew what to say. She wanted to thank him for what he'd done that morning, but how did you thank a man for earning your daughter's trust? For taking charge of a situation that should never have been his problem in the first place? For putting aside his feelings without a second thought to be there for a little girl who wasn't even his?

"Will," she said finally. "I don't know what I would have done if you hadn't been there today."

"You would have managed," he said quietly. "You don't need anyone's help, Annie. Not even mine."

Annie drew in a breath. But she *did* need his help. For the first time in her life she had someone she could count on, someone she could trust. She'd been on her own for so long, she'd hadn't realized what she'd been missing until now. "You knew Riley would find her."

Will nodded.

"I'm going to get her a dog," she said, knowing the longer she kept talking, the longer he would stay. "Maybe an older one from the shelter, one that's already been housebroken. I'll probably end up regretting it, but I've seen what Riley has done for her. I can't take that away from her now."

"I'm sure she'd like that."

Silence fell between them again and Annie looked back out the window, where Della was standing at the edge of the dock dabbing at her eyes with a tissue. "Will, please tell me why Della is crying."

"I told her something she didn't want to hear."

Annie's gaze swung back to his. She didn't like the sound of that. "What's wrong?"

"Nothing's wrong." Will lifted a shoulder. "I got a call from my CO about fifteen minutes ago. I need to get back to San Diego. My team ships out in forty-eight hours."

"Forty-eight hours?" Annie felt all the breath whoosh out of her lungs. "But that's only two days from now."

Will nodded.

"I thought you had over a week left on the island?"

"Things change," he said simply.

"But...when are you leaving? Tomorrow?"

"This afternoon."

She felt a rush of panic. "This afternoon?"

He started for the door. "I have to get ready, settle some things back at the inn."

She reached for the counter to steady herself. He couldn't leave. He hadn't even given her a chance to explain yet. "Will, wait."

He turned, but his expression held no emotion at all. He was withdrawing, she realized. He was distancing himself from her, from Della, probably from everyone so he could prepare to leave.

She followed him out the door. He'd never said anything about keeping in touch after he left. He'd made himself clear from the very beginning. When it was time for him to leave, things would be over between them.

But how could she let him go when nothing had been resolved, when he still thought so little of her? "Will you at least say goodbye before you leave? If not to me, at least to Taylor?"

He nodded, but she caught the flicker of hesitation in his eyes right before he turned. She stood in the doorway, watching him walk away.

Somehow, she knew it was a promise he wasn't going to keep.

TWENTY-ONE

*W*ord spread quickly about what had happened that morning. By lunchtime, most of the islanders had come into the café asking if there was anything they could do to help. Tim Foster had come in personally to ask if Taylor was all right. After Joe had explained the situation, Tim had agreed to stop hunting on his property for the next few days.

Annie was grateful, but they both knew her daughter's fear of guns couldn't shut down the entire hunting season.

Tim's blind was the closest one to the island—aside from Will's, which no one used—but there were hunting spots all over this area. Taylor was going to have to get over her fear. Joe had offered to take her over to Tim's farm in a day or two, once she calmed down, and walk her around the blind so she could get used to it.

So she would know what to expect when the gunshots went off next time.

It was the same philosophy Annie had used on Halloween. As long as Taylor was prepared, she would be able to get through this. They would both be able to get through this.

It was worth a try, at least. That's all they could do—keep trying until they got it right.

Walking the last of the dishes into the kitchen, she set them in the sink, taking a moment to lean her palms on the edge of the counter and just breathe. For the first time since early that morning, she was alone in the café. She'd sent Della home a half an hour ago, around the same time she'd begun to give up hope that Will was going to say goodbye to them. She'd been watching the door all day, listening for the sound of his footsteps on the porch, hoping he'd come, if not for her, at least for Taylor.

But he was probably halfway to the airport by now.

She was going to have to break the news to Taylor tonight.

Pushing away from the counter, she paused when the bell on the front door jingled. Maybe he'd only wanted to wait to say goodbye until everyone else had left. Nerves danced up her spine as she stepped out of the kitchen, but her heart sank when she saw who was at the door.

It wasn't Will.

It was Blake, the one person who hadn't bothered to stop by at some point today to make sure Taylor was okay. Everyone else on the island had offered to lend a hand, but Taylor's own father hadn't bothered to lift a finger. "Nice of you to finally show up again."

"I figured you wouldn't want me around, that I'd only get in the way," Blake said, closing the door behind him.

Annie picked up a rag, running it over the tables. He had an answer for everything, didn't he?

"How's she doing?"

"She's fine."

He walked across the room, brushing aside the sugar that had spilled on the counter before turning and leaning against it, perfectly content to do nothing while he watched her work. "Last night, I asked if you and Will Dozier were friends."

Annie moved to the next table, lifting the salt-and-pepper shakers to clean under them. "So?"

"You never answered me."

She set down the salt, looking up at him. "My friends are none of your business."

"Is that all you two are?" He lifted a brow. "Friends?"

"Like I said," she repeated. "It's none of your business."

"I think we should talk about it."

Annie threw the rag down. "What do you want from me, Blake?"

"I'd like to know what kind of relationship this man has with my daughter."

Anger curled like whips inside her, threatening to snap. "In the few weeks Will has known Taylor, he's been more of a father to her than you will *ever* be."

Blake regarded her coolly. "Then you'll both be interested to know that he agreed to sell the inn to me this morning."

"What?" Annie froze. No. He would never sell the inn to Blake. She picked up the rag again, moving on to the next table. "I don't believe you."

"He agreed to my terms this morning."

She shook her head. "Will would never sell the inn to you."

Blake smiled, his gaze shifting to the porch as someone walked up the steps. Annie felt a prick of fear when she spotted Spencer holding a bottle of champagne. He opened the door, stepping into the café with a ridiculous grin on his face. He lifted the bottle. "Time to celebrate."

Annie took a step back. This wasn't happening. This couldn't be happening. "Did Will sign the contract?"

Blake held out his hand to Spencer, and the two men shook hands. "We had to add a few clauses to the contract," Blake answered, "but Spencer drew up the new terms and sent it off to him this afternoon. He's going to sign it and send it back as soon as he arrives in San Diego."

Hope sprang in Annie's heart. It wasn't official yet. There was still time to stop him.

Spencer popped the cork. "I don't know how you did it, Blake."

Blake walked into the kitchen, rooting around for champagne glasses. "I made him an offer he couldn't refuse."

The sight of Blake in her kitchen, rummaging through her cupboards, pushed her over the edge. "Get out."

"What?" Spencer turned, his smile fading.

"Get out." Annie's fingers curled around the rag. "Both of you."

"Why?" Spencer asked, confused. "I thought you wanted this?"

"I did." Annie struggled to keep her voice under control as she strode to the door, holding it open. "Things change."

Blake's eyes met hers from across the room. "Annie."

"I said, *get out.*"

Setting down the glasses he'd found, he walked out of the kitchen. "You don't want to do this."

"Actually, it's all I've wanted to do since the moment I laid eyes on you yesterday."

Blake paused in the doorway, leaning down and lowering his voice. "You're going to regret this."

"Oh, really? Why?"

"You can't keep my daughter from me."

"You don't care about Taylor, Blake. You don't care about anyone but yourself. I don't know what you came here for, but it sure as hell wasn't to get to know your daughter."

Blake's eyes narrowed. "I bet a judge would be interested to know that you moved Taylor to an island famous for hunting after she was traumatized by a school shooting. That doesn't show very strong mothering skills, does it?"

Annie shoved him, hard, out the door. "Get. Out."

"This isn't over," he said, straightening his jacket and stalking down the steps.

Oh, yes it is. Annie slammed the door, digging her cell phone out of her apron. There was no way Will would have accepted Blake's offer unless he'd lied about something. Blake had to have spun some kind of elaborate story to convince Will to change his mind. Will would never have sold simply because Blake had upped the offer.

She punched in the number of the first friend she had made on this island, the one person she knew would do everything in her power to stop this sale.

Grace picked up on the third ring. "Annie?"

"Grace," Annie said, gripping the phone. "I need your help."

WILL PULLED to the curb outside the Governor's Mansion in Annapolis. Putting the SUV in park, he turned to Colin. "Thanks again for coming down and helping out."

Colin nodded, gazing at the traffic crawling around Church Circle a block away. "I know there's nothing I can say to change your mind." His hand rested on the door handle, making no move to open it. "But you should know that Becca said some things after you went upstairs last night...things about Annie."

"Did she?" Will asked indifferently.

"Becca's on your side, man. We all are."

Will watched a woman in a business suit and high heels dash across the street in front of them, ducking her head against the wind.

"Della told her what happened between Annie and Blake,"

Colin said. "She was hoping Becca would talk to you, since you wouldn't answer her calls."

"Look, Colin," Will said. He needed to get to the airport. At this rate, he was going to hit some serious rush-hour traffic heading out of downtown Annapolis. "I know you mean well, but I need to hit the road."

"Della left a ton of messages on your phone last night," Colin went on. "Will you at least listen to them before you sign the papers?"

Will tapped his fingers over the steering wheel. If he didn't say yes, Colin might make him sit here for another ten minutes. "Sure."

"That didn't sound very convincing."

"Do you want me to listen to them now, while you're sitting here?" Will started to pull out his phone.

"That's tempting, but no." Colin shifted in his seat to face him. "I have something else I want to talk to you about."

Something else? Will checked the clock on the dashboard. He still needed to fill up the gas tank and return the car to the rental lot before heading to the airport. Why hadn't Colin gotten these things off his chest during the hour-long drive?

"I've been doing a lot of thinking over the past few days," Colin began.

Will leaned back into the seat, tempering his frustration. This didn't sound like the start of a short conversation.

"I know what I want to do after my father's campaign ends next fall."

"What?" Will asked, surprised. He knew his friend had been struggling with this for some time. He wished he'd brought it up earlier, but he was glad he'd made a decision.

"I want to open a rehab center for wounded vets—sort of a transition center for injured service members who've been discharged from Walter Reed but aren't ready to go home yet."

Intrigued, Will let his hands drop away from the wheel. "But you don't know anything about medicine aside from the emergency training we used out in the field."

"I'm not talking about opening a hospital. I'm talking about a place where a handful of vets could come and stay for a while, a place where they could do some volunteer work and learn some new skills while they figure out what to do next. They might still need physical therapy, but I could bring someone in for that a few times a week, or hire drivers to take them where they need to go. I'm talking about a place for the ones who are physically ready to be discharged from the hospital, but aren't ready to reenter society yet. The ones who need a safe place to land until they can get back on their feet."

It was an interesting idea, Will thought. There were a few organizations offering services like this to veterans now, but not nearly enough. Even if Colin could only help a dozen vets a year, it would be that many more who wouldn't be struggling harder than they needed to be, who wouldn't eventually end up on the streets. "With your father's connections, you wouldn't have any trouble finding funding for an idea like that."

"I agree." Colin let the words hang between them. "And I know the perfect place for it."

Will pulled his gaze slowly from the windshield, where he'd been watching a thin branch bend at an impossible angle in the strong winds. "You want to buy the inn?"

"No." Colin shook his head. "I want you to be my business partner."

Will stared at him.

"There's something about that place, Will. It makes you feel better. I don't know how to explain it; it's like there's something in the air on that island. You can breathe easier. You can think more clearly. You can get from place to place in a matter of minutes. The people who live there; they're real people—the kind of people who understand us, who understand what we've been through. It's the kind of place I wish I'd gone after I got discharged from the hospital."

"But you came here." Will gestured out the window to the stately brick home. "To the Governor's Mansion. You had people waiting on you hand and foot."

"That's the thing. I didn't want people waiting on me. I didn't want my family doting on me, hovering around me, feeling sorry for me. I wanted to get up in the morning and do something that mattered. I wanted to get my hands dirty, work on a project, do something besides answer questions about how my leg felt that day. I know it might sound selfish. I have a great family. We have plenty of money. It's not like I needed anything, but I still felt lost. I wanted my team. I wanted my guys. I missed the camaraderie, that sense of belonging, of knowing what my mission was."

Will thought about how he would have felt if he'd been stuck in a home for months where he didn't have anything to do to get his mind off his injury and what he had lost.

He would have gone nuts.

But it didn't change the fact that he already had a job, one he wasn't ready to give up. "You're asking me to walk away from the teams, Colin."

"I'm asking you to consider your options," Colin said. "We could give these guys a solid start at a new life. We could get them out on the Bay, helping Ryan with his environmental projects, helping with whatever other projects need to get done on the island. I could tap into my networks in Annapolis and D.C. to help them get interviews and find jobs. You and I could both work with them on physical training to get them back in shape. I could start securing the funding now to open by next fall."

Will looked out the windshield, at a group of tourists huddled together under a sycamore tree, trying to read a map that was flopping around in the wind. "You've done a lot of thinking about this."

Colin nodded. "That first night, when you went home with Annie and I went back to the inn on my own, I stayed up all night researching private rehab centers for vets. There aren't that many, but the ones that exist are making a real difference in people's lives."

"It's a great idea, Colin. One I could get behind if circumstances were different. But there are other vets in the area. You shouldn't have any problem finding someone else to partner with."

"I don't want to partner with anyone else, Will. I want to open this place with you. I want you on my team again." Colin opened the door. "Will you at least think about it?"

Will nodded. What else could he say? "I'll think about it."

ANNIE GRABBED the phone on the first ring. "Grace?"

"Hey, Annie." Grace was short of breath, as if she'd been running. "I have news."

"Where are you?"

"On the hill, by the Capitol. It's murder in heels. Hang on."

Annie could hear horns honking, traffic whizzing past.

"Sorry. I'm back."

"Are you walking home?"

"Yeah," Grace said. "From the bar. I just had drinks with two of Blake's old fraternity brothers."

Annie sat up on the sofa. "You're kidding?"

"You'd be amazed at how much information you can find on an alumni website."

Annie stood and tiptoed across the living room, peeking in at

Taylor to make sure she was still sleeping. Careful not to wake her, she crept down the stairs to the café. "How'd you get them to meet you?"

"I pretended to be a member of one of the sororities they used to party with. We all got a good laugh about the fact that they couldn't remember me. Then we each ordered a Hurricane, for old times' sake."

"Wait," Annie cut in, concerned. "How drunk are you right now? Should you be walking home alone?"

Grace laughed, brushing her off. "I'm fine. I only drank a quarter of mine. Oldest trick in the book. Anyway, after we caught up with each other, we started gossiping about all our old friends."

Annie pulled out a chair at the closest table, sinking into it. "Did they have anything to say about Blake?"

"They had all kinds of things to say about Blake," Grace said. "Turns out, he owes them money—a lot of money."

"That doesn't make any sense. Blake has plenty of money."

"Maybe he did when you knew him before, but he doesn't anymore. According to the two guys I met with tonight, he has a serious gambling problem and he's up to his ears in debt. We're talking hundreds of thousands of dollars, Annie."

"Oh my God."

"Tell me about it. But that's not all. Apparently, his father got wind of it and he's threatened to cut him off if he doesn't shape up. He sent him up here to close the deal with the inn, to prove he cared enough about the company for his father to give him another chance."

"This is unbelievable," Annie breathed. "But what does Blake want with me and Taylor if he doesn't have any money? It's not like we'd be able to help him pay off any of his debts."

"His mother wants a grandchild."

"What?"

"Apparently, she's been after him for months to get married again and settle down. She wants a little girl to dote on."

"Taylor," Annie breathed.

"Yep."

Annie stared out the window, at the wind chimes spinning in the wind. "When he found out Taylor was his child, he thought he could close the deal with the inn, and get a wife and a child at the same time—all so his parents wouldn't cut him off."

"Exactly," Grace said. "But you know what really pisses me off?"

"There's more?"

"Oh, there's more," Grace said. "I made a few calls to the management team at Morningstar this afternoon. Every staff member assured me they have no plans to move into the eco-resort business."

"I knew it." Annie said bitterly. Grace had told her about the eco-resort when they'd spoken on the phone a few hours ago. Grace had found out from Ryan, who'd called his sister that morning to fill her in on the news. As soon as Annie had heard why Will had agreed to sell, she'd known Blake had made it up. But she hadn't had any proof until now.

"I've been trying to call Will ever since I found out," Grace said. "Ryan's been trying to call him. Becca's been trying to call him. He won't answer any of our calls."

"Della and Joe have been trying to reach him all day, and he won't answer any of their calls either," Annie said. "He's probably in the air by now, but what if he won't listen to any of the messages when he lands? If he won't pick up his phone, how are we going to stop him?"

"Someone's going to need to do something drastic."

"Like what?" Annie asked.

"Like get on a plane and go after him."

Annie went very still.

"Do you love him?" Grace asked.

"What?"

"Do you love him?" Grace asked again.

Annie's heart began to pound. What was the point in denying it anymore? "Yes."

"That's what I thought."

"I can't get on a plane right now, Grace. I can't leave Taylor. Not after what happened this morning."

"I thought you might say that."

Annie jumped at the knock on the door. Rising slowly, she spotted Della, Joe, Becca and Ryan through the glass. "Grace?" She waved them in. "What's going on?"

Becca walked into the café, holding out her hand for the phone. "Is that Grace?"

Annie nodded.

Becca took the phone. "Hi...yes... We're here. It's all set. Right...okay...see you tomorrow." She hung up the phone and pulled an envelope out of her pocket, handing it to Annie. "We got you a seat on the first flight out of BWI tomorrow morning."

Annie stared at the envelope. "I'm the last person he wants to see right now."

"You're wrong," Della said, taking the envelope from Becca and putting it in Annie's hand. "You're the only one who can change his mind, Annie. I know you're worried about leaving Taylor, but Joe and I will watch her. We won't let anything happen to her."

"What about the hunters?" Annie protested. "What if more guns go off? What if she needs me?"

Behind Della, Joe cleared his throat. "I talked to most of the local guides today. They agreed to steer clear of the area, just for the weekend."

"Why would they agree to something like that?"

Joe shrugged. "Most of them owed me a favor."

Annie gaped at him. Did every person in this county owe Della and Joe a favor? Looking back down at the envelope, Annie shook her head. "If I do this, I'll have to close down the café for the weekend."

"That won't be necessary," Ryan said, dipping his hands in his pockets. "Becca and I are going to cover for you."

Annie looked up at Ryan. "You're going to cover for me?"

He smiled. "I waited tables at Rusty's for two summers when I was in high school. As long as you can give me a crash course in how to work that espresso machine tonight, we should be good to go."

"I don't know what to say."

"Say yes," Becca urged.

At the sound of a child's footsteps padding down the steps, they all turned. Taylor was wearing her pink flannel pajamas, with a fleece blanket wrapped around her shoulders. Riley wagged her tail when she saw the crowd gathered in the café.

Taylor paused at the bottom of the stairs, blinking up at them. "What's going on?"

Della walked over to her. "How would you like to spend the next couple of nights with Joe and me? We could have a slumber party and stay up late watching movies and eating ice cream."

Taylor looked over at Annie. "Are you going away?"

Della brushed a hand over Taylor's hair. "She's going to see Will."

Taylor hugged her blanket tighter. "Will's gone?"

Annie nodded.

Taylor gazed up at Annie, her eyes widening. "Are you going to California to bring him back?"

Annie swallowed. She was going to California to convince him not to sell the inn. She didn't know if she had the power to bring him back. "I don't know, sweetie."

Taylor walked over, tugging on Annie's hand. "You have to go get him and bring him back."

Annie looked over at Della, who was blinking back tears. Taking a deep breath, Annie lifted Taylor up and set her on her hip. "I don't know what's going to happen, but I promise I'll try."

Della walked over, putting her arms around both of them. "Bring him back, Annie," she whispered. "Bring him home."

TWENTY-TWO

*W*ill parked on a side street off Orange Ave in Coronado, a few blocks away from the ocean. Normally, he would have looked forward to meeting his teammates at McP's Irish Pub—one of the popular SEAL hangouts close to the base. He would have enjoyed watching the younger guys hit on the women who hung at the bar specifically to meet Navy SEALs. Hell, he probably would have ended up hitting on one himself before the night was over.

The rest of the guys on his team, the ones with families, had gone home to spend the evening with their wives and children.

For the first time in his life, he envied them.

A warm breeze blew in from the Pacific and he turned his gaze toward the beach. Slipping his sunglasses on, he followed the sound of crashing surf to the stretch of white sand in front of the Hotel del Coronado. He'd spent the day on the base, getting briefed on the mission to gather intelligence on an Al Qaeda training camp in Yemen, getting supplies ready, checking and double checking his gear, touching base with each member of the team to make sure they were mentally prepared to leave first thing in the morning.

But the real question was: was *he* prepared to leave?

Stepping onto the beach, he took in the familiar scene: women lounging in bikinis, dogs chasing tennis balls through the surf, teenagers catching waves on their boogie boards, parents helping children build elaborate sandcastles that would be washed away by morning.

Reaching into his pocket, his fingers brushed unconsciously over the yellow ribbon his sister had given him so many years ago. A few hundred yards down the beach, a BUD/S trainer was shouting at the newest class of SEALs. Thirty guys had dropped to the sand, counting out a series of push-ups before scrambling to their feet and resuming their evening run.

When he'd first joined the SEALs, he'd been so focused on going after the people who'd killed his mother and sister that nothing else had mattered. Nothing any of the trainers could have said would have intimidated him or tempted him to quit. Most of the guys in his class had been equally driven, with 9/11 still fresh in their minds. They'd all been desperate to get out there, to hunt down the terrorists who'd attacked them at home.

But none of them had expected the wars in Iraq and Afghanistan to last over ten years. None of them could have predicted the effect those two wars would have on over two million returning service men and women back home now and struggling with how to deal with what they'd experienced.

He'd like to think they'd made the world safer. They'd captured Saddam Hussein and killed Osama Bin Laden, but there were still plenty of terrorists actively recruiting, forming cells, planning senseless attacks on innocent people. The War on Terror wasn't going to end anytime soon.

A few yards in front of him, a little girl in a pink dress was scooping sand into a plastic bucket. Her father was digging a mote around her sandcastle, and she squealed every time it filled with water.

Slipping the knotted ribbon out of his pocket, he held it in his palm. It was faded now, stained with dirt and blood, unraveling at the seams. He wondered what his sister would say if she could see him today. Would she be happy with the path he'd chosen? Would she be happy he'd spent the past ten years avenging her death?

What would his mother say if she found out he'd just walked away from the first woman he'd ever truly loved?

He'd taken Colin's advice and listened to the messages on his phone last night. If what Della had said was true, then Annie couldn't have been behind the plans for the resort. She hadn't even been in contact with Blake since before Taylor was born.

He would never forget the look on her face when he'd accused her of seducing him.

All she had ever wanted was to be left alone.

But he hadn't listened, had he? He hadn't left her alone—not once. Almost from the moment he'd laid eyes on her, he hadn't been able to stay away. He was the one who'd seduced her. He was the one who hadn't been able to take no for an answer.

And, yet, at the first sign of trouble, he'd cast all the blame on her.

His gaze fell back to the ribbon. Waves curled, crashing over the sand. Seagulls circled overhead, their cries piercing the salty air. He heard a child's laughter gliding over the wind as he slowly began to pull the ribbon apart. The knot gave way, revealing two silver threads hidden inside.

They sparkled, glinting in the fading sunlight.

As bright as the first day his sister had given it to him.

He knew what he had to do.

"This is it." Annie thrust several crumpled bills over the seat. "Thanks. Pull over here. Right here's fine."

She didn't bother to wait for the final tally, her left arm already looped through the handle of her overnight bag. She pushed open the door, stepping out. "Keep the change."

The taxi sped away, leaving her alone on the curb.

She took in the six-unit apartment building in Ocean Beach. Colin had given her Will's address, but he, like everyone else, had expected her to arrive over six hours ago.

She hadn't counted on missing her connection in Denver, or on having to wait so long for another flight.

What if she was too late? What if he'd already signed the papers and she'd come all this way for nothing?

Gripping the handle of her bag, she scanned the numbers beside each door, searching for apartment #4. When she found it on the second floor, on the left-hand side, she headed for the stairs. Taking them two at a time, she could smell the ocean a quarter mile away. The freeway traffic hummed in the distance.

By the time she made it to the door, her hands were shaking and her palms were damp. She knocked three times, holding her breath as she listened for the sound of his footsteps.

What if Della was wrong? What if he didn't want to see her? What if he slammed the door in her face?

The door swung open and all words failed her.

Will's eyes widened. "Annie?"

He was wearing a white T-shirt and worn jeans. A shadow of stubble covered his jaw. Behind him, inside the apartment, a flat screen TV flashed the highlights of a sports game. The muffled voice of the announcer spilled out the door.

She'd rehearsed her speech a dozen times since last night, but now that she was here she didn't know what to say. Now that she was here, all she wanted was to walk into his arms and spend the rest of the night there. "I know I'm the last person you want to see right now—"

He grabbed her, yanking her to him. His mouth was on hers before she could get another word out, hot and raw and demanding. Her bag slipped from her fingers, landing on the floor with a soft thud.

Will.

She had come here to apologize, to stop him from selling the inn, to ask him to come back to the island with her. But what did any of it matter as long as he forgave her? As long as he still wanted her?

All her life she had been searching for a place to put down roots, a place to settle in, a place to call home. But what if *he* was her home? What if the only place she and Taylor truly belonged was with him?

Palm tree fronds rustled in the salty breezes as she eased back, looking up at him.

"I can't believe you're here," he said.

"I would have been here sooner, but I missed my connection in Denver."

"I've been trying to call you for hours."

"I left my cell phone on the first plane by accident. By the time I realized it, the plane was already gone." She took a deep breath, gazing up at him. "I'm so sorry, Will. For everything."

"You have nothing to be sorry about."

"I think I do." She stepped back. He wasn't going to be happy when he found out about the inn. She still needed to tell him about the eco-resort. If he'd already signed the contract, he might not be so willing to forgive her. "I heard why you agreed to sell the inn. Grace told me about the new offer. It's a lie, Will. Blake made it up. There isn't going to be an eco-resort."

"I know."

She blinked. "You know?"

Will nodded slowly. "I knew it was a lie as soon as I read the contract Spencer faxed over last night. They switched a few paragraphs around to make it look like a different document, but they didn't add in any of the language I asked them to. They probably assumed I wouldn't read it."

"So, you didn't sign it?"

He shook his head, watching her carefully. "Is that why you came here? To stop me from signing the contract?"

"Yes."

"You flew all the way to San Diego to stop me from selling the inn?"

She looked up at him as a thousand butterflies unfurled their wings inside her, fluttering around her heart. "I came because I love you, and you didn't give me a chance to say goodbye."

He pulled her to him, kissing her slowly this time, so slowly and tenderly he didn't have to say the words for her to know he felt the same way.

"We want you to come back to the island," she whispered.

"Who?"

"Everyone—Della, Joe, Grace, Ryan, Becca, Colin, Taylor." She eased back. "But I know how much being a SEAL means to you. I know that your career is here, that this is where you have to be. Maybe we could split our time between the two places. Maybe we could find a way to make it work."

He touched his forehead to hers. "I put in for a transfer to Virginia Beach today."

"Virginia Beach?"

He nodded. "I don't know if they'll accept it, but I talked to my CO this evening and told him everything. I am going out with my team tomorrow, Annie. But it'll only be for six weeks. And it'll be my last time overseas."

A glimmer of hope stirred inside her.

"My CO's going to make some calls while I'm away. He's

going to try to find me a position on base in Virginia Beach until my contract with the Navy is up next summer."

Annie held her breath. "Then what?"

"Then I'm coming home."

"To Heron Island?"

"To you and Taylor." He brushed a thumb gently over her cheek. "If you'll have me."

She pressed her lips to his, pouring her answer into the kiss.

"I'll take that as a yes." He laughed when they broke apart. "And by the way," he said, lifting her into his arms and carrying her into the apartment. "I love you, too."

TWENTY-THREE

SIX WEEKS LATER...

*A*re you sure you're ready for this?" Annie asked, squeezing Taylor's hand.

"I'm ready," she said bravely.

Standing outside the entrance to Taylor's old school, Annie struggled with a rush of conflicting emotions. She didn't want to be back here. She had never wanted to set foot in this building again. But Taylor had wanted to come.

Ever since they'd heard that Mount Pleasant Elementary had reopened two weeks ago, three months after the shooting in September, Taylor had been asking if they could make the trip.

Her counselor had said it would be a good idea, that it would give Taylor closure. She'd be able to visit with some of her old friends and teachers and see that everyone was getting back to normal, or at least a new kind of normal—one that included two security guards stationed outside the doors.

They nodded to Annie, stepping aside so she and Taylor

could walk through. Looping Riley's leash around her wrist, Annie was glad they'd decided to bring the dog. Not that they'd had much choice. Riley rarely left Taylor's side now.

When Annie had mentioned to Ryan that she was thinking of getting Taylor a dog from the shelter, he'd laughed and told her he'd given up hope of ever getting Riley back weeks ago. Taylor wouldn't know that Riley was officially hers until Christmas Day, but it was clear the dog had chosen her own family.

A few steps into the school, Taylor paused, gazing around in wonder. Sparkly garlands hung from the ceiling. Strings of paper snowflakes were strung along the walls. A huge paper mache snowman wearing a top hat and a goofy grin stood outside the entrance to the auditorium. Every locker had been painted a different shade of winter blue.

At the sound of footsteps, Annie turned to see Taylor's old principal walking toward them.

"Taylor." Sally Vaughn opened her arms to give her a hug. "It's so good to see you."

Taylor hugged her back, the ribbons tied to the end of her broom brushing over the floor.

"I see you brought a friend." Sally pulled back, patting Riley on the head.

"Her name's Riley," Taylor said.

"I bet I know a few people who'd like to meet her." Sally smiled, straightening and giving Annie a long hug, too. "I'm so glad you could make it."

It was amazing, Annie thought, how much she'd dreaded this moment. And, yet, now that she was here, she felt a strange sense of peace. Every person in this building had been affected by this tragedy, and they had all managed to walk back through the doors, return to their classrooms, and slowly begin to pick up the pieces. Together they were facing down this evil, and finding the courage to move on. She pulled back, smiling up at Sally. "The hallway looks beautiful."

"Wait until you see the classrooms." Sally waved for them to follow her. "We had volunteers working around the clock."

They made their way down the hall, passing several classrooms filled with students, until they came to the last room on the right. A huge banner hung across the top of the door with the words: "Welcome Back Taylor!"

A lump formed in Annie's throat as they stepped into Taylor's old classroom. Comfortable couches and armchairs had replaced the rows of desks. A colorful woven rug stretched across the linoleum floor. Blankets and beanbags were piled up in the corner beside a shelf overflowing with books. The walls were covered in student artwork. A Christmas tree twinkled in the far corner, decorated with white lights, sparkly ornaments, and seventeen paper angels—one for each of the students who'd been killed.

"We wanted to honor their memory," Sally said quietly, "but at the same time we wanted to create a place where we could come together—parents, children, teachers. A safe place where we could say anything, and there would always be someone to talk to."

Speechless, Annie could only nod. There were a few other parents in the room, along with a handful of students. The counselor—the same woman who had been with them from the beginning, and who they still spoke with once a week on the phone—rose from the couch where she'd been talking to one of the parents and came over to give Annie and Taylor a hug.

"This is..." Annie swallowed, trying to force the lump back down her throat. "It's..."

"I know." The counselor sent her an understanding smile and led her to the sofa as Taylor and Riley went to play with the other kids.

Throughout the next hour, Annie spoke with several of the parents. Two of the mothers who she'd been friends with before promised to make the trip to Heron Island as soon as the weather got warmer. By the time Taylor and Riley came back over, it was almost time to head to the airport.

Will had arrived back in San Diego a few days ago from his last overseas mission. He'd been gone for six weeks and Annie had been a nervous wreck the entire time, but he'd found out the day before that he'd gotten the position on the base in Virginia Beach. He'd be re-stationed in January.

Somehow, on top of everything, he'd managed to finagle a few days off for Christmas.

His plane would land at BWI in less than an hour.

Annie picked a piece of glitter out of Taylor's hair. "Are you ready to go?"

"Almost," Taylor said softly, her fingers curling around the handle of her broom. With Riley beside her, she turned and walked to the closet—the one where she'd hid from the shooter three months before.

Annie pushed slowly to her feet. Surely, this wasn't necessary. They had done what they came here to do. They didn't need to face down every demon on the first visit. "Taylor..."

The counselor stood, putting her hand on Annie's shoulder. "It's okay."

Taylor reached for the door. Silver Christmas bells hung from the knob, and they jingled as she opened it. She paused, for only a moment, before placing the broom inside and closing the door.

She turned and sent Annie a small smile. "I'm ready to go now."

ON CHRISTMAS EVE, two days later, Annie and Taylor pulled

up at the inn. Will had been strangely mysterious about his plans for the evening, but he'd told them to head down to the dock as soon as they arrived. The sun had set over an hour ago and it was a cold, clear night. A full moon cast a soft glow over the lawn as they stepped out of the car.

The inn was one of the only homes on the island that wasn't lit up with twinkle lights and draped in pine-scented garlands, but it brought Annie comfort to know that this was the last Christmas it would sit empty. This time next year, the rooms would be filled with veterans and their families.

Colin had already acquired a handful of investors, and Will had hired Jimmy Faulkner and his crew to start working on the renovations in a couple of weeks. Annie was looking forward to making sure Jimmy stayed on task and off his favorite barstool at Rusty's.

A faint buzzing from inside her jacket pocket had her fishing out her cell phone.

"Who is it?" Taylor asked.

Annie smiled, handing the phone to her daughter. "It's your grandmother."

Taylor answered the phone and Annie bent down, adjusting the red velvet bow on Riley's collar. Maria Hadley called every day now at five o'clock to talk to them. A few weeks ago, in a last ditch effort to save himself, Blake had told his parents about their grandchild, fabricating a story about how Annie had tricked him all those years ago to keep Taylor from him.

His announcement hadn't been received quite the way he'd expected.

Maria and Lance Hadley had flown up to the island the following day. They had introduced themselves to Annie and asked her to please tell them the truth, which she did. When they'd found out what Blake had done, Lance had apologized over a dozen times on behalf of his son and Maria had cried.

Lance and Maria Hadley were nothing like the snobs Blake had made them out to be. They were kind and compassionate and generous, and it hadn't taken long for Annie to agree to let them meet Taylor. They'd stayed on the island for three days to get to know their granddaughter, and before they'd left, they'd already made plans to come back a few days after Christmas to visit again.

The last any of them had heard about Blake, he was floating around some tourist town in Mexico—jobless, friendless, and still in debt.

He wouldn't bother Annie or Taylor ever again.

Taylor finished the call and handed the phone back to Annie. "She said, Merry Christmas."

Annie smiled, slipping the phone back in her pocket. She had no doubt they would both talk to Maria again tomorrow, at five o'clock, on the dot. "Come on," she said, taking Taylor's hand and leading her around the side of the house. "We better hurry. Della will never let us hear the end of it if we're late for dinner."

Ducking under the knobby branches of the hackberry tree, they both stopped short when they saw the dock.

"Mom," Taylor whispered. "Look."

Annie gazed at the lights wrapped around the pilings and strung along the edges of the pier. Will's grandfather's sailboat twinkled from the highest point of the mast to the tip of the bow. Strings of white lights gleamed like sparkly ropes along the sides of the hull to the stern, and a huge Christmas tree blazed at the end of the dock.

Taylor let go of her hand, running across the lawn with Riley on her heels. Annie followed, making her way slowly down to the water as moonlight streamed through the bare branches of the tulip poplars. Will met them at the edge of the dock, helping them into the boat.

He smiled as Riley curled up beside Taylor, sniffing at the

two presents on the seat. "Go ahead." He nodded for Taylor to open the present with her name on it. "You first."

Taylor tore into the paper, her eyes lighting up when she saw the purple fishing rod. "You remembered!"

"Of course, I remembered," Will said. "I told you I'd get you your own rod the night we went out on Ryan's boat. As soon as the weather warms up, we can start catching perch off the dock."

Taylor held the rod up. "I'm going to catch the biggest fish at next years' Rockfish Tournament."

Will laughed. "That's the spirit."

Taylor looked back at the other present. "Who's that one for?"

Will sat back, wrapping his arms around Annie. "It's for your mother."

Taylor handed Annie the present.

Annie took it, feeling suddenly nervous. Her fingers fumbled with the tape as she unwrapped it, lifting the lid of the small velvet box.

Inside was a gold ring, with three diamonds sparkling on an antique band.

"It was my grandmother's," Will said softly.

Annie looked up at him, her heart in her throat, as he took the ring out of the box and slipped it on her finger.

"She would have wanted you to have it," he said.

Annie looked down at the ring, then back up at him.

"I want to spend the rest of my life with you, Annie." He held out his hand for Taylor. "With both of you."

Riley barked, wagging her tail.

Will smiled. "And Riley."

Taylor climbed onto the seat beside them, tugging on Annie's sleeve. "Say yes, mom."

"Yes," Annie whispered.

Will's lips found hers and she closed her eyes. A cool breeze blew in from the Bay, and the soft tinkling of copper chimes drifted into the air. It was the same sound she'd heard over a dozen times since the first night she'd met Will.

She opened her eyes and spotted the tiny wind chime looped around a ring on the mast. The strings were twisted and tangled, the flattened pennies clinking together as the boat rocked back and forth.

She sat up slowly, reaching for it.

There was no way she could have heard this chime from the café. Will's property was at least a mile outside of town. But this was definitely the one she'd been hearing.

Untangling the strings until each gleaming red-orange piece dangled on its own, she looked back at Will. "Where did this come from?"

"I'm not sure," Will said. "I think it was one of the first ones my sister made. It's been there forever."

Forever, Annie thought, letting her hand fall away from the chime. Maybe Will's sister had been trying to tell them something. Threading their fingers together, she laid her head on his shoulder and smiled up at Taylor.

She could handle forever.

THE END

A NOTE FROM THE AUTHOR

Dear Reader,

I hope you enjoyed *Wind Chime Café*. Annie and Will's story holds a very special place in my heart. I grew up in a small town similar to Heron Island on the Eastern Shore of Maryland. I will always consider the Chesapeake Bay to be my home.

The Wind Chime series continues with Becca and Colin's story, *Wind Chime Wedding*, which is available now. Read on for a special preview. For updates on future books, please sign up for my newsletter at sophiemossauthor.com. Also, many of you have asked if I'm planning to share any recipes from *Wind Chime Café*. On the next page, you'll find the recipe for Della's Sweet Rolls and I've posted several more on my website.

Lastly, I have a small request. If you enjoyed the story, it would mean so much to me if you would consider leaving a brief review. Reviews are so important. They help a book stand out in the crowd, and they help other readers find authors like me.

Thank you so much for reading *Wind Chime Café*!

Sincerely,

Sophie Moss

DELLA'S SWEET ROLLS

Ingredients for the dough:
  ¾ cup whole milk
  ¼ cup water
  1 ¼ ounce packet active dry yeast
  ¼ cup sugar
  6 tablespoons melted butter
  1 egg
  1 teaspoon vanilla
  2 ¾ cups flour
  1 teaspoon salt
  ¼ teaspoon nutmeg

To make the dough:
  Warm the water and milk in a saucepan. Remove from the heat and add the yeast. Sprinkle ½ teaspoon sugar on top. Let sit for five minutes, or until foamy. In another bowl, mix the melted butter, egg and vanilla. Add the yeast mixture to the butter mixture and whisk until combined. In a bigger bowl, mix the

flour, sugar, salt and nutmeg. Add the yeast mixture to the flour mixture and stir. Place the dough onto a floured surface and knead for a few minutes. Shape into a ball and place in a large lightly buttered bowl. Cover the bowl with plastic wrap and let the dough rise at room temperature for about an hour, or until it has doubled in size. Take the dough out of the bowl, knead for a few seconds to remove excess air and then put it back in the bowl. Lay a piece of buttered plastic wrap directly over the dough, then cover the bowl with plastic wrap and refrigerate for at least 4 hours.

Ingredients for the filling:
   1 cup brown sugar
   1 teaspoon cinnamon
   ½ teaspoon nutmeg
   1 stick melted butter
   ¼ teaspoon salt

To make the filling:
   Combine brown sugar, cinnamon, nutmeg, melted butter and salt in a large bowl. Stir until smooth. Remove the dough from the refrigerator and transfer to a floured surface. Roll into a 9x13 rectangle and then spread the filling mixture onto the dough, leaving a little room at the edges so it doesn't spill out. Roll the dough into a log, using the longest edge to roll. Cut off about half an inch from each end and discard. Then cut eight to ten one-inch pieces from the log and lay in a buttered baking dish. (They will rise in the oven so leave some extra room in the dish. I fit eight pieces in a 9x13 dish and saved the rest of the log in the fridge for later.) Bake at 325 degrees for 30-40 minutes, or until golden brown.

Ingredients for the icing:
  ½ stick melted butter
  2 cups powdered sugar
  1 teaspoon vanilla
  2 teaspoons milk
  1 cup toasted pecans

To make the icing:
  Combine melted butter, powdered sugar and vanilla in a bowl. Add 2 to 3 teaspoons milk, depending on the consistency you want. Spread the icing on the sweet rolls about ten minutes after they've come out of the oven, so they're still warm, but not so hot that the icing drips off. Sprinkle with toasted pecans and serve warm!

For more *Wind Chime Café* recipes, visit my website at sophiemossauthor.com.

ACKNOWLEDGMENTS

Thank you to my mom and dad for your constant support and encouragement. Thank you to my editor, Martha Paley Francescato, for helping me bring this story to life. Thank you to my first readers—Juliette Sobanet, Rachel Kall, Audra Trosper, Christine Fitzner-LeBlanc, and Joy Ross Davis—for taking the time to read early drafts and provide valuable feedback. Lastly, thank you to all the men and women who have served in our military. I am so grateful for your sacrifice and for everything you do to keep this country safe.

Sophie Moss is a *USA Today* bestselling and multi-award winning author. She is known for her captivating Irish fantasy romances and heartwarming contemporary romances with realistic characters and unique island settings. As a former journalist, Sophie has been writing professionally for over ten years. She lives in Maryland, where she's working on her next novel. When she's not writing, she's testing out a new dessert recipe, exploring the Chesapeake Bay, or fiddling in her garden. Sophie loves to hear from readers. Email her at sophiemossauthor@gmail.com or visit her website sophiemossauthor.com to sign up for her newsletter.

BOOKS BY SOPHIE MOSS

Wind Chime Novels

Wind Chime Café

Wind Chime Wedding

Wind Chime Summer

Seal Island Trilogy

The Selkie Spell

The Selkie Enchantress

The Selkie Sorceress

Read on for a special preview of *Wind Chime Wedding*!

WIND CHIME WEDDING

CHAPTER ONE

"Miss Haddaway?"

Standing in the doorway to her classroom, Becca Haddaway glanced down at eight-year-old, Luke Faulkner. He was clutching a piece of paper in his hands and shifting self-consciously from one foot to the other. "Hey, Luke. Is your mom running late again?"

"I don't know." He looked down and pushed the paper toward her. "This is for you."

Becca's heart melted when she unfolded a pencil drawing of a bunny with big floppy ears in a field of clover. "This is so sweet. Thank you, Luke... But wouldn't you rather give this to your mom? I'm sure she'd love to have it."

He shook his head. "I want you to have it."

Becca scanned the crowded hallway filled with parents and students heading out for the long weekend. She didn't see his mother anywhere. "Why don't you stay and hang out for a while? I picked up some colored pencils at the store the other day. You could do another drawing for your mom, and then I could walk you home afterwards."

"That's okay." He dug the toe of his sneaker into the tile. "She'll be here."

Becca frowned when she spotted the holes in his shoes. His grass stained jeans looked like they could use another spin through the washing machine, and she was pretty sure he was wearing the same sweatshirt he'd worn yesterday.

Bending down to untangle the frayed laces of one of his shoes that had come untied, she glanced back up at his face, watching him for a reaction. "You've been quiet in class this week."

His small mouth thinned, his hands tightening around the straps of his backpack.

"I know things have been hard at home since you lost your father," Becca said gently, leaning back on her heels after she finished tying his shoe. "I'm always here if you want to talk, even outside school hours. You know I only live a few houses down from you. If you ever need anything, all you have to do is knock."

He nodded, avoiding her eyes.

Most schools would caution teachers to not get so involved in their students' personal lives, but this was Heron Island—less than three miles wide, with a population of only eight hundred year-round residents. People made it their business to know what was going on in their neighbors' lives, as much to look out for one another as for the gossip. More than one person had mentioned being concerned about how Luke might be getting on at home these days. It was her responsibility to make sure none of her students slipped through the cracks.

The sound of a rattling muffler drew her gaze out to the parking lot. A small, beat-up sedan pulled up to the entrance of the elementary school and Luke's mother jumped out of the driver's seat, rushing toward the glass doors.

"I have to go," Luke said, already jogging down the hallway to meet her. "Happy Easter," he called back over his shoulder.

"You too," Becca said, rising slowly back to her feet.

Courtney Faulkner pushed through the entrance. Her face was pale. Her dark blond hair was piled in a messy knot on top of her head. And she was still wearing her black hairdresser apron. She caught Becca's eye and mouthed, "*I'm sorry,*" as she grabbed Luke's hand and pulled him back toward the car.

Becca watched them drive away. She knew Courtney was doing her best. She was probably in a hurry to get Luke home and fed and shuttled over to her brother's house so she could race off to her second job, where she worked as a night shift housekeeper at one of the hotels a few towns over.

Looking back down at the paper in her hand, she wondered if Luke had given her the drawing because he thought his mother was too busy to appreciate it. She knew Courtney was far too proud to ask for help. And as much as Becca respected her independence and determination to pick up the pieces after her husband's death, everybody needed to lean on someone now and then.

Walking back over to her desk, she slipped the drawing into her purse and surveyed the mess from the surprise party she'd thrown for her class that afternoon. The tables and chairs had been pushed into a haphazard circle. The floor was covered in plastic eggs and candy wrappers. A questionable sticky substance was smeared across several flat surfaces, which she could only hope was leftover from the marshmallow bunnies that had almost incited a riot when she'd passed them out earlier.

Smiling at the memory of her students' excited squeals when she'd announced that instead of practicing double-digit subtraction they were going to have an Easter party, she spotted Shelley Needham walking down the hall. "Shelley," she called out to the

Heron Island Elementary School principal. "I've hardly seen you around all week. Where have you been?"

Shelley paused in the doorway. Her short, curly gray hair was slightly mussed. Her hazel eyes were distant and troubled. "Meeting with the board."

"Why?" Becca asked. "What's wrong?"

"Nothing." Shelley offered a ghost of a smile. "Routine stuff. Planning for next year." She reached down, snagging a pink plastic egg off the floor. "I'm surprised you had time to throw a party today. Don't you have enough on your plate with the wedding and the move?"

Becca ignored the sudden twinge of apprehension. She was getting married to her high school sweetheart, Tom Jacobson, in three weeks and moving to D.C. after their honeymoon. She should feel excited about her new life...not anxious. Reaching for the broom propped against the wall, she started to sweep up the sparkly bits of green plastic grass. "I found time."

"That reminds me..." Shelley fished out a piece of dark chocolate from inside the egg. "I still haven't gotten your letter of resignation."

"Oh, right." Becca's gaze landed on the envelope that had been burning a hole through her desk for two weeks now. She had given Shelley plenty of advance notice, but she hadn't made it official yet. Taking a deep breath, she picked up the letter. What was the point in putting it off any longer? Crossing the room, she handed the envelope to Shelley. "I keep forgetting to give it to you."

Shelley took it, slipping it into her pocket. "Thanks."

Becca paused when she noticed the dark circles under the other woman's eyes. "You look tired."

Shelley forced another smile. "I'm fine."

"Are you sure?" Becca set the broom down, gesturing for her to come further into the classroom. Shelley had been like a second mother to her since she was sixteen. She could usually tell when something was wrong.

Shelley's gaze drifted out to the playing fields. "I really didn't want to burden you with this."

Becca closed the door behind them. "What's going on?"

Shelley sighed, running her hands down the front of her wrinkled suit jacket. "I guess I'm going to have to tell everyone on Monday anyway. I might as well tell you now." She looked back at Becca. "The board is thinking of shutting us down."

"What?" Becca's eyes widened. "Why?"

"The state cut the education budget for next year."

"But we've survived plenty of budget cuts in the past. Our district always finds a way to come up with the money."

"This time it's different," Shelley said. "A few of the board members have been pushing to shut us down for a while now. They're convinced that the county could save a lot of money by consolidating. The governor's decision to reallocate the funding for next year has motivated them to explore their options."

No way, Becca thought. There was no way the board would actually shut down the school. Heron Island Elementary had been open for over sixty years. She had gone to school here. Her father had gone to school here. Almost every person on this island had gone to school here. There had to be another way to balance the budget. "What about the renovations the board approved for the gym—the ones that were supposed to happen this summer? Can't they be pushed back?"

"I've spent the past six months convincing the board that those renovations had to happen. They think the gym won't be safe for the kids if we don't get the work done this summer. And even if we did try to delay it, it still wouldn't make up even a fraction of the cost that it would save by shutting us down."

"Where will all the kids go?" Becca asked.

"St. Michaels Elementary."

"But those classrooms are already overcrowded."

"I know," Shelley said. "I wish I had a better solution. I've been trying to talk them out of it, but it's not looking good."

Becca sat down in one of the kids-sized chairs, staring at the sticky marshmallow goo smeared across the table.

"I know it's a small consolation," Shelley said after a long pause, "but you picked a good time to leave."

A good time to leave? Becca lifted her gaze to the wall covered in construction paper bunnies that her students had made that day. It was one thing to leave her job as a teacher, but the thought of the school closing down completely...?

This classroom had been her mother's classroom when she was a second grade teacher. All Becca had ever wanted was to follow in her mother's footsteps. She would have been happy to teach at this school for the rest of her life. She had agreed to move to D.C. to be with Tom because that's where his job was now, but she had secretly hoped that he might want to move back here one day, that he might tire of the city after a while and want to work at one of the smaller firms in Easton or St. Michaels. She had hoped that, maybe, after a few years, she might be able to come back and teach at this school again.

Becca looked up at Shelley. "I might be leaving, but this island is still my home. I wish you had told me what was happening. I could have been doing something to help. Why don't you let me talk to the board? If nothing else, I could raise the issue of Taylor."

"I already have." Shelley pulled out the chair across from her and sat down. "Dozens of times. They said they're planning to hire more counselors next year, that it would be good for her to get used to the structure of how the larger schools work for when—"

"For when *what*?" Becca cut in. "When she has to go to middle school? That's three years from now. Taylor will be in third grade next year. She still has a long way to go before she's ready to face a classroom of thirty-plus kids. She needs to be here, where we can give her the attention she deserves. Where she can be taken care of, and where all the teachers care about her progress, not just one counselor who might be able to fit her in between all her other appointments."

"Becca," Shelley said softly. "I know. Believe me, I've said all the same things to the board."

Becca met Shelley's gaze across the table. It wasn't just Taylor who would be affected. If this school shut down, Shelley and all the other teachers would lose their jobs. "What will happen to you?"

Shelley picked at the yellow sugar stuck to the marshmallow goo with her fingernail. "I've started putting out feelers to some of the other schools in the area, but no one's hiring right now. It might be time for me to retire, or find something else to do..."

"Are you ready to retire?"

"No, but neither was Della when she got laid off last year. She worked as a receptionist in that law firm in Easton for thirty years and now she's a chef at the café. I've never seen her so happy."

"That's not the same," Becca argued. "Della loves to cook. She didn't want to answer phones and manage calendars for the rest of her life. This is your passion, Shelley—kids and teaching. You've been working here your whole life. You can't just let that go."

Shelley smiled sadly, covering Becca's hand with her own. "We always knew this could happen one day. I'm just glad you decided to leave before it happened to both of us."

A mile down the island, Colin Foley stood inside the waterfront inn his friend, Will Dozier, had inherited from his grandparents last year. Pulling his gaze from the thin crack snaking through the wall beside the fireplace in the family room, he glanced over at the contractor. "How much is this going to set us back?"

"We need to replace the drywall and repair the damage to the foundation," Jimmy Faulkner answered. "Two weeks worth of labor. Maybe a few extra grand, probably closer to five."

Colin ran a hand through his hair. He wasn't worried so much about the money. He was worried about the delay. He'd already told several key donors that they would be open by Memorial Day.

He couldn't go back on his word to the first people who'd invested in him, or to the families of his former SEAL teammates who'd already made plans to travel out to the island for the opening.

It would be the first time they'd all gotten together since the devastating mission in Afghanistan that had ended with two of their youngest team members being flown home in body bags and an extended stay at Walter Reed National Military Medical Center for him.

When he'd returned home from that career-ending deployment over a year ago with the lower half of his left leg blown off by a grenade, he'd struggled for months to figure out what to do with his life. It was a trip to Heron Island last November to visit his former team leader that had sparked the idea to open a rehab center for wounded warriors on the island.

Colin had managed to convince Will to go into business with him, and as soon as his friend's contract with the Navy was up in a few weeks, he'd be moving back to Maryland to help run the place.

This inn had been in Will's family for generations, but at the moment, it was Colin's responsibility. He didn't take that responsibility lightly. "If you need to hire more men to get the job done faster, hire more men. We need to open by Memorial Day."

Jimmy removed his red trucker hat, rubbing the heel of his palm over his scalp. "What about Becca's wedding?"

Becca's wedding? Crap. He'd completely forgotten about that. Will had promised Becca that she could hold her wedding here the week before they opened. They couldn't go back on their word now. "We need to have everything finished and cleaned up before then."

"It's going to be tight," Jimmy warned.

Reaching into his pocket for his phone when it buzzed, Colin glanced down at the screen, then back up at Jimmy. "Whatever you need to do, just do it."

Jimmy nodded and Colin turned, picking up the call. "Hey, Dad."

"Colin," his father's deep voice came through the line. "I understand you cancelled your seat at the Victory PAC fundraiser in Baltimore tonight."

"I had to make a last minute trip down to the island." Colin stepped over a pile of paint cans on his way out to the porch. "Something came up at the inn."

"Is everything okay?"

"Just a minor setback, nothing we can't handle."

"Good," Nick Foley said. There was a pause and Colin heard a muffled voice in the background, most likely his campaign manager or one of his assistants. As the Governor of Maryland, his father rarely went anywhere without an entourage of assistants.

When his father came back on the line, his tone was rushed. "Are you still planning to attend the dinner at The Dockside in Annapolis on Saturday night?"

Colin looked out at the wide sloping green lawn that led down to the Chesapeake Bay. The last thing he wanted to do was sit through another fundraiser dinner, but part of the agreement he'd made with his parents when he'd committed to work on his father's campaign through May was attending at least two social events per week. "I'll be there."

"Natalie wants to know who you're bringing."

"I'm sure she does."

"Colin—"

"Put her on, Dad."

"What?"

"Put her on," Colin repeated, leaning his shoulder against the unpainted doorframe. "I know she's sitting right next to you."

There was another long pause before his stepmother's smooth, cultured voice drifted through the line. "Colin, honey, I need to know who you're bringing to the dinner Saturday night."

"Hi, Natalie."

His stepmother sighed. "Why do you insist on making this difficult for me?"

Colin smiled. "Because I don't need you to set me up."

"But I have so many friends with nice *single* daughters."

"I don't need you to set me up," he repeated.

"But what about Priscilla Davenport's daughter, Julie—remember her? Your father said you two went to pre-school together."

"Oh?" Colin said. "Were we an item back then?"

"Please be serious, Colin. Julie just moved back to the area and she's recently divorced. I think you two would really hit it off." She added a note of hope into her voice. "I could arrange for you to sit together on Saturday night..."

"Natalie." Colin pushed off the doorframe. The woman was relentless. "I'm bringing someone."

"Who?" she asked, surprised.

"You'll meet her on Saturday."

"Won't you at least tell me her name?"

"No."

His stepmother lowered her voice to a whisper. "She's not one of those women you pick up at the bars, is she?"

Colin choked out a laugh. "What?"

"I know what goes on in downtown Annapolis on the weekends," she huffed. "I hear things."

Colin rolled his eyes. "I'm not bringing a woman I picked up at a bar."

"Then who is she?"

"Someone you've never met before."

"How...mysterious."

Yes, Colin thought. She was. She was so mysterious she didn't even exist yet.

"You'd better not be making this up," Natalie warned. "Last time you told me you were bringing a date, you came alone, and there was an empty seat beside you all night. We had to put your father's jacket on the back of your chair so it didn't look like you'd been stood up."

Colin shook his head, smiling. No one at that party had thought he'd been stood up. But appearances were everything to his stepmother. And ever since she'd taken it on as her life's mission to find him a wife, he hadn't had a moment's peace. If he had to spend one more night talking to a woman who made him want to claw his eyes out from boredom, he'd lose it. "There won't be an empty seat this time, I promise."

"I wish you would tell me who you're bringing," she said. "What if I forget her name when I'm introducing her to people?"

"You won't forget her name," Colin said. Natalie Foley never forgot a name. "I'll see you on Saturday." Ending the call, he slipped his phone back in his pocket.

Jimmy walked out to the porch, unscrewing the cap off a tarnished silver flask. "I made a few calls. Looks like I can get a bigger crew here to start on Monday."

"Thanks," Colin said.

Jimmy handed him the flask.

Colin took it, walking down the steps to where a pile of raw lumber sat under a blue tarp. He lifted the tarp with the toe of his boot, inspecting the quality of the wood.

"I saw your picture in the paper last weekend," Jimmy said.

"Yeah?" Colin said distractedly.

"Who was that woman you were with?"

"Last weekend?" They were all starting to run together at this point. Letting the tarp fall back into place, he glanced back at Jimmy. "Christy Caraway, maybe?"

"Christy Caraway of Caraway's Crab House? The heir to the biggest chain of seafood restaurants in the Mid-Atlantic?"

Colin nodded, taking a sip from the flask.

Jimmy whistled. "I'm impressed." Leaning back against the house, the contractor dipped his hands in his pockets. "Nice rack, too. Have you seen her naked?"

Colin smiled. "She's easy on the eyes, but that's about all she's got going for her."

Jimmy grinned. "She looked pretty good in that picture."

They all looked good in the pictures, Colin thought. Every woman his stepmother set him up with was the same: attractive, wealthy, well connected, and only interested in him for one reason—because he was the governor's son.

He'd been engaged to a woman who'd only wanted him for his status before—for being a SEAL. He hadn't realized it at the time, but his ex-fiancée had made it perfectly clear when she'd broken up with him a week after he'd returned from Afghanistan without his leg, saying she couldn't marry an amputee.

Gazing out at the wide expanse of water, he watched the late afternoon sunlight glint over the surface. He could hear the water lapping against the rocks along the shoreline, the wind whipping at the layers of plastic covering the gaps in the walls where a few of the downstairs windows were being replaced.

There was no going back, no point in remembering what he'd lost or who he'd once been. This place was his future. And the first step was opening by Memorial Day.

Nothing was going to get in the way of that.

Screwing the cap back on the flask, he tossed it to Jimmy.

Now, all he needed was to find a date for Saturday night.

75594080R00182

Made in the USA
Middletown, DE
06 June 2018